FOREVER DEVOTED

FOREVER BLUEGRASS #8

KATHLEEN BROOKS

LAURENS PUBLISHING

COPYRIGHT PAGE

To my dad. Thank you for instilling my love of books by reading All Things Great and Small to me as a child every night. That love of reading grew into a passion for writing. I love that you sneak into the library and move my books up front and are just as excited to read my books as I am to write them. I love you.

Forever Concealed

Forever Devoted

Forever Hunted - coming April/May of 2017

Women of Power Series

Chosen for Power

Built for Power

Fashioned for Power

Destined for Power

Web of Lies Series

Whispered Lies

Rogue Lies

Shattered Lies

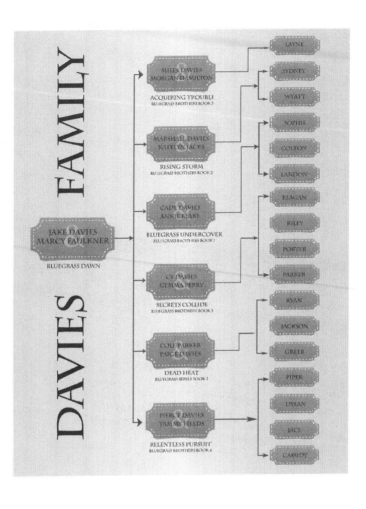

DAVIES FAMILY

JAKE DAVIES & MARCY FAULKNER
BLUEGRASS DAWN

MILES DAVIES & MORGAN HAMILTON
ACQUIRING TROUBLE
BLUEGRASS BROTHERS BOOK 5
- LAYNE
- SYDNEY
- WYATT

MARSHALL DAVIES & KATELYN JACKS
RISING STORM
BLUEGRASS BROTHERS BOOK 2
- SOPHIE
- COLTON
- LANDON

CADE DAVIES & ANNIE BLAKE
BLUEGRASS UNDERCOVER
BLUEGRASS BROTHERS BOOK 1
- REAGAN
- RILEY
- PORTER
- PARKER

CY DAVIES & GEMMA PERRY
SECRETS COLLIDE
BLUEGRASS BROTHERS BOOK 3
- RYAN
- JACKSON
- GREER

COLE PARKER & PAIGE DAVIES
DEAD HEAT
BLUEGRASS SERIES BOOK 1

PIERCE DAVIES & TAMMY FIELDS
RELENTLESS PURSUIT
BLUEGRASS BROTHERS BOOK 4
- PIPER
- DYLAN
- JACI
- CASSIDY

DAVIES FAMILY FRIENDS

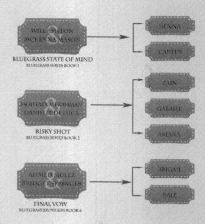

WILL ASHTON
MCKENNA MASON
→ SIENNA
CARTER

BLUEGRASS STATE OF MIND
BLUEGRASS SERIES BOOK 1

MOHTADIM RAHMAN
DANIELLE DE LUCA
→ ZAIN
GABRIEL
ARIANA

RISKY SHOT
BLUEGRASS SERIES BOOK 2

AHMED MULEZ
BRIDGET SPRINGER
→ ABIGAIL
DALE

FINAL VOW
BLUEGRASS BROTHERS BOOK 6

1

Three weeks ago. Atlantic Ocean near Nigeria . . .

THE ROOM WAS dark as the large screen flashed with the image of the large American cargo ship named *The Caribou*. The light from the image illuminated the room filled with men. Chief Petty Officer Walker Greene was a member of the US Naval Special Warfare Development Group, which everyone in the military just called DEVGRU. Civilians still called it SEAL Team Six even though that name was no longer used by the military. Walker leaned forward as his lieutenant commander pointed out the breach points on this ship.

"*The Caribou* was taken hostage by Nigerian pirates an hour ago," Lieutenant Commander Stephens told the eight men of the DEVGRU's Red Wolves squadron. "The captain was able to send an SOS before the bridge was stormed."

"How many pirates?" Jud Melville asked. He was the senior chief petty officer and leader of Walker's team. His mind was meticulous when planning a rescue.

"Eight," Stephens responded.

Walker's brow knit as his commander turned to the blueprint of the cargo ship and laid out the plans for the rescue. "It's strange, isn't it?" Walker asked after they discussed their mission. "The Nigerian pirates typically don't try to steal a ship. They usually take the crew ashore and ransom them to the ship company. But in this case, they're taking the ship with them. What's on the boat?" Walker asked. It had to be something big for the pirates to try to disappear with a massive cargo ship. They had to know that the longer they were at sea, the more likely they'd be caught. A new picture came up and Walker let out a low whistle. It was the ship's manifest. Platinum, gold, and diamonds were just some of what was on *The Caribou.*

"They'd just picked up cargo from South Africa. They stopped in Nigeria to pick up their last bit of cargo before heading back to the United States. They were attacked after exiting the harbor. Reports show the ship is now heading south. There are some known pirate hangouts in the region, and we believe they will be going there to unload. We've been called in to rescue the crew of *The Caribou.* We're diverting our course since we're so close. Our original assignment has been sent to another platoon. Be ready for RIB deployment in fifteen minutes," Stephens ordered as the men all stood. The RIB, or Naval Special Warfare Rigid Inflatable Boat, could operate in heavy seas and carry all eight members of the Red Wolf squadron.

"What do you think, Greene?" Senior Chief Melville asked as they walked as a group to get ready to deploy.

"It's a big ship, which means there're plenty of blind spots to board. They're fifty miles out, so we can come in dark and quiet. They won't expect us so soon since no one knows we're here. They probably figure they have time to stash the boat and cargo before local enforcement realizes they can't handle it and calls for international help. Patrols are down since we put a dent in the Somali pirates, so they will think they have time on their side," Walker said, opening his locker and peeling off his shirt.

At six foot one, Walker was one of the taller SEALs. Melville stood four inches shorter and thirty pounds lighter than Walker. The prospect of boarding a hostile ship wasn't new to them. They'd done it before, and if Walker were honest, this sounded like an easy in and out. As a SEAL, you go in knowing you'll come out alive. But if you can't, you'll go out taking as many bad guys with you as you can.

"What is that, Greene?" Shane Wecker, Walker's best friend, laughed at the small Roman numeral tattoo Greene had gotten on his biceps. "That's what you ended up getting?"

Walker looked down at the tattoo that represented the year he became a SEAL and shrugged. "I'm too sexy to cover up this body." The team howled with laughter since Shane's back and chest were covered with as many tats as the Navy would let him have. Shane softly punched Walker in the stomach as he laughed. Walker blew out the playful punch and started to pull on his gear. He loved these guys. They were his brothers, and there was no one better to tease than family.

"Your sister doesn't have a problem with them," Wecker said with a grin as he held out his arms to the *oohs* of the other men.

Walker shook his head as he finished strapping on everything he would need for the rescue. "It's a damn good thing you love her or I'd have to kill you. I'd hate for my little sister to be a widow at thirty." Edie and he were four years apart and had become inseparable since their parents passed away ten years before. He'd attended her college graduation, and she'd encouraged him to follow his dreams after his second combat deployment with the SEALs to try out for this elite group made up of the best of the best of combat tested SEALs.

When Walker became a SEAL, his sister had moved from their small hometown of Shadows Landing, South Carolina, to Virginia Beach to be closer to him. After joining DEVGRU, Walker had introduced her to his squad. Shane had gone from bad boy to loving husband in less than a year. Their second anniversary was in three days.

"Okay, enough harping on Walker for being a coward when it comes to needles," Jud Melville teased as everyone quieted down for their orders. "Cal, you and Larson take the bow. There you'll trigger the fire alarm, but I don't want a big explosion, just something that will bring some of them to us."

"You got it," Larson nodded as he double-checked his pack for the tools he'd need.

"Walker, you'll take the starboard entrance a quarter of the way up the bow while Shane will insert at port side. Rick, starboard beam and Joe, port beam. Perry and I will take the stern nearest the bridge. We'll move in a wave pattern, building up to breach the bridge."

Walker nodded. He would board and wait for the fire to be set. Then Cal would reach him and Larson would reach Shane. Together they'd moved forward, meeting up and spreading out with Joe and Rick and taking out any of the pirates who came to check the fire. They'd split off quietly and join Jud and Perry to regain control of the ship.

"Let's go, men! Tomorrow we'll look back on tonight and it will seem like an easy day," Jud said as they walked through the ship to board the RIB. A three-man crew would be with them to drive the boat and man the onboard weapons. Walker took a deep breath, closed his eyes, and said a quick prayer to Saint Michael before climbing on board.

~

THE LARGE CARGO vessel loomed as if it were a ghost ship. The lights were off, and no one was visible on the bridge near the stern of the ship. Jud made the motion to ready themselves as the throttle lessened to hide the noise of their arrival. They sliced through the waves toward the ship as Walker and the rest of the men pressed themselves against the RIB and tried to disappear from sight.

Spray from the ocean splashed Walker and his team, but they didn't mind. They were frogmen. Being in the water was second nature to them. The RIB slowed, and at Jud's silent order, Cal and Larson scurried up the bow and went to work setting their trap. Less than a minute later, Walker began to climb the rope one of the crewmen had secured, with Shane right behind him.

The cargo ship didn't echo their silent footfalls as one by one each member of the Red Wolf team boarded the hostile vessel and moved toward the bridge along the rail. Huge containers towered over them like skyscrapers, covering them in shadow until they emerged at the stern of the ship. As Walker scanned the bridge with his scope, he saw Jud and Perry move into position. "It's a go," Walker whispered. Cal nodded and pressed the remote detonator. A second later a distant fire alarm could be heard.

"Something's not right," Shane said as he scanned the area. "No one is moving. No lights, no people, no pirates."

"We're moving in," Jud said over the coms. They had

climbed the ten stories up, but the plan was for them not to move in until the pirates had shown themselves.

"Wait for us," Walker replied as he gave the order to climb.

Jud didn't answer back as he and Perry breached the bridge. Walker cursed and took off up the metal stairs, rifle in hand, as he continually scanned for hostiles. The metal stairs groaned and creaked at they raced up them. At the top, Walker held a fist to stop his team. He held up three fingers and motioned to the far side of the bridge. Cal, Larson, and Joe took off for the far door to the bridge while Walker, Shane, and Rick got into position.

"We're in position," Cal's hushed voice said over the coms.

"Go." Walker ordered as he flung the door open. Shane and Rick entered with guns pointed.

Walker stepped into the bridge after his teammates and scanned the area. The lights were off. The glow was from the computers covered with blankets. Everything was wrong. "Abort!" Walker yelled, but it was too late. Gunfire from under the desks, from a closet, from all around them erupted. Walker returned fire as he stepped back toward the door.

The smoke from the gunfire filled the room quickly, making it hard to see as he fired blindly in the direction of the hostiles. "Shane, Rick, you're clear back!"

But no one followed him as he stepped from the smoke-filled air and out onto the deck. The gunshots stopped, and in eerie silence, Walker held his rifle at the ready. His heart beat faster, but he wouldn't give into the fear. He had a job to do. And so long as he was still breathing, he'd do it.

The smoke began to clear and a black form could be

seen. Walker put the sights on the head and his finger on the trigger.

"Walker! Shane! Anyone!"

Walker released the pressure on the trigger and pushed his night vision goggles back up onto his helmet. "Jud! I'm here. Are you injured?"

"Walker, thank goodness," Jud said, relieved as he appeared in the doorway. But he didn't appear alone. Moving past him were armed hostiles. "Thank goodness you're the only one left. It was easier than I thought to take out the best of the best."

Ice froze in Walker's veins as he registered what Jud had done. Walker took a step back and hit the metal rail of the bridge that overlooked the water some 120 feet below. "What have you done?"

"Done? I've become a multimillionaire in ten minutes. Do you have any idea how much all of this is worth on the black market? Further, as the lone survivor of the heroic yet devastatingly tragic rescue operation, I'll get a book deal, a movie deal, and everything I've ever wanted."

"You did this for money and fame?" Walker asked, disgusted and completely baffled.

"You think they pay us enough for our jobs? We make nothing. Less than a freaking person sitting safely in a cubicle all day. We put our lives on the line every day, and we get nothing. I'm tired of it. I want it all, and I'm taking it all. 'Poor Walker Greene was the last to die,' I'll say tearfully to the world as I tell them how bravely you fought and died. Now smile for the drone one last time." Hidden from sight in the bridge, Jud tossed out two smoke bombs blinding the drone, and turned to the man next to him. "Shoot him."

Walker didn't think. He'd already devised his escape. He did it the instant he boarded the ship. They were trained to think that way, and Jud should have seen it coming as Walker flung himself backward over the rail. Gunfire ripped into his thigh, sending him flipping in the air so his booted feet slammed into the water first. The impact was so hard it felt like he had landed on solid ground as bullets tore through the water. The force of his sixty miles per hour drop sent him plunging deep into the ocean's depths.

Walker's lungs burned and his body hurt, but he forced his arms to move as he swam for the surface. The waves carried him up and down and crashed over him as he struggled to swim away from the cargo ship. Walker tried to use his radio coms but got nothing but interference. Jud must have jammed them at some point.

But then Walker heard the motor from the RIB as people shouted on the cargo ship. He could hear Jud issuing orders from inside the bridge and knew he had to make it to the RIB or he would die out there.

It was a sight from heaven when the RIB tore around the end of the cargo ship as the crew laid cover fire. Walker waved his arm and swam toward them as they raced to his rescue. Walker swam with all his strength as a sniper from the bridge saw him and fired. The RIB returned fire on the bridge as they closed in on him. Walker swam for all he was worth and finally a hand came out toward him, urging him the last twenty feet. Walker froze at the sudden loud thundering boom and a high-pitched whistle as a shoulder launcher fired. Walker only had enough time to see the man in shadows against the rail, hidden by the stacks of shipping containers before the RIB exploded.

Walker's heart plummeted as he dove under to protect himself from the explosion. Fire glowed above him as the dead bodies of his compatriots floated among the debris. Part of the RIB sunk slowly by him, the glow from the fire still burning on the surface of the water to illuminate the small hold of the boat now split in half. It was used for storage . . . and for an emergency raft.

Suppressing the urge to surface for breath, Walker kicked his legs as he chased the sinking debris. His lungs burned, pain stabbed his leg, and there were black spots in his vision. But those spots didn't change the fact that he saw the bright orange of the life raft crammed into the hold.

The boat seemed to sink further and further away as Walker stretched his fingers toward his only chance at survival. With one last burst of strong kicks, Walker surged against the depths and his hands closed onto the small handle of the raft. With a final yank to free the raft, Walker swam for the surface. Holding onto the straps for dear life, Walker used one arm to frantically push through the water and into the night air.

Walker filled his lungs the second he breached the water's surface. He pulled the small rectangular package holding the boat to his chest and breathed until the dizziness subsided. It was then he noticed no more shots were being fired. Looking around, he saw he had drifted further from the ship and was in the middle of a debris pile drifting away with the current.

Walker took an assessment of the situation. The smoke was clearing. He pulled his night vision down on his helmet and watched as Jud, standing at command in the darkness of the bridge, called the men together outside. Suddenly one man shot in toward Jud, but Walker couldn't see what happened to Jud. The next thing he knew, a wave of bullets washed over the pirates from inside the bridge. Jud staggered from the bridge with his rifle in hand and kicking the guns away from the pirates who hadn't fallen dead overboard. Jud collapsed to his knees and pulled two flares.

He waved them at the drone Walker knew would be flying high above them, reporting their mission back to Lt. Commander Stephens. Walker had seen enough. He needed to get in touch with base before Jud. Because from what would be captured by the drone, it would look like Walker died before the smoke bombs covered the ship. And then the drone would report back with the clearing smoke, a now visible pirate shooting someone, and then Jud saving the day by killing all the pirates.

Tearing the compression sleeve from his arm, Walker wrapped it tightly around his leg, slowing the bleeding as much as possible. He took a breath and began the combat sidestroke as he swam in the direction of his ship and his commander. When he was in training, he had done a five-and-a-half-mile night swim. Only this time his leg was bleeding and the possibility of shark attack rose exponentially.

WALKER LOOKED BACK, and once he was out of sight of the cargo ship, he pulled the life raft from the valise and pulled the auto inflate. Tired and exhausted, he tried to compartmentalize the fact he'd lost his team, his best friends, and his brother-in-law at the hands of his team leader. He dragged himself into the orange raft and collapsed. He groped for his coms, but hope died as he saw his pack was riddled with bullets. Through the adrenaline of the moment, he hadn't felt those shots lodging into his pack and bullet proof vest.

Walker sat near the opening of the raft's canopy to keep a lookout for friendlies as he stripped off his gear. He had cuts and bruises, but his leg was going to be the major problem. He was lucky the bullet had gone through his thigh about six inches up from his knee, but it was bleeding badly, and he knew he wouldn't last too long.

Walker grunted in pain as he dug through his things for his first-aid kit. He cleaned it the best he could, pressed quick-clotting gauze to it, and wrapped pressure gauze around his leg. It would do until he could get help. Only help never came.

2

It had been five days since the tragic events on the cargo ship. The bleeding had stopped, but an infection had set in as Walker's life raft bobbed along the ocean waves. He'd heard no planes nor seen any helicopters. No one was looking for him, and he knew why—Jud. Jud's plan had worked, and right now getting revenge was all that was keeping Walker alive as he battled the delirium that came with the infection and dehydration.

As day six came and went, Walker's resolve did not waiver. He slept and he hallucinated, but he never gave up. He focused on keeping his wound as clean as he could. He used his knife and managed to catch a fish. In his hunger, he ate the thing practically whole, but it was enough to get him to day seven. And on day seven, everything changed.

WALKER AWOKE the seventh evening to see his sister crying. She sat on the other side of the raft, cast in an orange glow from the almost completely set sun through the canopy door. Her knees were drawn to her chest as she wrapped her arms around her legs and cried. Edie rocked back and forth as pain contorted her face. Her brown hair was pulled back in a ponytail, but strands were falling out and covering part of her face. She was in her NAVY T-shirt and jeans shorts with no shoes.

"Edie?" Walker's dry voice cracked as his parched tongue tried to lick his split lips.

His sister's electric blue eyes looked up from where they'd been buried against her arms. Tears streamed down them but didn't diminish the brightness of her eyes that were almost identical to his.

"Are you alive?"

"Yes, Edie. I'm here," Walker said, using all his strength to pull himself toward his sister.

"Don't leave me alone, Walker. I'm so scared."

"I'll never leave you, Edie."

"It's getting dark," she reminded him. "Turn on the lights."

Walker looked around, his eyes landing on the flare. "I don't have any lights, but this will be just like camping out. We'll pretend to roast s'mores, just like we used to do when we went camping."

"You always look out for me, Walker," Edie smiled as she wiped her tears.

Walker looked down at the flare. "It's my only one," he muttered.

"Light it, Walker," Edie demanded, her tone turning serious.

"But," Walker started to say, but Edie shook her head.

"No, light it now. *Now!*" Edie screamed so loudly Walker fell back.

"Okay, okay. Move over so I can light it."

"Light the flare now!" Edie continued to yell as she

moved from the door so Walker could lean out the raft to ignite the flare. "Now! Now! Now!"

The spark lit and the flare glowed brightly in the quickly darkening sky. He turned back to Edie. "There, you're safe now."

Edie smiled and cupped his cheek. "Come back to me, Walker. Fight with everything you have. Promise me. Promise me you'll fight."

Walker nodded his head. "I promise. Now, come here and we can pretend we're camping."

Edie scooted next to him at the door as he held his hand holding the flare in it out over the water and lay down. He felt Edie's fingers comb through his hair as his eyes closed.

When Walker felt the hands of a stranger on him instead of his sister's, he reacted with instinct despite his condition. His knife was to the man's neck before Walker even opened his eyes. When Walker did open his eyes, he could barely focus on the person who was leaning over a small boat rocking Walker's shoulders.

"Who are you?" Walker croaked, but when the man answered he couldn't understand him. "I don't understand."

"Help," was the only word Walker finally understood as he gave into the sturdy pair of hands along with oblivion.

WALKER'S EYELIDS felt like sandpaper rubbing across his eyes as he forced them open. He took in the lighting, the metal walls and ceiling, and the bed he was lying on. He was on a ship in what passed as a medical room. An IV was in his arm and an old man sat working at a desk ten feet away.

Walker continued to look around at the posters when it came to him. This wasn't his ship. He was on a Greek ship.

They must have rescued him. "Hello," he said slowly, finding his voice was stronger than it had been the night he was pulled from the water.

The old man's head snapped around to look at him. His skin was olive, his hair white and combed back, and he had a big smile on his face. Walker evaluated the situation quickly. He wasn't in danger.

"Ah! Hello. Hello. Okay? Okay?" he asked as he shuffled over to Walker.

"Where am I?"

"Okay!"

"How long have I been unconscious?"

"Yes, yes. Okay, okay." He smiled as he took Walker's blood pressure and stuck a thermometer in his mouth.

"Do you speak English?" Walker asked around the thermometer and got an immediate reprimand in Greek. He didn't need to understand it. Every kid heard it growing up. Don't talk until the thermometer is done taking your temp.

The thermometer beeped, and the man took it out and his smile grew. "Yes, yes."

Apparently Walker's fever had broken. "English?"

The man nodded and pulled up the bed sheet. Walker jumped. "Okay, okay," he smiled as he checked Walker's wound and frowned. Walker tried to say something else, but the man held up a finger, went to his desk, and picked up a phone. He spoke quickly into it before hanging up and coming back with a world map.

"Hello?" the man asked, pointing to England, Canada, and the United States before looking for Australia.

"United States," Walker said, pointing to the map. The man smiled largely.

The man pointed to himself. "Costa." Then he pointed to Greece.

"Walker," Walker said, pointing to himself.

The door opened and the captain walked in. He was in his fifties with dark hair and a friendly smile. Costa began speaking rapidly, and Walker heard his name and country before the captain nodded and pulled a chair to Walker's bed.

"I am Captain Kyrkos. We pull you from water three days ago," he said slowly in heavily accented English.

"Thank you for the rescue. Where are we?"

The man nodded and Costa handed him the map. The captain pointed to the Atlantic Ocean. "Going to Char-less-ton, U-nited States."

Home. Walker let out a deep breath. Shadows Landing was thirty minutes or so upriver from Charleston. Better yet, there was an Air Force base, a Coast Guard base, and a naval base all nearby.

"Soldier?" Captain Kyrkos asked and held out his phone.

Walker began to say no when Kyrkos pointed to his phone. It was on an international news site, and there was a picture of Jud Melville hailing help with the flares. Walker grabbed the phone and scrolled through the story. The story recounted Jud's heroics, and there were even pictures from the drone of Melville taking out the pirates. Walker felt his jaw clenching and relaxed it as he noticed the captain watching him. *All bodies had been retrieved from the ocean except that of Chief Petty Officer Walker Greene, who is presumed dead.*

"You," the captain simply said. "Walk-her Green-ey"

Walker didn't bother correcting the pronunciation. "Have you called anyone?" Walker asked, setting down the phone. His mind was already planning an escape.

"I say to myself. Must be reason not looking for own man. I no call. I wait to ask you." Captain Kyrkos looked him over closely as Costa began to speak. "The doctor says you need surgery on your leg. There's a, um, tiny piece metal in it. But he no knows how to do it. You call for help?"

"No. Don't call." Walker handed the phone back as the captain looked seriously at the article before turning off the screen. He wasn't going to drag his sister into this. His sister undoubtedly thought she'd lost her husband and brother in one horrific mission gone wrong.

"I see you need help. They try kill you, yes? What happened to you?"

Walker didn't know how to answer the captain so he settled on the truth. "Betrayal."

The captain nodded solemnly. "I have seen this in my life. I take you to Char-less-ton, but we will be boarded. Understand?"

Walker did understand. Customs would board first to see if they could unload and that's if the Coast Guard didn't decide to do a routine check. He needed to slip off the boat unseen before then. Jud, thinking Walker was dead, was the best thing that could happen until he could formulate a plan. "If your doctor can keep me well enough to swim, I'll be off the boat before you reach the dock."

Captain Kyrkos patted Walker's shoulder. "You okay. You strong. You fight for life. Kyrkos and Costa will take care of you. We arrive thirteen days."

~

WALKER CLENCHED his jaw in pain as Costa began to clean out the wound while pushing a steady dose of antibiotics into him. Kyrkos and Costa were the only ones who saw him. Walker worked on walking, doing pushups, crunches, and one-legged squats as Costa frowned on. Days passed as the image of Jud killing Shane and his team ran on a loop over and over again. He had a plan, but first his leg needed to heal. Walker had given it much thought over the last twelve days. He was going to sneak back into Shadows Landing and have his best friend, Dr. Gavin Faulkner, remove the shrapnel. Gavin would keep him hidden until he was healed. Then he would go after everything Jud stole before taking the life of the man who had taken the lives of the ones he loved.

3

Keeneston, Kentucky...

"Mom, I think I have enough clothes packed for a conference," Layne laughed as her mother, Morgan Davies, brought in yet another bag of new clothes from the trunk of her car. "I'm going to be late if you don't stop showing me gorgeous clothes. It's a nine-hour drive, and I need to go."

Layne's mother didn't seem worried, and as an only child, Layne was used to her mother's ways by now. She didn't have a sister or brother to take the attention of two very attentive and loving parents away from her. As a result, she had probably learned a lot at a young age. Her mother was a PR spin doctor and had brought Layne to work anytime she was home from school. Her father, Miles, was the CEO of his own company, and before that a team commander in the Special Forces. Which Special Force was up for debate. Her father had said Army Rangers, but Delta Force seemed more likely, although he never talked about it.

He simply taught her how to kill someone with her pinky by the time she was twelve.

However, the smothering love of her parents was the reason Layne was so excited for the business trip. Normally she would be nervous about presenting a speech at a medical conference on the use of some of her new techniques in physical therapy to treat wounded veterans, but not when it meant she'd be able to spend four days in Charleston, South Carolina. She'd splurged and rented a beach house on nearby Isle of Palms and was looking forward to some Layne time.

"It's Charleston," her mother said, pulling out a beautiful bright pink sundress. "In the summer. You need something pretty and breezy. Those doctors won't know what hit them."

Layne rolled her eyes. "So, that's why you bought all of the new clothes." Layne let out a long suffering groan. "I'm not going there to meet a husband. I'm going there to escape the pressure of meeting a man. And maybe, just maybe, find a hot man, have crazy sex, and *not* have Dad scare him away in the morning . . . or before we can even have sex."

Her mom dropped the bikini she was shoving along with the third dress and, admittedly, a cute pair of shoes, into Layne's already packed bag. "Um, well. I mean, I know you're twenty-nine and you've—" Morgan blushed under the same raven black hair as Layne. "And I know your father scares away all men, but I won't scare so easily. Even with shock tactics. So, find a sexy man, bang his brains out, and then marry him."

"I'm leaving," Layne said, frustrated as she tried to yank her bag away from her mother.

Her mother let go of the bag, but not before stuffing

another dress into it. "I love you. Have a great time, dear daughter."

Layne leaned over and kissed her mom's cheek. "I will. I'll see you in a few days."

Layne and her mother walked out of Layne's small house in Keeneston as her little white Maltese dog, Fluffy Puppy, followed. The daughter of a family friend had named him when he was a little white cotton ball of a puppy. The description fit, so Layne had kept it. She called him FP for short. His long flowing white hair was pulled away from his eyes with a small camouflage bow as the rest of his hair brushed along the grass before he spotted her father, Miles, leaning against her car. Fluffy Puppy yipped with joy and bounded toward her father.

"I see we're rat sitting," her father said, trying to hide the smile he had for FP. FP, on the other hand, was on his hind legs dancing around in a circle for her dad. Miles took her bag and carried it around to the back of her SUV. FP followed adoringly and her mother laughed. The little dog loved her dad and her dad secretly loved the little dog. He would come over in the middle of the day to walk FP, or possibly plant a bug to spy on his daughter, all without telling Layne. But Layne was her father's daughter and had her own spy equipment, which caught her father opening the front door and bending onto the ground to catch a running fur ball in his arms. Oh, her father may be a super soldier who, even at his age, was still in fighting shape, but give him a fluff ball of a dog and he was all baby talk.

"Now," her father said, coming to the driver's door. "I want you to be careful. Let us know when you get there."

"I will," Layne said before leaning out the window and kissing her mom once more and then her dad. "Wish me luck."

"You'll be wonderful," her mom gushed as Layne started the car.

"We're proud of you, Layne." Layne blew a kiss at her father before backing her car out of the driveway. When she looked back, her father had FP in his arms.

"Four stress-free days, here I come!"

~

CHARLESTON WAS HEAVEN. She'd woken to the sun streaming in her window and the sound of waves crashing along the shore. Inspired by the view, Layne had taken a run along the beach before exploring Boone Hall Plantation on her way into Charleston. That morning she was picking up her welcome package for the conference before going to a meeting with the board of doctors who had invited her to speak the next day. She'd follow that up with a little shopping on King Street and then spend the afternoon on the beach. And then dinner . . . oh, she was looking forward to dinner. Charleston was a town for foodies, and Layne wasn't a woman who shied away from food.

"Can I help you?" a woman behind registration asked.

"Davies, Layne Davies." Layne waited as the woman rifled through packets. She looked around the historic hotel's conference area. There was a vendor selling gourmet coffee and a small restaurant on the side opposite the row of doors leading to various meeting rooms. The lobby area was filled with men and women wearing matching lanyards.

"Ah, here we go, Dr. Davies. You're tomorrow morning's keynote speaker. Be here by eight-thirty; you go on at nine. You'll be in the main room right there." The woman pointed to a set of doors and then handed her a tote bag filled with all the materials she'd need for the conference.

"Thank you." Layne smiled as she stepped out of line and dug into the bag for her nametag. Yup, time to get used to answering to Dr. Davies. She had completed her Doctor of Physical Therapy degree years ago, or DPT as everyone called her degree, around the same time her cousin Piper received her Ph.D. Only Piper liked to play with viruses and nanotechnology while Layne liked to play with muscles and bones.

"Dr. Davies!"

Layne turned as she heard her name called. A group of men walked quickly toward her. Three were around her dad's age and the one waving was somewhere in his early thirties.

"I'm so glad we ran into you here. We were just on our way to meet you for brunch. We can walk over together. I'm Dr. Luke Benningford," the younger man said, holding out his hand.

"Oh! Well, thank you so much for suggesting me for the keynote. I'm interested to hear what you military doctors are seeing as areas we could work together on," Layne said, suddenly glad she'd worn one of the new dresses her mom picked out. Hello, Mister Conference Fun. And by the way Luke was checking her out, Layne thought this may be the best conference she'd ever attended.

WALKER SHOOK Captain Kyrkos's hand as Costa smiled and moved in for a hug. Walker wrapped his arms around the little man whom he'd spent the last thirteen days teaching English, and who had kept the infection at bay long enough for Walker to get home.

"Thank you, both, for saving my life."

With one last nod of thanks, Walker limped to the rail, swung a leg over, and climbed down toward the warm waters of Charleston Harbor. With a splash, Walker disappeared into the water before the captain docked his container ship for customs to board.

It felt good to be home, even if that meant swimming up the Cooper River. He'd grown up swimming these waters. And he knew where weekenders kept their boats. But it wasn't a boat he was after. Those would be noticed if he took one. No, it was one of those plastic kayaks he wanted.

Walker kept his stroke steady as he made his way across the river toward the apartments he knew many people stayed at on the weekends. When Walker he dragged himself out of the water, he realized how hurt he'd been, and despite the regimen he'd kept himself on, how out of shape this wound had made him.

Staggering up the sandy beach, Walker kept his eyes peeled, but no one was around at midnight on a weekday. It was easy to reach the cabana that housed the kayaks and took only seconds to pick the lock—thank you, U.S. Navy, for teaching him that trick. He picked out a dark red boat, and in less than three minutes, was back in the water, happily paddling toward home.

Walker spent an hour and a half winding his way up the Cooper River until he turned onto a small branch of the river. Shadows Landing wasn't far at that point. The small offshoot was wide and deep and meandered back to join the Cooper River farther up. That's what had made it perfect for bootlegging in the old days. Shadows Landing may might be small, but it had a colorful history. More importantly, Gavin's office and house were located right on the river.

Walker sniffed the air. He was home. No, it wasn't the

smell of the woods that gave it away, it was the smell of barbeque. The town had a barbeque rivalry to end all rivalries. Walker smiled at the scent. It had been two years since he was last home to visit. His life was in Virginia Beach now, but that hadn't stopped him from hanging out with Gavin. They met once a month at different beaches along the coast to surf or play golf and get caught up on all the hometown gossip.

Walker paddled harder as Gavin's dock came into view. He coasted up to it and reached for the ladder. As soon as his feet were on a rung, he kicked the kayak as hard as he could. The currents would take it back to Charleston.

Silently, Walker climbed the dock, unscrewed the light in the post to better hide in the shadows, and walked through the dark night to the house. Gavin kept a spare key hidden behind a surfboard bolted to the house with FAULKNER written across it. Reaching under the surfboard, Walker felt around until he found the key.

Gavin wasn't married, so that made breaking in easier. No pets. No wife. No problems. Walker closed and locked the door leading into the kitchen before creeping through the house. He found Gavin asleep on the couch with a movie's credits rolling on the television.

"Gavin," Walker hissed, looking around to make sure they really were alone. "Wake up."

"Do I have a patient?" Gavin muttered, pulling a blanket tighter around him.

"No, it's me, Walker. Wake up. There's an emergency."

Emergency was any doctor's trigger word. Gavin's moss green eyes popped open. "Walker? What the hell are you doing here? Alive? In my living room? In the middle of the night?"

"I'm in trouble," Walker said. Relief filled him as he sat in his friend's leather armchair. He finally had someone he could talk to.

"No shit. There've been guys here, looking for you. And the news has been reporting you're dead for *weeks*," Gavin said, jumping up.

"It took that long to swim the freaking Atlantic Ocean," Walker said as he closed his eyes and winced as he adjusted his leg.

"You're hurt." Gavin was already heading toward Walker's leg to examine it.

"Shot. Weeks ago. By that son of a bitch claiming to be a hero."

"Jud Melville shot you?" Gavin exclaimed as he motioned Walker to follow him into his adjoining office.

"Wait until you hear what else he did." Walker filled him in on the mission, the rescue, and his time on the Greek boat. By the time Walker was done, so was Gavin. He'd numbed the wound, cleaned it, debrided the lingering infection, and removed the shrapnel lodged in his leg.

"This Costa did a good job keeping it clean and feeding you antibiotics. Good thing he gave you a tetanus shot, too. Now let's feed you and think about how to handle this," Gavin said, holding out his arm to help Walker from the surgical table. What had been a dining room and a formal sitting room had been converted into his offices. The formal sitting room was an exam room and the dining room was a space for performing small surgical procedures. Gavin's cousin, Ridge, was a builder and had added a reception room on the side of the house, which led into the exam room.

They hobbled through the door connecting the surgery room to the rest of the house. The morning sunlight warmed the kitchen as Gavin brewed coffee and reheated some leftover pulled pork. "Can I stay here for a while? I need to heal before I can go after Jud and fix all the wrongs he committed."

"Of course. Have you called Edie yet?"

"Not yet. I thought I better be somewhere she could get to me before telling her I was alive."

Gavin smiled at that. "She's a force of nature, that's for sure. She'd have found a way to helicopter out to you." His smile slipped. "She called me. She was being pressured to have a service for you—to legally declare you dead. She wouldn't do it."

Walker smiled as the doorbell to the doctor's office buzzed through the house.

"I better get that. I'll be right back." Gavin wound his way through the house as Walker grabbed a fork and took a big bite of pulled pork.

"I'm telling you, you have no right to be here and if you don't leave this instant I'll call the sheriff."

Walker didn't freeze. He was already moving. He slipped silently into the garage and under Gavin's sports convertible before he even heard the footsteps he knew would be coming.

He didn't have to wait long. Three minutes later the door opened and booted steps stopped near him as the man opened the car door. "I told you, no one is here. The sheriff is on the way."

"The sheriff has no jurisdiction here. This is a military matter. You will notify me immediately if you hear anything from Walker Greene," a voice commanded.

"Walker Greene is dead. He died a hero. Why are you here?" Gavin demanded.

"I just need to make sure he's dead so he can be buried.

You never know when there's a traitor in your midst. This isn't public, but Walker Greene died a traitor."

4

"We need to get you out of here," Gavin said ten minutes later while pacing the kitchen.

"Just give me some supplies. I can hike out and steal a car a couple towns away," Walker said as he ate quickly.

"Not with your leg. You need—" Gavin paused and ran to the counter. He shoved some papers around and pulled out a booklet of some kind. "You need someone who specializes in rehabilitating wounds. Someone like this."

Gavin slammed the open booklet in front of Walker. He looked at a picture of a striking woman with black hair loosely curled around her shoulders, hazel eyes, and a girl-next-door smile. Under her picture it read, *Dr. Layne Davies, DPT*.

"This is the medical conference I'm going to this morning. She's speaking in two hours."

"And you think she'll help me? Do you know her?"

"Um," Gavin stalled. "Not technically. Hold on, I need to call the group."

"What do your sister and cousins have to do with this?"

"Everything," Gavin said before sending a group text.

"DAVIES, AS IN OUR COUSIN?" Gavin's sister, Harper, asked twenty minutes later. Everyone was there except Ryker Faulkner, who worked in Charleston and usually only came home on weekends.

"That's what you're most surprised about after hearing this whole thing?" Wade asked his cousin as he messed with his short, buzzed hair. Trent, Wade's brother, similarly shook his head at their cousin. "I've been asked by the Navy to search all incoming ships for stowaways. Now I know I was looking for my own friend." Wade was part of the Coast Guard, which was how Gavin knew when he needed to get off the container ship and where to swim to avoid detection.

"You poor thing," Tinsley said, squeezing his hand.

"What can we do?" Tinsley's brother, Ridge, asked.

Harper crossed her arms and looked worriedly at her family as Gavin pulled out the family scrapbook. "I know Great-aunt Marcy Faulkner, now Davies, doesn't want anything to do with us, but maybe this feud she had with our grandfathers and Great-Grammy won't matter to cousin Layne."

"Doesn't matter to me," Trent shrugged.

"Well, it matters to me. Great-Grammy said Marcy chose her husband over her family and didn't want anything to do with us. Why would this cousin of ours help our friend, someone in a very dangerous situation, when they've ignored us our whole lives?" Harped demanded.

Ridge let out a sigh. "Look, Harper, you're the youngest and were only ten when Great-Grammy died. She was the only one who made a big deal about it. I asked both my Grandpa Kevin and your Grandpa Scott decades ago, and they said it was just one of those things that happened over time. Marcy was happier in Kentucky and had her own life."

"Let's call them," Harper insisted.

"Harper, come on," Trent snapped. "You know both of them are at the nursing home and don't need this kind of stress."

"The way I see it," Tinsley said softly, "this isn't about Layne Davies, our cousin. This is about Dr. Layne Davies, the top doctor of physical therapy for veterans in the country. The real question remains—is there anyone better to take care of Walker?"

The room was silent. Walker didn't want to get into the middle of a family feud, but he needed help, and he needed it now. Further, Charleston sounded a lot safer than hanging around here. And, if he were honest, having someone as beautiful as Layne Davies nurse him back to health wasn't lost on him.

"She's the best," Gavin said simply.

"Then there's your answer," Wade said simply. "I have to go back to the base. You want me to take Walker?"

Gavin shook his head. "No. I'm scheduled to attend the conference, so no one will question me heading there or talking to Layne."

Ridge got up and walked out of the kitchen and into the living room. He picked up a book and headed back into the kitchen. "That guy is still out there."

Gavin grimaced and Walker knew what he was going to say before he said it. "How do you feel about riding in the trunk?"

"No problem. I'll climb in while you all say a very public goodbye. Thanks for all your help."

Tinsley was the first to hug him. "Stay safe. I'll be thinking of you."

"Me too," Harper said, joining in the hug.

Wade, Trent, and Ridge shook hands with him as they all walked slowly to the front door. The local anesthesia was wearing off and Walker's leg throbbed as he made his way to the garage. He hobbled to the trunk and sighed. It was so small. He opened it and shoved things aside before curling up on his side. He had to tuck his knees to his chest to fit. He closed the trunk and sat in the darkness trying not to concentrate on his wound. He heard people talking and then the garage door open from the outside.

Gavin was still calling out to his family as he got into the convertible and backed out of the garage. He pulled onto the street and then stopped again.

"Seriously? I'd like to see some identification," Walker heard Gavin say, his voice tight with barely controlled anger.

"Where are you going today, Dr. Faulkner?" the same man from before asked.

"Medical conference. Or maybe I just wear this annoying badge for fun."

"Come on, I need to get to the base!" Walker heard Wade yell before honking his horn.

"Keep a look out for Walker Greene and call me if you see him."

"Why would I look for a dead man?" Gavin asked again but didn't wait for an answer. He gunned his convertible, and at this speed, they'd be in Charleston in no time.

LAYNE FOLDED up her notes as she answered questions from the doctors surrounding the podium. Her speech had gone very well and the response was better than she'd hoped. Dr.

Benningford, or Luke, as he wanted Layne to call him, was beaming proudly beside her.

Speaking of proud . . . *Excellent speech! You nailed it. And who is Luke?* Dad! He'd activated the microphone again on her phone, only this time she was glad her parents listened to her speech. But now they had to go. Layne continued to answer questions as she reprogrammed her phone and set new passwords. It wouldn't keep her dad out forever, but it should hold him the rest of her trip.

"Let's get brunch and celebrate," Luke smiled at her as he placed his hand at the small of her back and guided her around the crowd.

"I'll be in the lobby during the break if anyone has any more questions. And my contact info is in the program," Layne told those still waiting to talk to her.

"I'd like to join you for brunch if you don't mind."

Layne looked up from resetting the final password on her phone to find a pair of green eyes looking at her. Layne was five foot eight, and this man had to be six foot two. His dark brown hair looked windblown, and unlike Luke, his body was muscled in a natural way that indicated he exercised outside of a gym. God, she loved Charleston. And the accent! That slow seduction sent her stomach flipping.

"Sure," Layne smiled as Luke frowned. Competition was good for him. "Layne Davies," she said, holding out her hand.

"Dr. Gavin Faulkner. It's a pleasure to meet you."

"You too." Layne grinned.

"I don't know if we can get a table for three," Luke said, suddenly sounding immature to Layne.

"I won't take much of your time. I actually have a case I'd like to discuss with Dr. Davies privately."

"Layne, please. My cousin Piper is the doctor in the family," she said, giving her best flirty smile.

"Medical?" Gavin asked, seeming to relax.

"PhD. She works with viruses and nanotechnology."

"Our table—"

Layne tried not to snap at Luke so instead she smiled sugar-sweet. He was a southern man. He should get the warning. "Why don't you get the table, and I'll be right there after I hear about this case Dr. Faulkner needs my help on." Luke tightened his jaw, but turned away without complaint. If only he'd chosen to flirt instead of pout, she would have acted on his interest. Now he seemed boyish compared to Gavin.

"Interesting family you have. A DPT and a PhD," Gavin said, leading her to a quiet corner of the lobby.

"Yes. And a big one." Layne rested her hand on Dr. Hottie's arm. "But it was really my dad who inspired my work. See, he was in Special Forces when he was younger and taught me firsthand how the injuries soldiers receive are very different than from what a normal ER would see. It really shaped me growing up, and that's why I do what I do. So, Dr. Faulkner . . . you know, I think I have family around here named that." She laughed as Gavin paled slightly. No! Oh, no, this couldn't be happening.

"Um," Gavin hedged.

"Do you have a Marcy Faulkner in your family tree? I can't remember what her brothers' names were, but I recall Grandma telling us they were in the Navy."

Gavin took a deep breath and Layne felt her stomach preparing to drop. "Actually, I'm your cousin. My Grandpa Scott is your grandmother's brother."

"Shit," Layne cursed as she felt her stomach plummet.

Gavin's face got red as he put his hands on his hips. "Just

because you want nothing to do with us doesn't mean we're bad people. And I have someone who needs serious help, so I won't let this stupid feud prevent him from getting the help he needs."

Layne stopped shaking her head and held up her hand to stop his rant. "Wait, what? Grandma always hoped to know you. She made my uncles look you up online. It was your grandfather, great-uncle, and especially our great-grandmother, who didn't want to have anything to do with my grandmother."

That stopped him. Damn right it should. It was his family's fault for the rift, not hers.

"Then why did you curse if it wasn't because we're the dreaded Faulkners?" Gavin asked, confused.

"First a priest and then my own cousin," Layne muttered as she buried her face in her hands.

"Okay, I'm confused."

Layne peeked over her fingertips at her cousin. "I hit on a priest without knowing he was one. Now I'm flirting with my own cousin. My family is never going to let me live this down."

Gavin's lips twitched as he fought the smile.

"Go on, give in," Layne said, letting the humor of the situation outweigh the embarrassment.

Gavin tossed his head back and laughed long and hard. Layne's own lips turned upward as she shook her head. "I swear, I have the worst luck, and I will do whatever it is you need my help with if you swear you won't tell anyone about what just happened."

Gavin stopped laughing and held out his hand. "Deal." They shook and Layne looked back into the restaurant to see Luke pretending not to watch. "But what you do mean by 'my grandfather's fault'? Great-Grammy always told us

Great-Aunt Marcy chose her husband over her family and didn't want anything to do with us."

Layne's head shook automatically. "That's not what happened. Great-Grandma hated Marcy. She was cruel to her. She constantly berated her and told her she wasn't important. Uncle Scott and Uncle Kevin were what mattered. My grandmother had fallen in love with my grandfather and Great-Grandma didn't care. She just expected my grandmother to leave the love of her life because your grandfather got married or something. For the first time in her life, my grandmother didn't give in and do what was expected of her. She married my grandfather the second she turned eighteen. They've been together ever since. They had five sons and one daughter. My dad, Miles, is the oldest of the six children."

Gavin was quiet for a moment as he took in what she said. Layne wondered if he'd argue with her, but hearing what little she had, Layne was willing to bet their great-grandmother had caused the rift and kept it going, either for attention or to feel superior. Layne didn't know which, but her grandmother had described her mother as a very cruel-hearted woman who believed only sons had value. Layne and her cousins had always thought it an exaggeration, but now she wasn't so sure.

"It sounds as if there is a lot of family history that needs to be cleared up, but now isn't the time to hash it out." Gavin paused and looked back at Luke sitting in the open restaurant across the lobby. "I hate to keep your date waiting, but this is of a pressing nature."

Layne pulled out her cell phone and sent Luke a text to eat without her. She promised him she'd see him in an hour and then looked at her cousin. "I'm all yours for an hour. Tell me about this case."

5

Layne should have seen the family resemblance. Gavin looked a lot like Ryan and Wyatt, except he had green eyes instead of Grandpa Jake's hazel ones. He even carried himself with utter confidence like her cousins did.

"You say it was untreated for two weeks?" Layne asked as they stood in the Charleston heat. Tourists, Citadel cadets, and locals walked by as they talked. A man played a saxophone a block away on the steps of one of the many historical churches. Even though Layne wanted to listen and enjoy her time in this great city, Gavin's case had captured her interest.

"Yes. He, um, was on a vessel that didn't have a surgeon. But he was treated as best as he could have been."

Layne rolled her eyes. "Look, Gavin, I know you don't know me and probably distrust me based on our family history, but I know the military. I know classified information, and I know injuries. I also know that while you're not lying to me, you're leaving some very important details out. You may think I'm some hick from Kentucky, but

I can say with certainty, whatever it is this man has gone through, there is absolutely no way it'll shock me."

Gavin was quiet as he glanced down the street. Layne followed his eyes to a convertible and a man leaning against it. The man didn't look military, which told her he was special ops. His sable brown hair was similarly windblown to her cousin's and his muscled arms were crossed over a very muscled chest. Plus he was favoring his left leg.

"Or we could just go ask him," Layne suggested.

Gavin shot her a look and then back to the man. "How did you know?"

"Like I said, my dad and two uncles were Special Forces. My guess has always been Delta Force. Another uncle was a spy. I have a whole bunch of neat tricks up my sleeves. I'll help him, but I need the truth."

The man's head turned toward her in that instant, and his electric blue eyes pinned her to where she stood. Layne wouldn't have been able to move if her life depended on it. She surveyed the man as much as he surveyed her before he looked away.

"Then let's go meet him, but I have to have your word you won't tell anyone about him. Not Luke, not someone asking questions at the conference, not a police officer who pulls you over for speeding. No one," Gavin said, grabbing her hands and making her look at him.

"You have my word, Gavin. And to me, that means everything."

WALKER HAD THOUGHT Dr. Davies was attractive in her picture. In real life, she took his breath away. She looked back to Gavin, and then a second later they headed toward him. Walker guessed the good doctor was in.

He pushed himself off of the car and grimaced as the muscles in his leg knotted up. His leg worked, but it hurt, and especially after being in the trunk for part of the trip to Charleston. He only hoped the doc was half as talented as she was beautiful then he'd be ready to take on Jud in no time.

"I haven't told Dr. Davies anything yet," Gavin called out when they got within ten feet. "I'm leaving it up to you if you want to or not. She does believe she can help you."

"Where's the injury?" she asked. Her voice was light, with just a hint of a southern accent but full of confidence. The way she asked the question sounded more like an order, and Walker found himself answering automatically.

"Hmm, can you roll your pant leg up that high? I'd like to talk a look at it," Dr. Davies said, not taking her eyes off his leg. She took in the way he was favoring it, the way he wobbled, and the way he grimaced.

"It's a little high for that, Doc."

Her eyes flew up to his, and Walker saw the similarities to her Shadows Landing cousins. While her eyes were hazel, what green was in them was the same color as Gavin's. "How rude of me. I haven't introduced myself. Layne Davies," she said, holding out her hand. Walker paused, not knowing if he should use his real name or not. "My father was Special Forces if that helps you decide if you want to use your real name or not. I know how to keep a secret."

That both reassured Walker and worried him, but everything about Layne Davies screamed trustworthy. He didn't doubt for one second she could keep his identity a secret. But did he really want to drag her into something so dangerous?

"Okay, how about this," Layne started, "let me examine you and see what we're working with. You be honest with me about that, and I'll be honest with you about recovery. Then, if you feel more comfortable with me, you can tell me your name and what kind of trouble you're in. I will tell you, I won't blink an eye at whatever it is. I may not be a soldier, but I've seen plenty of action."

"In Kentucky?" Gavin asked as if she were telling a joke.

Layne smiled slowly and suddenly Walker worried about embarrassing himself if he had to take off his pants in front of her.

"Oh, you have no idea how much goes on in Keeneston," she said with a smile that made him think he was on the outside of an inside joke.

"You have a deal, Dr. Davies," Walker said.

"Layne, please. Is there anywhere we can go for an exam? I would offer my hotel room, but I rented a beach house on the Isle of Palms."

Gavin nodded. "Yeah, my cousin Ryker has an office a couple blocks away. We can go there."

"Gav," Walker warned. Ryker owned a shipping company along the Cooper River just a mile from downtown. And right now shipping companies were being searched for one Walker Greene.

"He has an office on Bay Street," Gavin said reassuringly, and Walker nodded. That would be very close and not as watched as the shipping yards.

"Then let's go. It'll be fun to meet a new cousin," Layne said with something near excitement and worry. If what Walker heard this morning were true, Ryker was the last cousin Layne should meet. Even Harper would be nicer.

LAYNE REMINDED herself to breathe as she followed Gavin to his cousin's office. The soldier struggled next to her, but

Layne knew better than to offer assistance. Soldiers like him would see it as an insult.

"Here we are," Gavin said as he pushed open a dark green door along the bluestone sidewalk in historic Charleston. The old house converted to offices was painted a Charleston blue/green color and a white sign hanging on iron over the door read *Faulkner Shipping*. "Don't worry about Ryker. He's usually at the shipping yard at this time of the morning."

"Yet here I am."

Layne tore her eyes from the historic maps of Charleston Harbor lining the entranceway to see a pair of cold green eyes narrowed at her. This was a man used to getting his way. A strict man who held his power in his coldness. Too bad for him, his stare had nothing on her father's.

"Hello, cousin!" Layne smiled extra wide just to needle him. She wasn't one to run and enjoyed the momentary shock in Ryker's face.

Layne was pretty sure Gavin's mouth hit the floor as she wrapped her arms around a frozen Ryker Faulkner. Her head only came to his chest, but she squeezed for all she was worth and discovering, contrary to his icy demeanor, Ryker was, in fact, warm-blooded.

"I'm Layne Davies, your cousin from Kentucky. It's so great to meet you." Layne smiled as she stepped back from Ryker. "But, now I need an office to examine my patient, so we'll have to play catch-up later." Layne patted his shoulder, grabbed the soldier by the hand, hauled him past a stunned secretary and into what she guessed was Ryker's personal office, and shut the door on her cousins. Not that being alone in a room with the soldier let her breathe any easier, but Layne turned off her hormones as she set her bag on the massive mahogany desk.

"Okay, mister. Take off your pants and have a seat. Let me see what kind of injury we're working with." Layne kept her back turned as she dug through her bag for a pair of latex gloves. She could tell he stood still for a moment before deciding to trust her. She heard his pants hit the floor and her face flushed. Taking a deep breath and putting on a clinical eye, Layne turned around.

The man sat in the dark brown leather chair with his injured leg outstretched. Layne's eyes went straight to the wound. In seconds, she was on her knees in front of him manipulating his leg this direction and that. The soldier would never tell her what hurt, but she could read his body well enough to get all the answers she needed.

"No fever?" Layne asked as she felt the muscles and soft tissue around the injury.

"Not anymore. The injury was three weeks ago. It was unattended for one week. By that time it was infected, and I was delirious. I was then able to get treatment. The wound was cleaned, and I was put on antibiotics. However, Gavin had to go back in and remove some debris that was preventing healing. He's done that and now I'm good to go."

Layne gave a brief chuckle under her breath. "You're not good to go. You're alive. But you need a lot of work on this leg to get it back to full use. I'll start with a compression wrap, then you'll need massage, specific exercises, stretching, and electrotherapy. You've had severe muscle damage at the wound site and your leg muscles have begun to atrophy."

"Can you help me? I need to get back to fighting shape."

Layne stood and looked down at him. "I can help you, but you have to help me. I need your name, who you are getting back into fighting shape to kill, and why it looks like you were shot by a military weapon. I'm guessing it was friendly fire since you're not reporting it and sitting in a base hospital somewhere getting treatment."

"It was anything but friendly," he muttered. "And I should warn you, if you're found helping me it could be trouble for you. It's only fair to let you walk away when all I can do is bring danger to your door."

"Then you picked the right doctor. Danger is something I can handle."

The man looked down to her soul. He searched her out and after several long seconds he seemed to see Layne was telling the truth. Her father had trained her for danger her whole life, and the threat of it only made her more determined to help.

"Then I'll take you up on it, doc. My name is Walker Greene."

6

The pretty doctor probably didn't mean to gasp, but she did. "You're supposed to be dead." Before he could reply with a smartass comment, he saw the wheels turning in her head. "Jud Melville tried to kill you," she stated as if it was clear as day.

Once again this woman left him stunned. "How did you possibly guess that?"

She shrugged and shoved her long black hair away from her face. "Easy. You don't want anyone to know you're alive, which means you were shot by someone you know. The only person alive from the mission you were on is your team leader, which means he's the one you're hiding from, and the only reason you'd do that is if he shot you."

"He killed the rest of my team," Walker found himself admitting. He thought she'd scream, deny it, say it wasn't so, but instead she just nodded.

"We figured something was fishy about that operation."

"We?"

"My father and I. As I said, he's former Special Forces.

When he listened to Melville's account of the mission, he said it didn't sound right."

Walker didn't know what to say. He wasn't expecting to be believed. "Thank you for believing me. And for helping me. There's one more thing you should know. There's someone looking for me."

"Figures, since your body was the only one not recovered. Melville wants to make sure you stay dead and buried. Well then, I guess we'd better keep you out of sight. I have to stay for one more day, then we can leave." Layne tore off her gloves and shoved them back into her bag as if this was no big deal.

Walker had the feeling he was suddenly no longer in control. "Leave?"

Layne nodded as she turned around and faced him. She seemed so innocent, how could he bring her into this? "We leave for Kentucky day after tomorrow."

"Kentucky? Wait," Walker said, struggling to sit up and pull up his pants. Layne instantly bent and handed him his pants. He saw her eyes heat up as they moved up his leg and past his wound before her face flushed and she looked away.

"Yes, the best place for you is at my home. I have all the equipment I'll need to start your rehabilitation. Melville and his minions won't think to look for you there. Plus, there's no place safer than Keeneston if they do manage to locate you. But right now, here's the key to my house I'm renting. I'll give Gavin the address. I have to get back to the conference. Lucky for you, there're more reps there than I can shake a fist at, so I can get a ton of stuff to bring back tonight to begin your treatment."

Walker reached out and grabbed Layne's hand as she moved to open the door. "Thank you."

She smiled at him, and Walker felt as if his whole world brightened. "Are you armed?"

Walker blinked and then smiled. This woman may be the death of him if he wasn't careful, because right now she seemed too good to be true. "No. I'm not."

Layne appeared shocked, but then she reached into her bag and pulled out a folding knife and tossed it to him. It was a freaking SOG knife. Who was this girl next door with a military blade in her purse?

"Sorry, but my guns are in the car. This will do for now. I assume you know how to use it."

If Walker were less of a man, he might be insulted. Instead he laughed. "Yeah, I think I can figure it out." The door opened as Gavin and Ryker practically shoved their way inside. "Is everything okay?" Gavin asked, looking from a perfectly unruffled Layne to him laughing.

"Yes," Layne smiled. "Can you drive Walker to my place? I'll start working with him as soon as I can leave the conference. We'll leave the day after tomorrow for Keeneston."

"We?" Ryker asked suspiciously as Layne filled him in on her plan.

"Mr. Faulkner, a man who says he's investigating the death of a Mr. Greene is here to speak with you. I'm afraid he doesn't have an appointment and won't leave." Walker shot a gaze to the closed office door as Ryker's secretary spoke over the intercom. Layne was already on the move. She had the window open and was motioning for him to hurry and join her.

Without question, Walker moved. There was something about Layne that invoked complete trust. "Take my car. It's parked in the back," Ryker whispered, handing the keys to

Gavin. "Drop Walker off and then come back. Leave the keys under the back tire."

Gavin nodded and Layne gave Ryker a wink. Walker saw Ryker shake his head, but his lips had twitched upward. His newfound cousin was beginning to make a dent in Ryker's wall.

It hurt hopping out the window, but Layne was there to help steady him. She didn't make a big deal about it, but she wrapped a surprisingly strong arm around him and practically propelled him into the back of the SUV. "Stay lying down until you're out of town. I'll see you in a couple hours."

With that, she silently closed the door and disappeared down the alley before Gavin had even left the small parking lot. "That sure is some cousin you have," Walker said from the floor of the backseat.

"It sure is. I'm starting to think my Great-Grammy caused some trouble that wasn't warranted. If the rest of the family is anything like Layne, I think we'll get along just fine."

Gavin stopped talking as he made his way down East Bay Street toward the Ravenel Bridge. It was hard to put his trust into someone he didn't know, but Layne Davies was a person Walker could trust with his life. Only this time he was putting it to the test.

"LUKE, you wouldn't believe the infection. Can you imaging hitting your leg with an axe and not getting treatment? I prescribed a physical therapy routine, but the old man may never walk without assistance again," Layne said, shaking her head as she took a sip of sweet tea. Luke had waited in the restaurant, and Layne had found herself lying easily to the man who no longer held any appeal for her.

"Do you want to come out to dinner with us tonight? There're a couple of great people I think you should meet," Luke asked, no longer wanting to talk about Gavin Faulkner.

"I don't think so. I'm exhausted and talked out," Layne smiled as she took another sip of her drink. "I didn't know conferences were so taxing. I'm kind of glad tomorrow is the last day. However, I will miss Charleston. I have fallen in love with it here."

Luke smiled and jumped at the opening she'd inadvertently given him. "Then you must come back to visit me, er, here. Next month is restaurant week. If you think the food you've had so far is good, it's nothing compared to all the restaurants trying to outdo each other for local awards." Layne's stomach agreed, but it wasn't fair to lead Luke on when her mind hadn't been able to get the image of Walker Greene standing in front of her out of her head. Piper, Reagan, and Riley, three of Layne's cousins back home, had teased her that all her pent-up sexual frustration would cause her to do something rash, like hit on a priest or an unknown cousin. Right now she agreed with them. Layne was having a very difficult time not thinking of all the things she wanted to do with Walker Greene.

"What is it?" Luke asked.

"Hmm?"

"You sighed out loud. Sad about leaving me, er, Charleston?"

"Oh, I was just thinking of the long drive back home. Maybe I'll leave tomorrow night to break it up."

"You can't do that! You'll miss the Medical Ball."

Luke may have been horrified at that prospect, but Layne thought it sounded pretty good. Out of the corner of

Layne's eye, she saw Gavin talking to someone in the lobby. He must have just gotten back, but he looked irritated. The man he was talking to didn't look like a doctor. Instead he looked like someone from the military, presumably looking for Walker.

"If you'll excuse me, Luke, I want to make it to the two-o'clock panel." Layne hurried from her table and straight at the man obviously bugging her cousin.

"I told you, I've been here all day. I just got out of a panel on wound care."

Layne pretended to trip and as she fell, she latched onto the man bugging her cousin. He was tall, lean, and had military police written all over him. Although, what was interesting was that he was older than the typical MPs.

"Oh my gosh, I'm so sorry!" Layne said, pulling the man's wallet from his pants pocket and slipping his business card from it before silently dropping his wallet to the ground. "Is this yours?" she said, bending to pick it up. The man looked at her suspiciously as he opened his wallet to make sure everything was still in it. Layne didn't pay him any more attention.

"Dr. Faulkner, what did you think of that last panel? Your question on wound packing was something I was wondering about, too." Layne looked seriously at Gavin as if she hasn't spent the afternoon with him.

"Thank you. I was just telling this man about the panel."

"Dr. Faulkner was in the previous panel, you say?"

Layne looked at him confused. "Yes. And he asked an excellent question." Layne turned away from the man and back to Gavin. "Are you attending the next panel, Dr. Faulkner? I'd love to hear your thoughts on it."

"Excuse me," Gavin said to the man before turning toward Layne and opening the door to the conference room.

"I think you may want to skip the last day of the conference," Gavin whispered as they took their seats.

"I was thinking the same thing."

WALKER STARED out over the ocean as the sun set behind him. His game plan had been to recover and get revenge. Now that he had the recovery part planned out, he turned his mind to revenge. He'd found a tablet and a laptop in the house but couldn't crack the security on either one. Instead, he'd been forced to turn on the 24-hour news stations. He'd spent hours listening to them. As he clicked through the stations, he found Jud doing everything from interviews on the news stations to daytime talk shows to appearing on one of the late night shows.

Jud had signed a multimillion-dollar book deal and it was rumored the film rights had already been snatched up for another couple million. He'd gotten the fame he wanted, but what had happened to the shipment of goods that disappeared? The crew of the ship had been found locked in a hold after it had been cleared out of some of the gold. Some platinum, all of the diamonds, and other gems were missing, too. All told, the ship's owner filed an insurance claim for one hundred million dollars. What had Jud done with the goods? Who was he working with? Couldn't be the pirates since he killed them all.

"How's your leg feeling after walking in the sand?"

Walker turned around and found Layne standing there in a violet bikini with a pair of black shorts on. She dropped two towels and a bag onto the sand next to him. "It's sore," Walker admitted.

"There's a study that shows exercise, especially low impact, helps cut down the time for wounds to heal."

"Does that mean we're going for a run?" Walker grimaced at the idea.

"Nope. It means we're going for a swim." She reached into her bag and tossed him a pair of navy-blue swim trunks with little green palm trees embroidered on them and turned around. "Put those on, and let's start getting you feeling better."

The house was on the end of the Isle of Palms in a private community. At this time of evening, everyone was inside having dinner. They were the only ones on the beach as Walker stripped off his pants and boxer briefs and stepped into the swim trunks.

"Do they fit?"

"Yeah, thanks. I don't really have any clothes with me."

Layne turned around and pointed to the bag on the sand. "I picked you up a pair of jeans, some athletic shorts, and a couple T-shirts. I guessed your size, but if the swim trunks fit, I think you'll be good."

"Thank you. I was getting tired of wearing the same thing," he said as he pulled off the worn and dirty T-shirt Costa had given him. He smiled to himself as he caught Layne staring. "So, what's first?"

Layne reached into her bag of tricks and stuck a waterproof bandage over his leg and smiled. "We swim. Doesn't have to be hard swimming, just enough to get the blood flowing."

Layne slipped her arm around his waist without saying a word. Walker felt foolish for leaning into her, and it wasn't because of his leg. He'd had his fair share of women. There were bars in Virginia Beach crawling with Frog Hogs, women who enjoyed the hunt of discovering and sleeping with SEALs. He couldn't disappoint them, after all. But the feeling of Layne's hand resting on his waist was more erotic than any of the stripper-like moves the Frog Hogs pulled off. Walker wasn't one to fall in love, but he could admit he was lusting for his cute physical therapist. Especially when the side of her breast brushed against him, making him think about slowly removing that bikini top and . . . Walker leapt into the water to cool his thoughts.

7

"Don't be such a baby," Layne said with a roll of her eyes. "It's a king-sized bed and you need good rest after the workout I gave you."

They had ended up swimming for an hour, and then Layne had helped Walker back to the one-bedroom cottage she was renting. She'd stretched and worked the muscles of his leg, cleaned the wound, and put a compression wrap on it. She'd also argued with him when she'd handed him a pair of crutches. Ultimately she'd gotten her way. Especially when she told him he didn't have to use them all the time. Only when his leg needed rest. But now it was time to go to bed and the stubborn man was trying to sleep on a couch that wasn't long enough for him.

"Are you a virgin? Is that why sleeping in a bed with me scares you?" Layne asked, knowing she was pushing him. The only other option was for her to sleep on the couch and, really, she would much rather sleep in a bed with a sexy man and pretend he desired her.

"A virgin?" Walker sputtered. "I was trying to be respectful."

"No, you were trying to be stubborn. Now, get into bed."

"Yes, ma'am," Walker said as he hung his head. Wow, this could really damage a girl's ego, Layne thought as she slid into bed and rolled onto her side, facing away from him.

"Goodnight," she said as she reached for the light and turned it off.

"Goodnight, Layne."

Layne practically groaned. A voice like that should be outlawed. Now she understood the panty-dropper hitting Keeneston who was mysteriously leaving panties all around town. But if Walker spoke sexy words to her in that deep, smooth accent, then her panties would drop, too.

THAT NIGHT LAYNE dreamed of Walker, his words, his voice caressing her, his rough hands cupping her breasts . . . Layne's eyes shot open. She wasn't dreaming. Or at least she wasn't dreaming about Walker's hand on her breast.

Walker had her tucked tight against him. Her head was on one of his arms and the other arm was flung over her side and cupping her breast. She also felt something very insistently pressing against her ass.

"Walker? I need to get up," Layne said even as she snuggled closer to him. She rubbed against his erection and his hand tightened over her breast, his fingers playing with her taut nipple.

"Hmm? Crap!" Walker yelled as he pushed her away. Layne shrieked as she rolled off the bed and landed with a thud on the ground. "Damn, I am so sorry."

Walker's head appeared over the edge of the bed and looked down at her. "That'll give a girl a complex," Layne muttered. "Wait, have you talked to my dad?"

"What? No, I don't even know your dad."

"Have you gotten an anonymous message threatening castration for touching me?"

Walker's brow creased, and he looked at her strangely. "Did you hit your head?"

"You mean when you were so horrified at finding yourself touching me that you shoved me out of bed without receiving a single threat? No, I didn't hit my head. But I now wish I had," Layne muttered as she stood up and darted into the bathroom, completely humiliated.

WELL, he screwed that up. Walker listened as the shower ran and flopped back against the pillows. He didn't want Layne to think he was taking advantage of her. That's why he pushed away from her. He didn't mean to push her off the bed. He felt like a complete idiot. But what did her dad have to do with it?

Walker pulled his knee to his chest and then straightened it out. He began the exercises Layne had taught him to do four times a day as he thought of a way to apologize. The door opened and Layne darted out wrapped in a towel.

"Sorry, I forgot to grab my clothes," she mumbled as she grabbed a dress from a hanger and ran back into the bathroom.

"Layne," Walker called out as he grimaced as he stood up. "I'm sorry. I didn't mean anything by it. I was just surprised."

The door was flung open and Layne walked out in a beautiful dark pink dress. Her wet hair was tied up in some sort of twist thingy. "I'll make an appearance at the conference while you swim in the pool. No ocean swimming when I'm not here. I don't want you to cramp. I'll be back in a couple hours, and we'll be on our way to Kentucky by lunchtime. Okay?"

"Sure," Walker said, slightly defeated. Layne wasn't about to forgive him and maybe that was a good thing. He needed to focus on healing and his plan to take Jud down, not the completely breathtaking woman who caused his heart to speed up and other parts to, um, throb.

"Great," Layne said with a fake smile as she practically ran from the cottage.

"Hey! Can I have the password to your tablet? I want to do some research," Walker called out as he wobbled after her.

Layne spun around, grabbed the tablet from his hands, pulled something up, and started typing before shoving it back at him. "There. You can get on the internet, but everything else is password protected."

"It's like you don't trust me."

"Said the man who shoved me out of bed."

Walker took the hit as Layne slammed the car door and was already a mile down the road before he could say anything. He was going to have to try to explain himself better when he saw her that afternoon. Walker sighed and took the tablet inside. After making a fresh batch of coffee, he sat down and began searching the news.

What's the matter? Why did you take down your password? Have you been hacked?

What? Walker looked at the messages popping up on the screen and then suddenly the green light turned on and a video call popped up.

"Who the hell are you?"

Walker stared at the older man who must have been the one sending the messages. "Who are you?"

"The dad."

Oh, this was starting to make sense. "I'm the patient."

The man's eyes narrowed, and Walker shivered. It was as if the man could reach through the screen and choke the life from Walker without blinking an eye. This man was scary.

"My daughter doesn't have any patients in Charleston. And you're not in Charleston; you're in Isle of Palms. And according to the IP address I just traced, you're at my daughter's house. Put Layne on now."

"She's not here, sir. She's at her conference," Walker gulped.

"Then what the fu—"

"Miles Davies! Get off your daughter's computer right this second!"

A woman with hair the color of Layne's appeared on screen, only hers was streaked with a little silver.

"But he's looking up—"

"I don't care what he's looking up." The woman turned to the computer and flashed an apologetic smile. "I'm so sorry, young man. My, what a handsome man you are. Anyway, we'll let you get back to it."

The man and woman glared at each other, but the woman won out when the man gave Walker one last snarling glare before hanging up. Walker was left staring at the tablet wondering if Mr. Davies were going to pop back on. He was already tracing what Walker was looking up, which worried him enough to set down the tablet. However, with resignation, Walker realized it was better for Mr. Davies to know what he was researching than anyone else. And if something did happen to him or Layne, at least her father would know where to point the investigation.

With resolve, Walker picked the tablet back up and began looking over Jud's schedule, his social media accounts, and digging around his connections to find a link

between Jud and the man Layne had discovered was private
security.

"WHAT ARE YOU STILL DOING HERE?" Gavin hissed as they
walked through the lobby toward the morning panel
together.

"Luke is creating a fuss, and I didn't want him to make
such a big one that Mr. Snyder took notice to my absence.
I'm leaving after this panel," Layne said, making sure to
smile and wave at the people around her.

Gavin looked back to where Darrel Snyder, the private
security Layne pickpocketed, stood in the lobby, watching
the comings and goings as if Walker would just magically
show up at a medical conference. "You'd better not be seen
with me anymore."

"My contact info is in the program. Feel free to call me
anytime. I'm really glad we got to meet, Cousin Gavin,"
Layne said with a wink before waving down a doctor she'd
met the first day.

Layne made sure she talked to as many people as
possible before the panel started. Luke made sure to sit next
to her as the panel began. Right on cue, her phone buzzed
with a text message from her cousin Piper. She'd called
Piper and ordered the emergency text.

*Really bad traffic predicted for tomorrow. Some festival in
Charleston. You may want to leave early.*

Layne leaned over to Luke and showed him the text
message. "What festival?"

"It's this big tour of homes. People come from all over
the South," Luke whispered back.

Layne let her face fall as she looked worried. "I have a

patient tomorrow afternoon that I can't miss. I'd better leave today."

"Today? But—"

"I'm so sorry, but I'd feel better if I did. Want to do an early lunch before I head out?"

"Sure," Luke said, the offer of lunch placating him.

LAYNE IGNORED Gavin for the rest of her time at the conference. She ate a quick lunch and tried not to appear too eager to leave. She promised Luke she'd stay in touch and pretended to leave reluctantly.

By noon, she was driving up the small driveway to the cottage to pack for the trip home. Layne was confident in her skills. She knew she'd be able to help Walker heal his leg, but she'd also been around enough soldiers at the VA to know that the mental trauma of having your team killed in front of you by a trusted leader was going to have a bigger impact on him. Right now he was focused on hunting Jud and healing his leg, but when all that was done, Walker was going to have to face his nightmares. Layne wondered if he'd let her be the one to help him through this trauma after he shoved her away from him.

SHE TURNED off the car and looked at the cottage. The door opened and Walker came to stand on the deck. He smiled tentatively at her and Layne wondered if he was trying to play nice so she'd treat his leg or if he really felt bad about kicking her out of bed.

"I met your father." Walker smiled, albeit a little wobbly.

Good. She hoped her dad made him piss himself. "What can I say? I'm a daddy's girl," Layne said with a shrug even as she was mentally composing the nasty text she was going to send her dad for snooping.

"Your mom seems nice."

"She can be scarier than my dad. She just wants grandchildren, so I'm sure she was on her best behavior." There, that should scare him a little more. "Yeah, she's desperate to get me married off—apparently that includes to a complete stranger." Layne smiled to herself as Walker paled a little. She was going to put the fear of her parents into him, not because she didn't like him, but because she did. She'd been drawn to him instantly. After this morning, it was clear the feelings were one-sided and she needed a major divider between them to protect her heart. She was already in lust with Walker; she didn't need to fall in love with him. And there was no bigger buffer than her parents. Talk of marriage, children, and her father's threatening antics was better than a cold shower to every man she dated.

"That must be nice to have parents that love you so much. It's just my sister and me now," Walker said, holding the door open for her.

Layne walked into the cottage feeling like a bitch. She hadn't known he had lost his parents. And while Layne sometimes felt the pressure of her parents, it was all because they loved her so much. "I'm sorry. I didn't know you lost your parents. Or that you had a sister. Where is she?"

"Edie is in Virginia Beach. She was married to my best friend, Shane Wecker."

Layne covered her mouth with her hand. "The news didn't report that she was also your sister. Oh my gosh, does she know you're alive?"

Walker shook his head. "After Darrel Snyder began looking for me, I didn't dare contact her. It's tearing me apart, not being there to console her. A widow at thirty, and now she thinks she lost not only her husband, but also her only family."

"You need to let her know. I can get you an untraceable phone."

"How could you get that?"

"Oh, I have my connections," Layne said, thinking of her family.

"Thank you, but not yet. The only way she's safe is if she thinks I'm dead. She already refused to declare me dead since they haven't found a body. I don't want to bring any attention or danger to her."

"I'm sorry, Walker. I know you probably won't take me up on the offer, but you can trust me if you feel like talking. It's a nine-hour ride to Keeneston, after all." Layne shoved the last of her clothes into her bag, not bothering to fold them. Walker leaned down and picked the bag up. "I'll get it. I don't want any pressure on your leg," Layne said quickly.

"Thanks, doc, but I've got it. See, I'm even using a crutch." In one hand, he carried one of her bags and with the other he picked up one of his crutches and used it to help him down the stairs and out to the car.

Layne picked up the other bag and did a quick look around the cottage, making sure she didn't leave anything behind. When she turned from locking the door, she looked to where Walker was holding the driver's door open for her. The sun shone in his hair, causing it to shimmer as brightly as his eyes. Damn. She needed to build those walls or she was in for the mother of all heartbreaks.

8

Layne and Walker drove in silence until they reached Columbia, South Carolina. Finally, she felt as if she could breathe a sigh of relief. She hadn't noticed any cars following her as they made their way west. It was time for a break. She normally wasn't one to stop after a couple hours of driving, but for the past twenty minutes, Walker had been quietly massaging his leg.

"What are you doing?" Walker asked as she pulled off the interstate.

"I thought I would top off the gas and get some snacks for the car. Do you want to pump the gas or get the snacks?"

"I'll pump the gas. But get me something with chocolate," he called out as she got out of the car.

"I wouldn't peg you as a sweets guy," Layne said, watching him hobble around the car. She inserted her credit card and he lifted the pump.

"I'm nothing but sweet." He grinned and gave her a wink.

Wall. Big, big wall was what she needed. Layne gave him a half smile and took off for the convenience store. In minutes, she was back with bottles of water and an array of snacks. Walker finished up while she put the bags into the car. "How is your leg feeling?"

"Tight." Walker grimaced as he moved without his crutch.

"Walk into the restroom and back. You need to warm it up if you don't want it cramping. Then when you get back, make sure to put your seat back all the way and see if you can get your foot up on the dash for a little stretch."

Walker didn't argue; instead he turned and hobbled away. By the time he was back in the car, he was looking better. "Why did you want to become a physical therapist?"

Layne got back on the interstate and tossed a chocolate bar to Walker before answering. "My dad suffered from PTSD. He got involved with therapy dogs. Since I was a little kid, I would join him at the hospital to visit soldiers with our dog. When I was eight or so, I saw a woman working with a soldier who had lost his ability to walk after being injured in an IED explosion. I watched the triumph in their eyes the first time he took a step after months of hard work. Over the next year, I watched them work together, and I was there when he walked out of the hospital. I wanted to do that. I wanted to help. To give hope where hope had been taken away. I can't make everyone better, but if I can improve a life in any small way, it's a job well done."

"That's you. I'm not surprised at all. You're someone who wills people to get better. I can tell by the way you're already looking out for me. So, you work solely with veterans?" Walker asked, letting Layne out of responding to his nice words about her.

"No. I wish I could, but I do all my work with veterans pro bono. In order to afford to do that, I'm on staff with the

Lexington Thoroughbreds," Layne said. "Plus, I have my own clinic."

"You work for a professional football team?"

"Yeah. One of my best friends is the team's sports psychologist. Her father owns the team along with another family friend. And the dad of the kids I used to babysit is the coach."

"Seriously? Are you talking about Trey Everett and Will Ashton? How do you know them all?" Walker asked, suddenly very interested.

"They're all from Keeneston. I grew up with them. I told you, Keeneston isn't like any other town out there. We may be small, but we're mighty."

"Tell me more about Keeneston," Walker requested, sitting back in the chair.

For hours Layne told him about her family, about the three old ladies who ran Keeneston, about the Ali Rahman royal family who lived in town, and about her aunt and friend both being pregnant at the same time.

"And I thought my dad was bad." Layne laughed as she told him about the fathers spying on their daughters. "But Abby said her dad, Ahmed, has sent drones after her."

"Drones—wait, Ahmed? As in the Ali Rahman soldier? *He* lives in Keeneston?" Walker asked, sitting up so fast he hissed as he unintentionally moved his leg.

"Yup. You know him?"

"Of course I know him. He's a legend. There's even a torture technique named after him. And he lives in Keeneston? And you're friends with him?" Walker asked with disbelief.

"Friends? He's like my uncle. He and my dad still work out together."

"Wow," Walker said with wonder. "I'd kill to work out with Ahmed. What he could teach me . . ."

"Well, if you let me work on your leg multiple times a day and do everything I tell you, you can work out with him in a couple weeks." Layne let that be a motivator.

"I'm at your command, doc. So, tell me more about your family."

Layne had already noticed Walker asked questions to stop her from asking her own. He'd talked a little about Edie, but it was clear it was painful for him to think of her on her own after hearing about her husband and believing her brother to be dead as well.

"Well, Sienna Ashton is the daughter of Will Ashton, the owner of the Thoroughbreds, and Judge Kenna Ashton. She's the one who's pregnant. She's married to my cousin, FBI Agent Ryan Parker. He'll come in handy for your situation."

"He'll help?"

"We're family. Of course he will," Layne said with certainty. "Then there are Zain and Gabe. Not family, but like brothers nonetheless. They're princes of Rahmi. Both are married now. Zain to a German interpreter named Mila and Gabe just got married a couple weeks ago to the nicest woman named Sloane. Gabe is on his honeymoon, and I think Zain is in Canada on some diplomatic trip, but he'll be back soon. Then there's my cousin Sydney Davies, well, McKnight now. She's married to a private investigator named Deacon. They have a dog named Robyn who scares Ahmed. It's really quite entertaining."

"Sydney Davies . . . the supermodel fashion mogul?"

Layne smiled. "Yes, and my cousin. As I said—"

"Keeneston is not like anywhere else. I'm beginning to understand that. Then you also have a cousin who works with nanotechnology. I've heard rumors of the military buying some clothes made with nanotech that stops bullets. It's a very big up-and-coming industry."

Layne grinned wider as Walker looked at her. "Let me guess, your cousin?"

She nodded. "Yup. That invention was all Piper. She discovered it worked when she gave it to Ahmed's protégé, Nash Dagher, who is married to my cousin Sophie. She's a weapons developer."

Walker laughed out loud. "I think I'm going to the safest town imaginable."

"That you are." Layne paused and decided to ask what had been on her mind since she first learned of who Walker Greene was. They'd been talking for hours; they were already into Kentucky, so she asked, "What happened that night?"

WALKER DIDN'T HAVE to ask what night she was asking about. She hadn't pressed him the entire seven hours of their trip. But now she deserved to know everything. "As you've figured out, due to the media coverage of the incident, I'm a SEAL. But not just a SEAL. I'm part of DEVGRU."

Layne nodded. "The famous SEAL Team Six. I kind of guessed that. I don't mean this to sound strange, but you remind me of my dad, and I think he was in something similar. I recognize the signs."

"We were in the Atlantic off the coast of Nigeria heading toward another mission when we got a call that an American crew had been taken hostage by Nigerian pirates. Since we were the closest team, we were rerouted while another team filled our spot on the original mission.

Everything was completely normal. We reviewed the boat and made our plan. Everything was fine until we approached and no one could be seen. Shane felt it was off. I did too. I should have followed my instinct and had everyone pull back, but I didn't. Then Jud appeared and lured us up to the bridge. We were sitting ducks as he and the pirates took everyone out. I was only left alive because I was the last in. I backed out and leapt over the bridge into the ocean after Jud ordered me killed."

Layne glanced over at him with a frown. He didn't want pity, and luckily it didn't appear as if she were going to do that. Instead, she looked as if she were thinking through a problem instead of talking to him about his survivor's remorse.

"But *why*? Why did Jud do all of this?"

"Money. He is the one who stole the goods from the ship. He couldn't have been acting alone, though. He told me he was going to sell the goods on the black market and become a hero. He wanted the attention and the money. But what I can't figure out is what happened to the stolen goods. There couldn't have been much time between when everyone was dead and when he signaled the rescue."

"So, that's even more reason for him to make sure you're dead. No body found is a loose end he can't afford," Layne said as they drove through the Appalachian Mountains heading toward Lexington.

Walker nodded and turned to look out the window. Layne read his mood instantly and simply turned on the radio. Before Walker knew it, he was on a narrow country road winding through horse farms. They rounded a corner, and he knew they must have arrived in Keeneston. Even though it was nighttime, the summer nights left a warm glow over the town now in twilight.

"If you don't want everyone in town knocking on my door tonight, you may want to get out of sight," Layne said as she slowed down.

"Seriously?"

"Seriously. That's DeAndre's state trooper car up there, and he's turning into an bigger gossip than John Wolfe."

Walker unbuckled and slid to the floor. His leg protested but bent. "John is married to a Rose sister, right?"

"To Miss Lily, yes. And we thought aliens talked to him or maybe ghosts because he knows things before they happen. However, much to John's displeasure, DeAndre is starting to beat him out. If DeAndre sees me with a man in the car, he'll text his girlfriend, Aniyah, who is best friends with my cousin Riley, the politician. Well, Riley will tell her twin sister, Reagan, who will tell Piper . . . well, you get the picture. We won't even be home before I'll have people asking who you are."

"It may be safer if no one knew I was here," Walker said slowly, thinking about the gossip tree and how that one slip could bring Jud here.

Layne smiled and waved out the window as she drove through the small downtown. She didn't reply until he could no longer see the streetlights. "We'll try it, but I give it two days."

"How long do you think my rehab will take?" Walker asked as he held his hidden position on the floor.

"Three to six weeks. However, with your athleticism and a strong will to recover, and with being with me 24/7 so we can have multiple sessions . . . I am thinking three weeks, tops."

"I can stay hidden for three weeks," Walker said confidently.

Layne chuckled and shook her head. "Have you not

been listening to who lives in Keeneston? Gossip, suspicion, and betting on said gossip and suspicion is what everyone lives for. Two days. Tops. But don't worry. If we fill them in, no one will say anything to outsiders."

Too bad their lives depended on it. Walker looked up at Layne. Her dark hair blended into the shadows, her smooth skin glowing in what sunlight was left. He'd do whatever it took to protect her. This was a woman who hadn't hesitated to put her life on the line for a man she didn't know, even if that meant leaving her and this town safely in Ahmed's hands. For if he was found out, Walker already had developed a plan to keep her safe, and that plan revolved around the infamously dangerous Ahmed.

9

Layne closed the garage door to her house and let out a sigh of relief. She'd at least made it home without anyone seeing Walker. She said two days, and that was optimistic. Her phone buzzed before she could open the car door.

"Who is it?" Walker asked as he slowly pulled himself off the floor of the SUV.

"My dad. He must have put cameras up again outside my house," she said, reading the text.

Welcome home. Will bring the little rat over soon. Unless you're too tired and then I guess we can keep him.

She texted him back to keep Fluffy Puppy overnight, promised she was fine and just tired. After a video chat as she walked inside her house to show her father she was quite all right, her father relented and agreed to bring FP by the office tomorrow.

"I'm taking it your dad doesn't know the meaning of boundaries."

"Nope. He's never heard of them." Layne chuckled. "I used to hate it. He scared away every single boyfriend I had, but now it's endearing. I always feel loved, even if sometimes it's a smothering kind of love."

"What does your boyfriend think of it?" Walker asked, not so subtly, as he helped carry what little luggage there was inside the house.

"Don't have one."

"I wonder why." He snorted.

Layne rolled her eyes. If she found a man willing to stand up to her father and not run like a scared little boy, she'd marry him on the spot. Layne walked into her kitchen from the garage and set down her bags. She saw Walker looking at the pictures she had of her friends and family and at the little dog bowl on a mat in the kitchen.

"Cat?"

"Dog. A Maltese."

Walker's eyebrows rose. "I didn't picture you with a little froufrou dog."

Layne shrugged her shoulder. "My aunt Gemma and uncle Cy had one, and I loved that little dog as a kid. When you meet him, don't tell him he's little. He thinks he's a Great Dane."

Layne nibbled on her lip, though, as she looked around the house. "We do have a little problem."

"What's that?" Walker asked, suddenly on alert.

"It's easier if I show you." Layne walked from the kitchen and Walker followed. "That is the dining room over there," she said of the open doorway leading to a front room. "And you can see the living room already," she said, pointing to the living room with the large-screen television, two damask club chairs, and a soft green couch with a large rectangular coffee table between the seating. Layne turned down a hall and pointed out the half bath, then the full bath. "You can use this bathroom. There're towels hanging up already. There are more in the closet."

Layne nibbled her lip again as she opened the first bedroom door. "This room is my office," she said, stepping into the room lined with a bookcase filled with medical texts and books. A large desk faced the window overlooking the backyard. The room was a small bedroom but was perfect for an office.

She walked out and opened the door to the second bedroom. "And this is my gym. We'll be able to do all your physical therapy here as well as at my office in Lexington."

"Nice," Walker said, walking around the room checking out the equipment. This room was a good size, and she'd been able to put in a treadmill, an elliptical, and a rowing machine along with some free weights. Different exercise bands hung from the wall and a television was hung nearby as well. "But what's the problem?" Walker asked.

"This way," Layne said, walking to the last door. She opened it and Walker stepped into her bedroom. It seemed strange to have him filling her space. And there was no doubt about it; this man filled her house with his presence.

She saw him checking out the king-sized bed covered with a teal comforter. The tan walls were covered with pictures, some of friends and family, others of landscapes from her cousin Jace's humanitarian travels, and some from around Keeneston she'd taken herself.

Walker moved around to the side of the bed and peeked his head into the attached full bathroom and then turned to look at her. "It's you. But what's the problem?"

"How many beds did you count in the house?"

Walker's eyes flew toward the door as realization set in. "Oh. I'll sleep on the couch. It's fine."

"I don't know if you'll fit," Layne said as bad memories of Walker shoving her out of bed flashed through her mind.

Walker didn't answer but instead headed for the living room. Layne followed, already knowing the answer. Her couch was six feet long, but take out eight or so inches from the two armrests and Walker wasn't going to be able to lie straight, which is what his leg needed. Walker lay down on the couch. He rolled this way and that, but it was clear. He wasn't going to fit.

"If you can stomach it, then you can share the bed with me. But no funny business and no kicking me out of my own bed," Layne offered, even though it was laced with a threat.

"About that," Walker started, but Layne stopped him.

"We will never talk about that humiliation again."

"Layne," Walker said with that voice that went straight to her hoohah. She was temporarily lost in a fantasy and didn't realize he'd done it to quiet her. "I didn't mean any insult. I was trying to be respectful of you and didn't want you to think I was pressing myself on you. Only, I forgot about my strength and am simply guilty being overzealous in my southern gentlemanly manners."

His voice caressed her breasts and danced farther south until she realized what he had said. "What bullshit. I'm not some delicate flower who will get the vapors if a man touches me. Geez, if that's the kind of women you've been dating, I'm not surprised you're a virgin."

Walker tossed up his hands in the air. "Virgin?"

"Only a virgin is that much of a prude," Layne countered back, placing her hands on her hips.

For an injured man, he sure moved fast. Layne didn't have time to gasp in surprise when Walker had her in his arms and pulled her flush against him. Her breasts were pushed against his muscled chest. His lips claimed hers in a searing kiss as his arms anchored her to him. When she didn't pull away, he loosened his grip and dropped one hand to her ass. He squeezed her cheek as he pulled her hips to his and ground into her.

Layne moaned with pleasure and frustration as she pressed herself closer to his body. She wanted to feel all of him. She wanted to rip his clothes from his body and feel the incredible chest and abs she'd seen when they were swimming. She wanted him to take her now and never stop. To make sure he didn't fling her across the room if some semblance of so-called gentlemanly manners returned, Layne speared her fingers into his hair and pulled him to her.

Walker obliged as she opened her mouth to him. His tongue was as slow and seductive as his speech as he explored her. Layne wasn't sure how much time had passed as his hands ran up and down her back and his mouth left her breathless and eager for more.

Slowly, he pulled away and brought his hands to her cup her face. He brushed back her hair and tucked it behind her ears, keeping his eyes locked with hers. "Would a virgin kiss like that?"

"Well, they better since they aren't doing anything else with a woman."

Walker's lips tilted up into a smile before he bent and placed a quick kiss on her lips. "I don't think I've ever met a woman quite like you before."

"Is that a good thing or a bad thing?" Layne asked.

"Good. It's nice not to play games. I like not having to guess what you're feeling or thinking."

Layne smiled innocently up at him. "And what is it that you think I'm thinking?"

Walker's tilted smile grew into a grin. "You're thinking about having me strip you naked, kiss every inch of your body, and then—" Walker leaned down and began to whisper what he'd do to her. His lips gently brushed against her ear, his hot breath and the words he was saying shot straight to her core, and Layne was pretty sure she was panting. Walker leaned back and smirked at her flushed face.

"How does a virgin know about that?" Layne asked breathlessly.

Walker's smile fell as he growled low in his throat. He had her shirt off and his mouth at her nipple before he registered she was smacking his head.

"The door!" she whispered frantically.

Walker made an inarticulate sound of annoyance as Layne's nipple popped from his mouth.

"Layne? What's taking you so long?"

Layne's eyes widened. "Oh my God, it's my father. Hide!"

Layne shoved Walker into the half bath's small linen closet and raced topless to the door. Crap! Her top.

"Layne?" Her father's voice became more demanding as she twirled around, looking for her shirt. She didn't have time to locate her bra as she pulled the shirt over her head and reached for the door.

"Are you hurt?" her dad called as she heard the sound of his key scraping the lock.

Layne flung open the door. "Dad! Geez, I was changing. I thought you weren't coming by tonight. And where's FP?"

Her mother's head peeked over her father's shoulder. "Somehow your father forgot him at home," she said with a grin as Miles pushed past her and walked into the living room. He was walking into the kitchen when her mother froze.

"What?" Layne whispered, but her mother didn't answer. Instead, she darted around Layne and kicked something under the couch. Something that was dark purple. Something that looked exactly like her bra.

"Who is he?" her mom whispered.

"I don't know what you mean," Layne said innocently as her dad took off down the hall. Layne held her breath as he turned on the light in the half bath, looked around, and then turned the light back off.

"I mean, the man you have stashed in your bathroom. The one who so carelessly dropped your bra in the living room."

"Mom," Layne said with a roll of her eyes. Her mother only smiled more.

"Don't *Mom* me. You're flushed, your bra was on the floor of the living room, your eyes practically bulged from your head when your dad went into the bathroom, and your shirt is on backward . . . and inside out."

Layne looked down at her shirt. Busted. Layne turned her back to her mom, ripped off her shirt, turned it the right way, and slipped it over her head right as she heard her father coming down the hall.

Miles stopped where the hall met the living room and looked back and forth between his wife and daughter. "Did I miss something?"

"No, dear. We were just talking about Layne's trip. We'd better let her get to bed now that you've searched the house for intruders. Sorry for the interruption, dear, but we are glad you're home." Morgan kissed her daughter as her father approached them.

"I'll bring the rat by your office tomorrow. We're real proud of you, Layne. The speech at the conference was outstanding." Her dad kissed her cheek before walking out the front door, leaving her mom behind.

"Have fun tonight." She winked and Layne rolled her eyes.

"Mom, come on. There will be no fun. He's a virgin, for crying out loud."

Morgan blinked and Layne wanted to slap her hand over her mouth. "Well, there are plenty of things virgins can do and do well. Um, goodnight."

Layne watched her mother walk down the front steps, shaking her head while she mumbled something Layne couldn't hear. She closed the door and rested her forehead against it when she really wanted to bang it with her head. Oh my God, she'd told her mom about Walker being a virgin. At least her mom wouldn't say anything to her dad . . . or she hoped.

"You can come out now," Layne called. She heard Walker squeeze himself out of the bathroom closet.

"I haven't done that since I was in high school. Don't you think you're a little old to be hiding your—?"

"My?"

Walker's jaw tightened as he looked up at the ceiling searching for words. "Patient?"

Crap. "You're right. You are my patient and this needs to stop. I'm not going to take your V card while I'm treating you. That's totally unethical. I'm so sorry, Walker. From now on, nothing but professionalism."

Layne went down on her hands and knees and pulled her bra from under the couch. "But—" Walker started.

"Nope. It's wrong for me to take advantage of you. I'll sleep here tonight. You take my bed."

"Take advantage? Layne . . ." Walker started as she hurried past him toward her bedroom.

"Just let me change and grab a pillow, then the room is all yours." Oh my God. How could she have done that? She'd practically thrown herself at a patient. It was wrong on so many levels.

"I'll take the couch!" Walker yelled after her.

"Nope, I will. Tonight you sleep in my bed. I insist, especially after a long car trip."

And that was how Layne found herself staring at her ceiling in the living room in the middle of the night.

10

Walker didn't sleep a wink. He could smell Layne all over the sheets. He probably should have been worried since he'd had an erection for over four hours and hadn't taken any medication. Why on earth did he mention being her patient?

With a frustrated punch to the pillow, he rolled onto his back. The sun was coming up, and he was still up . . . in more ways than one. There was only one solution to this . . . um, problem. Walker got up and headed for the bathroom Layne had told him he could use. He stopped himself from looking in on her in the living room and closed the bathroom door. He turned on the shower, stepped into the freezing cold water, and swore that no matter what it took, Layne would be sleeping with him later that night.

WALKER LOOKED up at the three-story new building Layne had parked behind. "I'm on the third floor," she explained as he slowly got out of the car. He didn't want to admit it, but his leg was sore.

"We'll go in through the back. And you'll spend the day with me. There's a television in the staff kitchen you can watch when we're not doing rehab. I'll fit you in around patients. Luckily, I don't have anyone until later this afternoon, so we'll be able to do a lot this morning."

Layne continued to ramble as they took the elevator to the third floor. The elevator opened, and across from it were two glass double doors with *LD Physical Therapy* written across the glass. Walker could see some patients already waiting inside and easily recognized the ones who were former soldiers. They had a completely different bearing from the others who seemed more, well, snobbish.

Layne didn't go in the double doors, though. She turned down the hall and used a key to unlock an unmarked door. Inside was the staff kitchen. A woman was in the middle of pouring coffee and looked up to see who had entered. She was around fifty with light blonde hair and a warm smile.

"Layne, we weren't expecting you until later. How was the conference?"

"Hi, Jill. The conference was great. I actually have a new client I'll be working with extensively, which is why I came back early."

Walker held out his hand. "Owen Selkey."

"Nice to meet you, Mr. Selkey. Um, I guess we need paperwork on him?" Jill asked, clearly thrown off by having Layne bring him in through the staff door.

"I'll take care of it. Mr. Selkey is a referral who needs intensive treatment, so he'll be around quite a bit for a couple weeks, so don't be surprised if you find him relaxing in here sometimes," Layne said completely professionally. "Come on, *Owen*. Let's go to my office and review your rehab plan and then get to work."

"Nice to meet you." Walker smiled kindly at Jill as she took her coffee and returned his smile.

"You too, Mr. Selkey."

Walker followed Layne through a maze of halls to an office in the back. There were no interior windows, but when she opened the door, one whole side was floor-to-ceiling windows.

"Nice office," Walker said, taking a seat on a loveseat pressed against the wall next to the door.

"Thank you." Layne reached into her desk and pulled out some papers. "Fill these out, then we'll get started warming up your leg. Leave your name or any identifiable markers blank."

Walker took the papers and filled out his medical history while she returned some phone calls. When he placed them on her desk, she reviewed them as she talked to someone named Sienna. Wait, he remembered that name. Was she a cousin maybe?

"I'm glad the morning sickness is getting a little better," Layne said, her eyes reading every word he had written down. "I can imagine Ryan is being a little overprotective."

Layne looked up and stared at his leg before looking back down at his paperwork. "I'm sorry, what did you say?"

Walker knew something was wrong in an instant. Her eyes went wide as her head came up to stare at him. She swallowed hard. "Family dinner? Tomorrow? No, no, I remember now. Okay, I'll see you then. Bye." Layne hung up and dropped her head to the desk. She softly banged it three times before letting out a long breath and sitting back up.

"Bad news?" Walker asked worriedly. Layne always seemed so put together that it was unnerving to see her upset.

"Um, I have a family dinner at my grandparents' tomorrow night that I forgot about."

"So?"

"My grandparents," Layne said, holding up one finger. "My parents," she said, holding up another finger. "Eight aunts and uncles," she said, reaching ten fingers. "And sixteen cousins . . . not counting spouses. And every single one will want to know what happened in Charleston and why I came home a day early. And why my bra was on the floor of the living room." Layne grimaced.

"How would they know your bra was in the living room?" Walker asked, thoroughly confused.

"My mom saw it and kicked it under the couch before my dad could see it."

"Okay, so what's the problem? Your mom thinks you're a slob."

Layne was already shaking her head. "I also, um, had my shirt on backward and inside out, and she caught me freaking out when my dad walked into the bathroom. She put it all together."

"Look, we have nothing to hide. I don't understand the big deal."

"Oh, you'll understand it if we're discovered."

"If what's discovered?" a strange male voice interrupted.

Walker was already up and ready to pounce on the man in black slacks and a French blue button-up shirt. His blond hair was cut like a politician's, which instantly made Walker wary of the man.

"Aaron!" Layne said suddenly, looking nothing but happy to see the man a couple years younger than Walker's thirty-four. "I'm so happy you're here. This is Mr. Selkey. He's a special case and will require a lot of attention. I was hoping you could work with him when I'm unavailable."

She handed him the papers Walker had filled out. "Mr. Selkey, this is Aaron Ornack. He's a physical therapist who works here and donates time to help with my veterans.

Aaron smiled up from the paperwork and held out his hand. "Nice to meet you. I see Layne has you all set on a plan, so it'll be easy for me to jump in and work with you when needed." Aaron turned away from him after shaking his hand and flashed a smile Walker easily recognized at Layne. "How about dinner tomorrow to talk about your conference? Jill's been fielding phone calls since your keynote."

"I'd love to, but I have a family dinner. We'll catch up in the break room."

Walker relaxed a little even as the man moved closer to Layne. Her body language was easy for him to read. She wasn't interested. Aaron propped a hip on her desk and leaned forward, effectively cutting Walker off from their conversation.

"I was hoping we could talk about our future as well," he said cryptically before the intercom went off.

"Layne, your dad is on his way back," Jill said a moment before her father strode into the room. Walker watched with amusement as Aaron leapt from the desk.

"Good morning, s-s-sir," he stuttered. "I better get to work." And like a coward, he fled the battlefield leaving Layne all to Walker.

Although, when Mr. Davies turned to look at him, a strategic retreat did seem like a good idea. "You look familiar. Have we met?"

"Dad," Layne said, jumping up from her chair. "You know HIPAA and all the regulations. Did you bring Fluffy Puppy?"

Walker snorted and tried to cover it with a cough. Mr.

Davies looked over to him with understanding. "I know, right?"

"A little girl named him for me, come on!" Layne said, throwing her hands up in the air, and Walker got the impression this conversation came up regularly. "Just call him FP like everyone else does."

"I prefer Rat," Mr. Davies said while sounding completely affectionate. He reached into the satchel he was carrying and unzipped it. A little white fluffy head popped out. "Here's mommy, Rat."

Walker tried not to smile and turned away as Mr. Davies lovingly picked up the little dog who was aptly named. The little dog's long haired tail wagged happily as his tiny pink tongue darted out and covered Mr. Davies's cheek with kisses before losing his little mind at the sight of Layne.

"See you tomorrow for dinner at the farm, right?" Mr. Davies asked reluctantly, handing FP over.

Layne gave the little dog a hug and then set him on the ground. The little dog danced on his hind legs for Mr. Davies and sniffed the air. He zeroed in on Walker as he seemed to float over to him.

"Watch out, he doesn't like strangers," Mr. Davies said. But FP didn't seem to mind Walker as he held out his hand. The little dog sniffed him, then pulled his black-lined lips back and smiled.

"Seems to like me just fine. He's even smiling at me," Walker said, leaning down to pick up the little dog.

"He doesn't smile for anyone but me," Mr. Davies whined as his eyes bore into Walker. "I could have sworn I've seen you before."

Walker just shrugged as he petted FP.

"Well, it's time to start your therapy," Layne said to him as she kept an eye on FP before turning to her father.

"Thanks for bringing FP. See you tomorrow." Layne jumped up and ushered her father from the office.

For the next two hours, Layne apparently took her family issues out on his leg. By the afternoon, his leg was throbbing as he iced it in the kitchen. He was also feeling rather dumpy with only two sets of clothes. However, the thought of asking Layne for money to get some new clothes grated on him. Especially when Aaron came strutting into the kitchen wearing his expensive clothes and looking like the type of man Layne should be with. Rich, smart, socially active, and someone who would never experience danger in his life. Someone she'd be safe with.

"The waiting room is out front," Aaron said condescendingly as he poured his coffee.

"Layne told me to come here and ice my leg, so I'm following doctor's orders." Walker repositioned his ice pack. "Mr. Davies sure is nice, isn't he?" Walker asked, knowing from Aaron's literal run from the room he was scared of the man. While Walker was too, he had the training necessary not to show it.

"Nice? He's a nightmare. But it doesn't matter. He'll come around once Layne and I are together."

"Excuse me, but my dad is not a nightmare."

Walker saw Layne standing with her hands on her hips staring Aaron down with the same look her father had given him over the video call. Damn, she was something else, and he wanted her more than he'd wanted any woman before. This woman would be his equal, his partner. She'd understand his life as a SEAL. Hell, with the look she was giving Aaron, she could probably train SEALs on withstanding interrogation. Aaron was about to grovel.

Layne held up a hand and cut him off. "Talking about

nightmares, your mother is out front to see you. She has Caro with her."

Aaron groaned. "They're in some charity together and Mom is determined to set me up with her."

"Well, as your mother just informed me, Caro is from the right family, went to the right boarding school and Ivy League college. Although I can't for the life of me figure out what she does."

Aaron stopped in front of Layne, and Walker leaned closer to hear. "I'm sorry for saying that about your father. Caro means nothing to me. You know I've wanted to see what happens if we go out, and I still want that. I'm just waiting on you to give me an answer."

Layne's hazel eyes quickly moved from Aaron's face to looking over his shoulder at Walker. Walker held his breath and gave her a small smile. He wanted to scream "No! Give me a chance," but this needed to be Layne's decision. Right now she wasn't going to give him any kind of chance since he stupidly reminded her he was her patient.

"I'm sorry, Aaron, but I don't want to mix business and pleasure. You have your clients, and I have mine. And we work well together. I don't want to jeopardize that."

Walker released a breath he'd been holding. He still had a chance. Well, as soon as he got his leg healed enough for her to discharge him.

Aaron lifted Layne's hand and placed a kiss on her wrist. Walker fought the urge to pummel him as Aaron slowly let her hand drop. "I respect your decision, but I hope you'll change your mind," he said softly, trying to make sure Walker couldn't hear.

Walker watched Aaron walk out the room, then looked at Layne standing there. Her jaw was tight, her hazel eyes had darkened in anger, and she clenched her fist. "Let's get back to work," she said briskly.

"Layne, are you okay? Do you want to talk about it?"

"I don't know how to say no more clearly. Every month he asks me out, and I always say no. I've told him he's not my type. He comes from an old Lexington family under the impression they mean something. He likes going to fancy events and being photographed in the local news. I don't. Look at me. I wear scrubs, not designer clothes. I work most nights until seven or eight and spend my weekends with wounded veterans or with my family—a family he's scared of."

Layne was pacing around the room now, her hands flying in all directions, "And he always harps on my dad. Look, I know my dad isn't the typical dad. He taught me how to kill someone with my pinky. However, he's my dad, and I love him. You weren't scared of him, were you?"

Layne stopped pacing and stopped in front of him. She looked at him practically begging him to like her father. "I'll always be honest with you, Layne. Your dad scares the shit out of me. But it's mostly out of respect."

Layne's whole body seemed to relax. "Thank you for saying that. How is your leg feeling?"

"Tired and sore, but I'll do whatever it takes to get it back in shape. Pain is just weakness leaving the body. I'm very comfortable with being uncomfortable. I learned that during SEAL training."

Layne gave him a smile, a real one that made her eyes soften, and Walker decided he'd go through whatever ordeal she wanted to put him through just to see her smile like that again.

11

Layne handed Walker his crutches and helped him into the house. He had had four sessions that day and would be very sore as his muscles got used to being active again. "Right into a hot bath for you."

"Bath? You know I don't really fit into a tub, right?"

Layne smiled at the image and then flushed as she thought about them both in the tub together. "I know, but you can sit in it and get your legs covered with the water. That's all that is needed. There's an old sore muscle remedy my Uncle Cy gave me that will make you heal faster."

"If you say so. Also, would you mind if I washed my clothes?"

"Oh, I didn't think about that. I can run out and get you some," Layne offered.

"No, please don't spend money on it. I already feel bad enough I'm having to live with you and can't even pay for dinner, much less for your services."

Layne looked at how tall Walker was and ran through all her cousins. Jackson was the same height, but Walker had way more muscles that Jackson. Walker was built like Dylan

. . . who wasn't in town. "I have an idea. Will you get the bath ready while I call my cousin Piper?"

"Sure. Can I do anything though?"

Layne shook her head. "I have it covered. I'll bring in the stuff for the bath in just a minute." She watched him hobble off with his crutches as she pulled out her cell phone.

"Hey, what's up?" Piper asked.

"Where are you?" Layne asked instead of answering.

"My parents' house having dinner. Why?"

"I need a favor, and it needs to be a cousin special," Layne said, dropping her voice in case Piper's parents, Tammy and Pierce, were listening in.

"Of course. You know I won't say anything. What do you need?" Layne could hear Piper walking away from her family.

"I need some of Dylan's clothes."

Piper didn't say anything for a second. "Okay, that wasn't what I was expecting."

"Please, no questions. I need some workout clothes, shorts, shirts, and jeans. And a pair of dress slacks and dress shirt, just in case."

"In case of what? Ugh. Sorry, a cousin special—no questions. Got it. It won't take me long. Mom is really tired with the baby right now, so she's already on the couch while Dad and Jace clean up. They made the mistake of mentioning Mom's age again."

Layne snickered. "You'd think they'd learn by now not to mention that." Tammy was in her early fifties and had accidently gotten pregnant. Uncle Pierce was sticking his foot in his mouth every couple of minutes. But to be fair, it was usually out of concern for his wife.

"Yeah, well, they haven't. Dad took Mom's dessert away, fearing gestational diabetes. Mom almost stabbed him with a fork. But I'll grab the clothes and be over in a minute."

"Thanks, Piper."

"Hey, what are cousins for?" Piper asked rhetorically before hanging up.

LAYNE HEADED into her bathroom and spent some time pulling out the right oils and salts to help his sore muscles. "Hey, Walker," she called out as she pushed the partially closed bathroom door open with her foot. Layne froze at the sight that greeted her—Walker's nude body. His back was to her as he reached for a towel. He spun in surprise and Layne's mouth fell open. She wasn't completely inexperienced, but with her father's overbearing way, she could count the men she'd been with on one hand and none of them looked like Walker.

Walker seemed to know she was appreciating the view of the muscled pecs, the little arrow of hair leading down the middle of a six pack down to his... Phew, it was getting hot in there. Layne waved a hand in front of her face. Her eyes couldn't seem to travel any farther from the clear evidence that Walker was getting very happy to see her. It just kept growing . . . "I didn't know they could be that size."

Walker chuckled, and that caused Layne to tear her gaze away from his Mr. Happy and back up to his eyes. "Did I say that out loud?"

"You sure did, sweetheart."

Layne felt her cheeks heat, but that was the last of her body to heat. Everything else was already panting for the man proudly standing naked in front of her.

"I, uh—"

"Want to join me?" Walker asked, taking a step closer to

her. He stopped when he was close enough for her to feel his body heat drawing her in.

The doorbell rang, causing Layne to jump back. "That must be Piper. I'll be right back. Um, stay here."

Layne practically ran to the door and flung it open. Piper's eyes went wide as she looked at her cousin. "What's up with you? Your face is flushed, and you're breathing hard. Oh my God! You have a man in there."

"I do not," Layne countered, grabbing the duffle bag from Piper.

"Is he naked? Is that why you needed my brother's clothes? And you said Dylan, and not Jace, so the guy must be more muscular. Can I meet him? Do I know him?"

"Piper! No questions. I'm neither confirming nor denying anything. But thank you for these." Layne slammed the door on Piper, who immediately moved to the window. Layne saw her face pressed to the glass. "Cousin special, remember?" Layne shouted as she pulled the curtain closed.

"Oh come on!" Piper yelled back, but after a minute Layne heard Piper's car start up. With a sigh, Layne headed back to the bathroom and knocked on the door.

"Come in," Walker said from inside. Layne walked in and found him already in the bathtub and swallowed hard. What she could do with the bottles in her hands . . . "I didn't want the water getting cold, and since you've already seen me naked . . ." Walker shrugged. Layne just stared. "Are you going to put those in the bath?"

"What?" Layne asked and then shook her head. She was a professional. She'd seen naked men before. She needed to stop thinking about getting naked and climbing into the tub with him. "Oh, yes. Here, I'll just add these, and you'll feel ready to go tomorrow."

Layne moved to his feet, sat on the edge of the tub, and

added the mixtures before turning on the hot water for one more minute to help the salt dissolve. She put her hand in the hot water and moved it around to spread the oils and salt, but before she could remove her hand, Walker's fingers closed around her wrist.

Without saying anything, he kept his gaze locked with hers as the water sloshed around him while he moved forward. He didn't let go of her wrist when he got near her either. Layne felt her breath catch as he placed her hand on his chest and leaned toward her. "Kiss me."

"I—"

"You want to. Kiss me," Walker coaxed as her fingers began to explore his chest all on their own. "Now."

Layne's hand moved to his sculpted shoulder as she bent forward. Everything in her body was crying to kiss him again. She wasn't sure if she was breathing anymore when her lips met his. Walker's wet hands captured her breasts through her shirt as he let her lead the kiss. Layne tried to go slow and to savor it, but when his hands began magically pulling every ounce of desire from her, the kiss deepened. Layne felt the switch go off—the switch holding her back. Pressing her breasts into Walker's hands, she moaned as one hand dropped from his shoulder to trail over his pecs. She felt the ridges of his abs contract as her fingers skimmed over his muscles headed for . . .

Walker pulled away, slightly breathless.

"What?" Layne asked, realizing she was almost in the tub.

"The doorbell."

"What?" Layne asked, so overcome with desire the words didn't make sense to her.

"The doorbell," he said again as she heard the chime. Layne muttered some curses she'd picked up from Dylan as

Walker chuckled. "That makes me feel like I'm back with the SEAL team."

Taking a deep breath, Layne stood and hurried from the bathroom, closing the door behind her as the doorbell rang again. "I'm coming!"

Layne threw open the door to find her cousin Reagan standing there. Reagan was the twin daughter of Uncle Cy and Aunt Gemma. The same ones who had gotten her to fall in love with the Maltese dog breed. Speaking of which, Fluffy Puppy shot past Layne and began dancing in front of Reagan.

Reagan scooped up the little dog and ran inside. "Quick, close the door. I've been here for the past two hours, okay?"

"What's going on?" Layne asked as she moved into the living room while Reagan turned on the TV, sat on the couch, and put her feet on the coffee table.

Reagan heard another car approaching and took a deep breath. "We've eaten pizza and have been hanging out watching TV for two hours, got it?"

"What is this about? Are you in trouble?" Layne asked worriedly.

"No more than you'll be if your dad discovers you have a man in the bathroom and you almost had bathtub sex."

"You wouldn't dare!" Layne hissed at her cousin.

"Two hours," Reagan said quietly as they heard a car door close.

"How did you know?" Layne whispered.

"There's two wet handprints on your boobs, your face is flushed, your hair is damp, and you keep looking at the bathroom door. My dad was a spy, remember? Which means if I figured it out, so will he. So stop looking at the damn door and introduce me to him after my dad leaves."

"Your dad's here?" Layne cursed as there was a knock on the door.

"Two hours, promise me. Cousin special."

"Fine," Layne swore as she stood to open the door. "Uncle Cy!" Layne smiled as she greeted Reagan's father. His head was still shaved short, and he looked ready to fight an army, just like her father, Uncle Marshall, and Uncle Cade had done in their younger days. They all worked out with Ahmed almost daily now. "What a surprise. What's up?"

Cy walked into the room and FP growled at him as Reagan smiled. "That damn rat hates me."

"He hates almost everyone; don't take it personally." Layne smiled.

Uncle Cy looked at her then. "Why is your shirt wet?"

"I splashed some of FP's water on myself when I was refilling his bowl," Layne said with a shake of her head. "Can I get you something?"

"No, I just wanted to check on my daughter. Her GPS . . . I mean, I was worried when she wasn't home for dinner."

Reagan crossed her arms and set her face. "Yeah, I disabled the GPS tracker you put on my phone." Reagan set down Fluffy Puppy who, to Layne's horror, ran straight to the closed bathroom door and began to scratch at it. "I'm so going to tell Mom."

"It's a dangerous world, and I want to make sure you're safe," Cy said, mimicking her hands-on-hips stance. "Look what happened to your sister."

A fellow politician trying to develop Keeneston with illegal dealings had attacked Riley. Riley had been kidnapped and was close to being killed when her now husband, Matt Walz, the new sheriff of Keeneston, with the help of Aniyah, Riley's secretary, helped to foil the plot. Uncle Cy had been even more overbearing since that happened. It didn't matter that Riley and Matt were blissfully happy and everyone was safe and sound.

"Well, I'm fine. Layne and I are having a girls' night since she's been away for a couple days," Reagan assured her.

"I see that now," Cy looked over to FP clawing at the door. "What is he going on about?"

"Nothing!" Layne and Reagan cried out as Layne raced to scoop up the dog.

"Is someone in there?"

Layne laughed. "Don't be silly."

"Okay, Dad. Now that you know where I've been . . . hey, how did you know I was here?" Reagan narrowed her eyes at her father.

"Every spy has his secrets," Cy said with a smug smile.

"Ugh! Can't you just be a normal father? For crying out loud, I'm almost thirty."

With hands on hips again, Cy looked at his daughter. "And you're still my baby."

That took the wind out of Reagan, just as it did when Layne's father said it to her. "I know, Dad, but you're smothering me. Let me have a life, please."

"No more lying to me because we both know you haven't been here more than five minutes. Your engine is still warm."

"Dad! This is what I'm talking about."

"I trust you, baby. I just don't trust anyone else."

Reagan rolled her eyes. "I'll see you at home, Dad." Reagan lived on their farm, and she knew her dad would wait up until she drove past the main house to get to her house at the back of the property.

"Okay, but then you need to tell me—"

"Dad!"

Layne thought she heard Cy growl, but he relented.

Instead, he moved over and kissed Reagan's cheek. "I love you."

"I love you too, Dad."

Uncle Cy headed over to Layne and placed a quick peck on the cheek before freezing. He leaned closer and sniffed. "You made my muscle recovery bath? There is someone in the bathroom."

"No," Layne laughed nervously. "I mean, yes, I made it. I was in the bath. My bathtub is covered with bras drying, so I used the guest bath."

Cy didn't look convinced and Layne knew without a doubt he'd call her dad the second he was in the car. "Well, I'll see you both tomorrow. Don't forget dinner at Grandma and Grandpa's."

"We won't," both girls responded as they watched Cy leave. They didn't say anything until they heard the car driving away. Then, like a bolt, Reagan took off down the hall.

"Stop!" Layne cried as Reagan threw open the bathroom door and skidded to a stop.

"Hi," Reagan said, blushing. "I'm Reagan, Layne's cousin."

"Yes, I heard." Layne heard Walker's deep southern voice from the bathroom.

"And you are?"

Layne peered over Reagan's shoulder and let out a small sigh of relief to see Walker standing with a towel slung low on his hips. At least he wasn't naked. He pulled on a T-shirt of Dylan's. "I'm getting dressed, if you'll excuse me."

Layne yanked on her cousin's arm, pulling her from the bathroom.

"Oh my gosh!" Reagan whispered with a huge smile on

her face. "I'm guessing Uncle Miles has no idea Mr. Hottie is here."

"That's right, and I would appreciate it if you didn't say anything."

"Of course not, but you know it'll be out soon enough. Someone will see something and say something to their friend. Then it'll be all over town."

"I know," Layne sighed as the bathroom door opened and Walker strode out with his wet hair combed back and dressed in a T-shirt and jeans.

"I believe you were about to introduce yourself," Reagan said, looking him over again. "You look familiar."

"I guess I have one of those faces," he shrugged, holding out a hand. "Owen."

"Nice to meet you, Owen. How did you and my cousin meet?"

"Okay!" Layne cut in. "You met, but now it's time to go." Layne shoved her cousin down the hall and into the living room as Reagan laughed.

"It was nice meeting you, Owen!" Reagan called out as Layne practically pushed her out the door.

Layne turned around to find Walker standing behind her. "Interesting family you have."

"They can be a little . . . well, a lot. A lot of everything. But I love them."

"Of course you do. Only a family that cares is so involved." Walker put his hands on her hips and pulled her close. "Now, where were we?"

12

Layne was stronger than any drug. Walker had had a taste of her, and he wanted more. He liked everything about her. She didn't back down, she loved her crazy family, she knew how to kill someone with her pinky, and then there was the feel of her body against his. Breasts big enough to spend hours caressing and kissing that led down to a flat stomach that showed she was incredibly active by her muscle structure, and then there was the sexy flare of her hips. Those hips drove Walker absolutely crazy. He wanted to grab onto them and . . . Walker took a deep breath to calm himself.

"Come to bed with me," Walker said softly.

"I want to, but I can't. As much as I would love nothing more than to strip you naked and have my way with you," Layne said as she shook her head. Walker couldn't stop from grinning. Only Layne would speak as if she were the aggressor when he was the one pursuing her. "I can't. You are my patient, and it's unethical."

"The second I'm healthy I'm picking you up, carrying you into your bedroom, and we won't stop making love until neither of us can move." Walker heard Layne's breathing speed up in response. Good. He wanted her to want him as much as he wanted her. He knew he could convince her to sleep with him, but he respected her too much for that. He could tell it would ruin whatever relationship they were building. "But for now, we'll just sleep. No more of you on the couch."

"Do you think we can?" Layne asked, nibbling on her lip. Damn, if she kept looking so edible he wouldn't be able to control himself.

"You have my word I won't make a move until you're no longer my physical therapist And if I have to, I'll fire you and hire that schmuck Aaron."

Layne laughed and Walker felt as if he were on top of the world. "Okay. Let's get you in bed, and I'll rub out your leg."

Walker didn't need help to walk, but when Layne put her arm around him to walk toward the bedroom with him, he simply took what she offered. He'd take every touch, look, and kiss he could get for now. And he was going to work like a man possessed to get his leg back to normal as fast as possible.

"Good morning, Mr. Selkey. You look so different, having shaved." Jill smiled as they entered the office early the next morning. Layne told Walker she had a patient at nine, so they arrived at eight so she could work with Walker first thing.

"Good morning, Jill. Thank you," Walker said, feeling where his facial hair had been. He'd shaved to help alter his appearance. He was also in new clothes and felt rejuvenated after the bath and then sleeping all night with Layne in his arms. True to his word, he didn't make love to her. He may have dreamed about it. How could he not when she was pressed against him all night? It had seemed natural to have her in his arms; he was reluctant to let her get out of bed.

"Oh, Layne," Jill called out. "You have a message from a Dr. Faulkner. He left a phone number for you."

Walker and Layne both stiffened. "Thank you, Jill." Layne took the paper with the message on it, and they both headed for her office.

Walker looked over her shoulder as he put the note on her desk. "That's not his phone number."

"Whose is it?"

Walker shook his head. "I don't know. Gavin's smart, though. It could be a burner phone."

"Close the door and let's find out." Layne took a seat as Walker closed the door. He came around her desk and leaned against it as she put her phone on speaker and dialed the number.

"Layne?"

"I'm here and so is a friend."

They heard Gavin release a worried breath. "Walker, you're safe?"

"Yeah, why?"

"That man, Darrel Snyder, stormed into my office last night. He broke down the door and tried to get into the medical waste container to look for blood samples. There was a fight, and luckily Ridge was over and came running in to help me when he heard the commotion. Darrel said he knew you were alive. He said I was going to be arrested. A friend of Harper's got me this disposable phone so I could call and warn you."

Walker looked to Layne. Gavin was worried and that

made Walker worried. "Is Darrel still in Shadows Landing?" Walker asked.

"No. He hasn't been back since. I'm worried he may have somehow found you," Gavin explained.

Layne's head rose to look at him as she put her hand supportively on top of his. "Why do you think that?"

"Because of Dr. Luke Benningford."

Walker watched Layne's other hand form into a fist before slowly releasing it as if she were trying to keep control of herself. "What did Luke do?"

"The conference ended last night. I was there keeping up appearances. I saw Darrel talking to Luke, and then they looked over at me. Two hours later he's kicking down the door to my office. I think Luke was spying on you and told him I had a patient I wanted you to see, and he possibly saw you with Walker."

"And my name and address is right there for everyone to see," Layne finished for him.

"I'll leave right now," Walker said, standing. But Layne held onto his hand, preventing him from walking away.

"Wait. There really is no safer place than Keeneston. Let's see how long we can throw him off the scent. I can handle him, and so can everyone else in Keeneston. Trust me." Walker looked into her eyes and saw she meant every word. But the feelings warred inside of him. He didn't want to leave Layne unprotected, but he also didn't want to stay and bring trouble to her.

"One week. Give me one week to work with you and to see how this plays out."

"I think you should. Since finding out who my family is, I've been looking them up. My uncles are badass," Gavin said over the phone.

"Our aunts are too," Layne pointed out. "And don't forget

Ahmed and Bridget. The two of them, not counting their children and my cousins, can overthrow a government during their lunch break. And if you need protection, you can go to Mo and Dani's farm. They're the prince and princess of Rahmi. Their house is an embassy and is well guarded."

"You have royalty in Kentucky?" Gavin asked with amazement.

"Yeah. And their children, Zain, Gabe, and younger sister Ariana, are good friends of mine. They'll help." Layne sounded so sure of herself and her town that Walker took the gamble.

"I'll stay. But we need to get to work. Thanks for the warning, Gav."

"Anytime, buddy. Stay safe. If you need me, call this number. You know we'll all come up at the drop of a hat if you need us."

Layne's smile faltered for a second as Walker thanked Gavin. "Gavin," she said softly, "you know you're welcome in Keeneston anytime you and your . . . I mean, our family . . . want to visit. I'm going to tell my grandmother tonight at dinner about meeting you. I know she'll want to meet all of you and so do I."

"Thank you. After talking to you, my cousins and I decided we're going to see our grandfathers and get the straight story from them. Then we'll talk and I'll let you know. Until then, stay safe."

"I promise I'll keep him safe," Layne swore as Gavin chuckled.

"I was talking about Walker keeping you safe, but I like your way better. Talk to you two soon. Goodbye."

Layne hung up the phone, picked up her intercom, and paged Jill. "Cancel all my eight o'clock, twelve o'clock, and four o'clock appointments for the next three weeks and block off those times."

"All of them?" Jill double-checked.

"Yes. I need to be with Mr. Selkey exclusively during those times."

"Are you . . .?"

"Jill, just do it. Now." Layne hung up and took a deep breath before looking at him. "Come on, we have a lot of work to do, and I fear not a lot of time to do it."

WALKER HAD ALWAYS THOUGHT he was a tough man. That was until he found himself limping inside Layne's house, dying to take one of her special baths. She'd worked him harder than a SEAL instructor, and he felt conflicted about it since she was so damn smart and sexy. Still, she'd hurt him. Badly.

"I'll get a bath ready for you, and then I need to change for dinner at my grandparents' tonight," Layne said as she set a bag of groceries on the counter for him.

Layne had been a woman on a mission, and he was that mission. She also seemed lost in thought, but Walker decided to give her time to herself. She'd come to him when she was ready to talk about whatever was in that beautiful mind of hers.

Walker put the groceries away as Layne started the bath and put in the mixture of oils and salt. Then she disappeared into her bedroom. With a deep breath to stop himself from going after her, Walker undressed as FP joined him in the bathroom. He sat in the tub with FP sleeping on the mat when the door was pushed open and Layne walked right in without knocking. To be fair to her, her hands were full.

"Are you planning on shooting me?" Walker asked, looking at the two guns she was carrying. One was a handgun he'd never seen before and the other was . . . "Dang, is that a HK 416 rifle?"

"Yeah, my dad gave it to me for my eighteenth birthday. I thought you may have used one in the SEALs."

"No, I used an enhanced M 14. Those are used by Delta Force."

"I knew I was right!" Layne smiled triumphantly before the smile slid. "I want you to have these while I'm gone. I have one I carry with me, but you're wounded and need all the firepower you can get."

"What's the handgun? I've never seen it before." Walker leaned over the tub to get a closer look.

"It's a gun my cousin Sophie made." Layne pressed something and held it by the barrel to him. "Put it in your hand as if you were firing it."

Walker dried his hand and palmed the gun. It had a good weight and excellent balance. There was a small beep noise and Layne nodded. "It's programmed to you now. You're the only one who can shoot it."

"Will you marry me?"

"What?" Layne chuckled with disbelief.

"You're smart, sexy as hell, can outperform a SEAL instructor, and you have the best guns I've ever seen. My heart is yours," Walker said, putting his hand to his heart.

Layne laughed, which was his intention, but Walker realized he wouldn't mind if she'd say yes. He hadn't slept with her yet, but he knew she'd be worth the wait. His body, heart, and mind were fully engaged. He was smart enough to know when that happened he was well on his way to falling in love.

"Take your bath." She chuckled again, leaving the guns on the counter. "I'm going to get dressed."

"Are you sure you don't want to take a bath first?" Walker asked seductively. He saw her shiver and flush pink.

"Three weeks," she said with a forced smile. "Easy, right?" he heard her mutter as she walked out of the bathroom, closing the door behind her.

Walker dropped his hand to scratch the top of FP's head. "Three weeks and she's all mine." FP stood and tried to jump in the tub. "You want a snuggle?" FP yipped happily as Walker picked up the hairy little dog and rested him on his chest. FP curled up with his nose buried in Walker's neck and promptly fell asleep.

WALKER HAD JUST CLOSED his eyes in the soothing bath when he heard a pounding on the front door a moment before it crashed open. Walker forgot about his bad leg as he moved FP to his left arm, leapt from the tub, grabbed the rifle, slung the strap over his shoulder, and picked up the pistol in his right hand.

When Layne screamed from the living room, Walker forewent the towel and charged out of the bathroom with FP in one hand and the gun in the other.

"Don't touch her!"

"Oh my goodness," he heard a woman gasp before he heard the deep feral noise coming from the man standing in front of Layne. A man he recognized, and a man who had murder in his eyes.

"Mr. Davies, nice to see you again." Walker lowered the gun and used Fluffy Puppy to cover his privates.

"You have my daughter, my dog, and my gun," Mr. Davies said through clenched teeth as he sneered at him.

"How lovely to meet a friend of Layne's," the woman said from behind Mr. Davies. "I'm her mother, Morgan."

"Nice to meet you, ma'am," Walker said with a nod of his head.

"I'm going to kill you," Mr. Davies said slowly and so softly Walker almost didn't hear him. A second later Mr. Davies charged, FP jumped, and Walker's gun went off as Mr. Davies tackled him to the ground.

"Dad!"

"Miles Davies!"

Walker dropped the gun that had taken a chunk out of the wall and held up his hands. "Take your hit. I won't fight back."

Miles rolled from the ground and sprang up. "Where's the fun in that? Get up, you deserter!"

"Deserter?" Layne and Walker asked together.

"I'm calling the authorities after I beat the shit out of you. I saw this coward on the news being declared legally dead after fleeing a battle where almost his entire team died. And then I remembered I saw him in your office. I came here to protect you, but he's already—" Miles took several deep breaths.

"Don't worry, dear. He's a virgin," Morgan said, putting a restraining hand on her husband's arm.

"*What?*" Miles and Walker asked in disbelief together.

"Jesus, Layne. You told your mom I was a virgin?" Walker asked with incredulity.

"Well, you are. You kicked me out of bed instead of touching me in South Carolina, and—"

Walker interrupted. "I was trying to be respectful!"

"You better pray to God you've been nothing but

respectful or I will kill you. And trust me when I say no one will ever find your body," Miles snarled.

"Now having seen him, it would be a damn shame if he were a virgin." Walker heard Mrs. Davies under her breath as he realized he was flashing her. Walker promptly covered himself with his hands.

"I'm not a virgin!"

"That's not helping you. Get up, you coward," Miles ordered.

"Dad!" Layne said again, only this time there was a threat to her voice as she tossed Walker a blanket from the couch. "He's not a deserter. I'm protecting him from Jud Melville."

Her father clearly didn't believe her. "It's true, sir," Walker said, using the wall to help himself up. His leg was killing him after all the action.

"You're injured," Morgan said, rushing forward and pushing the blanket aside. Could this get more embarrassing? However, that caught Miles's attention as he looked at the wound.

"You were shot," he stated.

"Yes, sir. Jud Melville tried to kill me to cover up the fact that the mission was really a robbery. He had my team killed. I only survived because I dove into the ocean from the bridge and was able to get a small inflatable lifeboat from the debris of what had been a RIB. Jud Melville killed my team, my friends, and my brother-in-law. And as soon as I get better, I'm going to kill him."

Miles was quiet for a moment along with everyone else.

"Unless Jud finds Walker first," Layne said quietly.

"What do you mean, finds him? They all think he's dead." Miles turned from Walker to look at his daughter. "What aren't you telling me?"

13

"Mom, can you stop pushing Walker's blanket aside?" Layne asked with a sigh. "Let him get dressed, and we'll tell you everything."

Her dad looked conflicted as her mother stopped trying to examine Walker's wound. Finally her father nodded with a grunt. "You've earned yourself a stay of execution, boy."

"Yes, sir," Walker said as if it were every day a dad threatened his life.

FP danced around Walker until he picked him up and headed back into the bathroom. Layne's mom rushed forward, "Oh, Layne. I had hoped you'd come back with a doctor, but he's much better. Even FP likes him, and FP doesn't like anyone except you, your father, and a cousin or two."

"Morgan," her dad said through clenched teeth. He was clearly unhappy. "She'd not dating him. She's saving him. Right?"

"Uh . . ." Layne didn't really know how to answer.

"Uh? What the hell does 'uh' mean?"

"Miles, dear, it's perfectly clear they like each other. A SEAL! Isn't that great? Someone you can relate to."

"No, it's not great. He's a frogman. And virgin, my ass. How could you think he was a virgin? Has he touched you? I'll kill him!"

"Uh," Layne managed to get out as her dad was reaching for a gun she didn't know he had on him.

"This will only take a second," he said, turning toward the bathroom.

"Dad," Layne said with a roll of her eyes. "I like this one. Don't shoot him."

Her mom clapped her hands happily together and then snapped her fingers at her husband before pointing to the chair in the living room. He thought twice about it, but then her mother narrowed her eyes and Miles sulked over to the chair.

"So, you like him?" Morgan asked, sitting in the other chair.

"I do. But I'm his doctor, so nothing more can happen until he's released."

"*Nothing more*?" Miles couldn't restrain himself.

Layne knew better. She should have kept her mouth shut. "Obviously we haven't done much since I thought he was a virgin. Now calm down and listen to what happened."

Her dad didn't look calm. In fact, he looked like a volcano ready to explode from the seat. Luckily, or not so luckily, Walker stepped into the living room with FP held like a football under one arm.

"You look as handsome in clothes as you do out of them," her mother quipped, and Layne about died of embarrassment on the spot.

"Thank you, ma'am," Walker said, taking a seat on the couch next to Layne.

"Call me Morgan. And this is my husband, Miles." Layne's father glared at him as her mom smiled as if she were in a meeting bringing in a new client. "Why don't you tell us how all of this happened?"

Walker looked at Layne, and she nodded. As he spoke of the mission, the days at sea, and his time on the Greek ship, she saw her dad change from glaring at Walker to considering what he was saying.

"When I made it to Shadows Landing, I snuck into my best friend's house to get the remainder of the treatment I needed on my leg. My friend is a doctor, Gavin Faulkner." Walker paused, and when Miles didn't say anything, he continued. "Gavin told me someone had been around town since I disappeared, asking questions about me. He told Gavin they had to make sure I really was dead to close the file on me. However, this man was pushy so Gavin wanted me out of Shadows Landing and someplace safe to recover."

"That's where I come in," Layne said, explaining how Gavin had approached her and how they had a run-in with the man at Gavin's cousin's office. "So, I pickpocketed him. His name is Darrel Snyder, and he works private security."

Her father was nodding now. "Cade and Nabi can look into him."

"Cade was Special Forces with my dad. They're brothers. And Nabi took over the security for the Ali Rahman family after Ahmed retired," Layne explained to Walker.

"But then this morning, Gavin called Layne to tell her his office had been broken into. This guy was trying to get into his medical waste receptacle and declared he knew I was alive. Gavin and his cousin fought the man off so he didn't get the evidence he was trying to find. Then Darrel disappeared. Gavin wanted to warn us that this other doctor had been talking to Darrel. The link between Gavin and Layne is the doctor who had the hots for her."

"He's on his way here to kill you," Miles said casually, leaning back in his chair.

"That's what we think," Walker answered as Layne put a reassuring hand on his knee. Her dad's lip snarled and she rolled her eyes at him.

"At least it sounds like you have good friends," Miles said with a grimace. "But you've put my daughter in danger."

Layne cleared her throat. "Uh."

"Dammit, Layne. What more can there be?" Miles asked with a huff.

"I'm glad you think Gavin is a good friend because that's not all he is," Layne said, trying to ease into the fact she was helping the other side of the family.

"He's Walker's boyfriend?" Miles asked with a hopeful smile.

"Uh, no." Layne said and her dad's smile fell. "Gavin Faulkner is your cousin."

Miles was up and out of his chair. "You're helping *them*? The same family who broke my mother's heart by exiling her?"

Layne held up her hands to stop him. "Funny thing is, he was told it was Grandma Marcy who did the leaving and wanted nothing to do with them. Obviously Great-Grandma—"

"Was a bitch," Morgan said angrily as Miles nodded.

"They really think we're the bad part of the family cutting them off?" Miles asked, sitting back down.

"Yup. Gavin's grandfather and great-uncle are in a retirement home. They both have congestive heart failure. He's going to speak with them now that we've met and he discovered we're not the ones who wanted the estrangement. He's trying to get to the truth."

Miles was quiet for a moment. "Mom will be very happy to hear this. Losing that connection to her brothers and having her mother cut her off was very hard on her, even if she rarely talks about it."

"Well," Morgan said cheerfully, "now that we know Walker is a respectable man and not a deserter, we better get to your mom's. It's after six."

"Crap, she'll tan my hide for being late. Let's go," Miles said, ordering everyone out and into his SUV.

"I still haven't decided if I like you or not. And I sure as hell don't like you even looking at my daughter," Miles said from the front seat as they sped down the winding, narrow country roads leading out to the Davies family farm, "but if you thought Hell Week during BUD/S training was bad, you might as well jump from the car right now."

Walker took Layne's hand in his and smiled at her. "I think I can handle it, sir."

Miles snorted. "At least this will be amusing," he told Morgan, who smacked him in return.

Layne hadn't prepared for this. She wasn't expecting to take Walker to a family dinner. This was a dinner where her uncles delighted in scaring off every date she or her cousins had ever brought. Most of the time they left before food was set out. And now she had a man most thought was dead or a deserter, and she wasn't really sure where they stood with each other. Amusing wasn't the word she'd use to describe it. More like terrifying.

The white farmhouse came into view, and she still wasn't prepared for it. Cars were parked everywhere. The uncles and some of her male cousins were sitting on the porch along with her grandfather when they pulled to a stop.

Her father turned and smiled at Walker. Although it wasn't the kind smile he always gave her. It was more a look of feral violence. "Let's see what you're really made of, Froggy."

Walker looked to her with confusion. "Is family dinner really that bad?"

"Uh," Layne said, trying to smile reassuringly even though she was pretty sure it came out as grimace. "Stay strong," Layne finally said, patting his arm before opening her door.

"Hey, Layne! Welcome back. How was the conference?" Jackson Parker, the middle child of Aunt Paige and Uncle Cole, asked. Jackson was with the FBI Hostage Rescue team and made it home occasionally. He was due to leave again in the morning.

"Good." She smiled. "Where's your brother?"

"Ryan's inside acting like a mother hen over Sienna. Apparently, there are dangers all around for a pregnant woman," Jackson teased, making his cousins and uncles laugh. That is, until the other door opened and Walker stepped out. Then there was silence, except for the scraping noise of chairs being pushed back as the Davies men all stood at once.

"Who's the grunt?" Uncle Marshall asked as his son, Wyatt, shook his head.

"I'm Wyatt. One of the many cousins," Wyatt said nicely with a wave as his dad smacked him.

"I'm Walker. Nice to meet you." Walker made his way around the car. He'd refused to bring his crutches so he limped slightly as he stood next to Layne. "And I'm not a grunt. I'm a Navy man."

"Ugh!" Uncle Cade groaned. "A squid. How could you tolerate that, Miles?" Cade and Annie's two sons, Colton and Landon, smirked as Walker took a deep breath.

"He's a froggy," Miles said as he walked up to join the other men. "At least he's not a squid."

"A SEAL? I thought you weren't supposed to tell anyone that."

"That's Uncle Cy. You met his daughter, Reagan," Layne told Walker.

"What the—Reagan!" Cy yelled as his daughter came walking out with her twin sister, Riley, and their cousin Sophie.

"What, Dad?" Reagan asked before looking up and smiling. "Oh hey, Layne. Owen."

"It's Walker, actually. Sorry for the fib," Walker grimaced.

"That's what. You know better than to withhold information. Wait, he was there yesterday when I stopped by, wasn't he?"

"Unlike those ground pounders in the Army, I know how to be quiet," Walker smirked.

"I like him." Sophie chuckled as her dad, Cade, gave her a look.

"Walker, this is Sophie. She made the gun I gave you."

"Well then, it is a pleasure to meet you. That's a great weapon," Walker said, stepping forward and meeting Sophie at the bottom of the stairs to shake her hand.

"And she's taken," her husband, Nash, said coldly from the top of the stairs.

"Bad ass," Cade whispered about his son-in-law to Miles with a smile.

Nash was a badass, but Uncle Cade's obsession with his son-in-law being the biggest badass of all the sons-in-law was something his brothers groaned about.

"And I'm not interested," Walker said, reaching back to grab Layne's hand. Nash looked between them and to the ribbing Miles was getting and smiled then.

"You have balls of steel for walking into a family dinner this early on. Good luck. Sophie, Piper wants—"

"Seriously?" Piper yelled as she pushed past the group standing on the stairs. "You didn't tell me *he* was the one I was getting Dylan's clothes for. And you didn't introduce me." Piper put her hands on her hips and tried to glare, but she didn't have a mean bone in her body.

"Whoa, what's this?" Uncle Pierce, Piper's dad, asked.

"I should have recognized that shirt," Jace, Piper's brother, said. "But why did you need Dylan's clothes to begin with?"

"I'd like to know that too. It sounds juicy." Aunt Tammy came out of the house with Layne's mom and the rest of the aunts.

"Honey, should you be so near the stairs? You're not as strong as you used to be and—"

Pierce didn't get a chance to finish as his brother Marshall punched him in the arm. "Ow. What did you do that for?" Marshall just shook his head.

"Goodness, you weren't lying about him being good lookin'," Grandma Marcy said to Morgan in what was supposed to be a whisper but wasn't.

"When you said you had a lot of family, I pictured lots of people, but this seems like so much more," Walker whispered into her ear as everyone began talking at once.

"And some aren't even here." Layne smiled back to him as the men hurried down the stairs to surround them.

"I think I need to introduce Walker to the family. Why don't you go inside and help Grandma with dinner?" Miles asked nicely, although she knew better.

Riley Davies Walz snaked through the crowd, closing in on them, and grabbed Layne's hand. "Come on. If Matt survived, then surely a SEAL can. Well, maybe."

"Traitors, all of you," Layne said, pointing to Nash, Riley's husband, Matt, and Sydney's husband, Deacon.

"We've been on the other side and this is the reward for surviving." Deacon grinned as he, Matt, and Nash joined in the interrogation that may or may not involve outlawed torture techniques.

"Come on in and tell us all about him," Sydney said, meeting them on the porch. "He'll be fine." Sydney caught sight of Colton on one side of Walker and Miles on the other as they corralled him out back. "Maybe."

"Why is he limping or is my eyesight going bad?" Grandma Marcy asked.

"He was shot," Layne said as they walked inside. Grandma didn't seem fazed. After raising five sons and a daughter, nothing really surprised her anymore.

"Who was shot?" Ryan asked from his place on the couch next to his pregnant wife, Sienna.

"The new boyfriend she brought to dinner," Riley answered.

Ryan shot out of his seat and was halfway across the room before he slid to a stop. "You okay, babe?"

Sienna rolled her eyes. "I've been fine. I am fine. I will be fine. Women have had babies before me, you know."

"Okay, just wanted to make sure." And then Ryan was gone with the slam of the door.

"Thank goodness you brought a diversion for Pierce and Ryan," Aunt Tammy said, taking a seat next to Sienna. A little round belly had appeared on her pixie of an aunt recently.

"I would kill him if he wasn't the father of my child,"

Sienna joked. "Although, it's sweet . . . in a completely smothering kind of way."

"Doesn't that sound lovely?" Katelyn, Sydney's mom, nudged.

"That's another year I'm waiting to have a child," Sydney shot back. Katelyn made a face at her daughter but then hugged her.

"So, tell us about this guy," Piper said excitedly.

"I think it's best to see if he survives first. There's a lot to tell, and it'll all be moot if he's dead." Layne looked through the living room and tried to see out the kitchen door, but had no luck seeing where the guys took Walker.

"*Pfft*, he'll be fine," Aunt Paige said with a wave of her hand. "Cole survived my brothers. Although, now there're cousins and sons-in-law too. Well, I'm sure it'll all work out . . . maybe."

14

Being hunted by Jud might be preferable to what Walker was going through at that moment. The Davies family was an undeniable unit moving as one. When one applied pressure, another told it would be over sooner if he just talked. Somehow, through the constant questions and the walking over the uneven terrain, which he was sure was done purposely to bring pain to his leg, the casual challenge was issued.

"I like bows myself," the one he learned was Landon said. His brother, Colton, however disagreed.

"Axes."

"I think we should make Froggy here jump a little. We all know the Navy has gone soft on their trainees." Miles grinned. Dear Lord, when he grinned he became even scarier.

"I like your thinking, brother." Cade nodded.

"A decathlon of sorts. If he passes, he can come inside. If not, well, we'll bury his body in Dani's garden. No one will find him on Rahmi embassy grounds," Marshall said to his brothers, who all nodded.

"Good plan. I like it." Miles ordered his nephews to round up ten weapons and suddenly Walker was left with just Miles and his brothers. "Now that we have the rookies out of the way, start talking."

A wall of Davies brothers and their brother-in-law formed shoulder to shoulder in front of him. "I can handle anything you throw at me, so give it to me," Walker challenged as he stood up straight and refused to give into the pain in his leg.

"Tell my brothers about Jud Melville," Miles ordered.

"I'd rather hear about his intentions with my niece," Marshall said before stopping and cutting his ice cold glare on Walker. "Damn, I didn't put it together until now. You're a dead man."

"Dead and buried if the news is correct. Some place in South Carolina. Your sister was on the news declaring that wasn't your body they buried in your hometown," Cade said, stepping closer to him. "Who the hell are you and what the hell are you doing with Layne?"

"I'm Chief Petty Officer Walker Greene of the US Navy's DEVGRU division. And I'm the only survivor who can tell what really happened on the mission that took the lives of my brothers at the hand of our senior chief, Jud Melville," Walker answered with a challenge in his eye as he looked at each and every one of them.

"SEAL team six, that's impressive," Cade said with a raised eyebrow as Marshall hit him.

"They're not called that anymore," Marshall said with a roll of his eyes. "How far behind the times are you?"

"Isn't anyone interested in what happened on the mission and how he ended up here?" Pierce asked. All the brothers returned their focus onto him.

"Tell them," Miles ordered. Walker obeyed and retold the entire story for the group.

"We're back in business." Marshall grinned after Walker finished. Walker didn't show his confusion but let them continue to talk among themselves.

"Wait a minute, this is my daughter we're talking about who is now in danger," Miles pointed out.

"And I will protect her with my life," Walker swore as the brothers cringed.

Miles rounded on him and slammed a fist into his chin. "She is *my* daughter, not *your* anything. I will protect her."

Walker didn't budge. He refused to. He absorbed the hit and let the pain fade with no reaction at all.

"To be fair," Cade said hesitantly, "your daughter is probably the most lethal of all our kids. If Sophie could take care of herself, Layne could do it with her eyes closed. Though Sophie did have the help of the biggest badass ever helping her."

"Oh, give it a rest," Cy groaned. "Matt is a badass too."

"Please, he just handled a drug dealer and politicians. *My* son-in-law single-handedly took down a terrorist organization," Cade said, puffing up his chest.

"And Deacon stopped a sex-trafficking ring. He's also a badass," Marshall defended.

"But—" Cade injected before Cy rounded on him with a punch to the gut.

Cole Parker held up his hands as his silver eyes sparkled with amusement. "I don't have a son-in-law in the game, but I think we should acknowledge Walker here just took a full-force punch from Miles without flinching. He has my vote of acceptance."

"Mine too," Pierce said, looking nervously back to the house. "I better check on Tammy. At her advanced age—"

All the brothers groaned. "She's going to kill you soon, and I'll help her bury the body," Cy said with a shake of his head.

"What? Having a baby at her old age is very stressful to her body and—"

"And you're supposed to be the genius," Miles said, rolling his eyes.

"Whatever. Good luck, Walker. I approve of him, but I better get back inside." The group watched as Pierce took off for the house as the young group including Ryan, Deacon, Nash, Matt, Colton, Landon, Jackson, Wyatt, and Jace came walking out of the barn and house carrying a variety of weapons.

"I'm withholding my vote until we see what you've got," Cy said smugly.

Walker shrugged. "No problem." He turned to Cade. "But what did you mean about Layne being lethal?"

Miles gave him a smile that sent a shiver up his back. "I trained her myself. You make one misstep, and you don't have to worry about me cutting off your balls. My daughter will do it with a dull spoon."

Walker felt his lips tilt up. He wouldn't say it, but while he knew Layne was his equal personally, he really loved the fact she may very well be equivalent to him physically. "I don't know about that. You know those Delta Force guys who are the Army's so-called counterpart to us DEVGRU guys . . . they're just a bunch of snake eaters. That's why our units overlap, because someone has to come in and save the day." Walker let his smile come then.

Miles, Cade, and Marshall glared, though Walker also noted the quirk of their lips. "I'd put my daughter up against someone whose whole basis of the English language revolves around the word *Hooyah*."

"But Miles, he's a hootin', lootin', parachutin' Frogman. What did you expect?" Cy asked sarcastically.

"Hooyah!" Walker called out.

Marshall laughed. "He has my vote. I like him."

"We vote on this stuff?" Wyatt asked, dropping two spoons on the ground. "Well, he already has my vote. Good luck with the spoons. Uncle Miles has weird knowledge on how to kill people with them. It would be frightening if you stopped to think about it."

Knives, spoons, handguns, assault rifles, sniper rifles, bows, axes, grenades, and a pair of boxing gloves. Surely his training would help him with this . . . maybe.

LAYNE LOOKED at her watch for the fifth time in twenty seconds. Time was moving slowly. Walker had been gone for an hour. Grandpa Jake said not to worry, most men who came to date Paige usually left alive. That hadn't helped.

"He'll be fine," her mother said, coming up behind her. Layne looked out the back window as two explosions were visible off in the distance. "Maybe."

People went on talking around her, but Layne didn't hear them. She looked behind her, and no one was paying her any more attention. They were all cooing over Sienna and Tammy's pregnancies. Her dad had always taught Layne to go after what you want, so that made the decision to break protocol easy. Layne slipped out the back door and ran silently through the night toward the explosions.

When she got close enough to see, she hid behind a tree and looked out. Her cousins and most of her cousins-in-law were all standing off to the side, looking defeated. Uncle Cy and Walker were lying on the ground, lining up a sniper shot. So this was what they did? For some reason it made her mad. What would have happened if she'd brought Luke home or something? He'd have pissed himself and run as fast as he could away from here.

That thought of having her choices taken from her is what propelled her out of the shadows and marching straight for her family. "I get the winner," she called out. It would have been humorous how everyone whipped around in surprise to find her ten feet behind them, except she was so mad right then she could hit someone.

"You're not supposed to be out here," Landon finally said.

"I beat the crap out of you before, and I'll do it again if you don't stand there and be quiet," Layne snapped.

Cy looked from where he was looking through the scope. "No problem, Layne. I'll be done with Froggy in just a sec, and then Uncle Cy will teach you a thing or two your dad couldn't."

"Do you need your glasses for the shot, Uncle Cy?" Layne asked sweetly. She was always the nice one, always there for people, the charity worker. But they'd gone and pissed her off now.

"Take your shot, sir," Walker said, having ignored Layne the entire time.

Cy let out a breath and caressed the trigger. A second later Walker fired his shot at his own target.

"Winner, Walker," Nash yelled a couple minutes later as he ran back from the targets set over a quarter of a mile away.

"Want a go at it?" Walker asked with a smile. He sounded as if he were having fun. But Layne had anger she needed to release, so she took Cy's rifle and lay down on the ground. She adjusted the sight, zeroed in on the target, took a breath, and when she exhaled she pulled the trigger back with certainty.

"Your turn to go get it," Nash told Deacon, who jogged away.

"What's next?" Layne asked with determination to beat her uncles into the ground for what they were putting Walker and her through.

"Spoons," Wyatt said, sounding very confused. "Can you kill someone with a spoon?"

"Yes," Layne, Walker, and Miles answered at once.

"Layne, honey, you've had your fun. Let us guys get back to this." Miles picked up a spoon and looked at the dummy target they had. "First one to get a kill shot wins."

"Argh!" Layne ripped the spoon from Walker's hand and rammed the handle up the dummy's nose and into the straw brain. "Done. Next?"

"W-w-winner, Layne," Wyatt announced, slightly stuttering over the words.

"For what it's worth, I was going to go for the ear," Walker said with a shrug before leaning forward and putting his lips near her ear. "You are sexy as hell when you're mad and handling weapons. Has anyone ever told you that?"

Some of the anger left her as she smiled. "Sorry for having taken your spoon."

"It's okay, but I think you crushed your father."

Layne looked to where he was silently holding his spoon. He looked like a sad boy who had broken his favorite toy.

"Winner, Layne," Deacon called back, holding both targets. Layne looked over and saw Walker's eyes widen. A smile returned to her father's lips. And Uncle Cy looked ready to cry.

"What's the score?" Layne asked happily.

"Layne, 2. Walker 7," Wyatt said, obviously enjoying seeing the uncles losing for once.

"Great, what's next?" Layne asked almost giddy now.

"Hand-to-hand," Nash said, stepping forward. "The last one goes to me."

"My son-in-law is the biggest—"

"Badass. Yes, I know," Layne muttered with concern. She grabbed Walker's hand and pulled him away from the group. His limp was severe now. While he gave absolutely no indications of being in pain, his leg said it all. "Are you okay? Is that a bruise on your face?"

"What? Oh, yeah, I'm fine."

"No, you're not. Your leg is almost in spasm. I can see the muscles constricting from here. You can't go up against Nash. This much activity will undo everything we're working toward to get you ready for Jud."

"But—" Walker started.

"Do you want to fight Nash or Jud, because you only get one." Layne put her hands on her hips and stared him down.

"Jud," Walker said sadly. "But I have to finish this. If I can do that, I'm accepted. And Layne, you're worth the pain."

Well, crap. That began to melt her resolve until she saw Uncle Cade pumping Nash for the fight. "I like you too much to see you hurt. It's not a fair fight, and you know it."

Layne left Walker there to hobble back as she stopped in front of her family. "Y'all love me, right?"

"Of course," came the immediate reply.

"And if Nash loses the fight, you'll accept Walker as my boyfriend and will stop this macho shit?"

"Well, what do you mean, stop?" Marshall asked confused. "Like all the way?"

Layne stared him down.

"If Nash loses, we'll welcome Walker to the family. That is if he's intending to stick around for a while," her father replied, looking past her to Walker. Layne looked behind her to find Walker standing there. He put one hand protectively on her shoulder.

"As I told you before, sir, I plan on sticking around, and I'll protect Layne with my life. Although, after seeing her kill a dummy with a spoon up the nose and a clean shot to the brain of a target, she may be the one protecting me."

Layne relaxed upon hearing him, sounding proud as opposed to insulted that a girl beat him.

"Done. However, I refuse to stop calling him Froggy," her father said stiffly. Layne felt Walker chuckle behind her.

"Good." Layne bent and picked up the boxing gloves and pulled them on her hands.

"What are you doing?" Nash asked, looking confused.

"As Walker's doctor, I can't let him further injure his leg. So I'm his fill-in. The deal was if Nash lost, not who won."

"You can't do that," Cade cried.

"She can. Good luck, honey."

"Thanks, Dad." Layne turned to Walker who tied the gloves on.

"Are you sure about this?"

"Absolutely."

15

"Where have you been? We were so worried!" Morgan cried when the entire group traipsed back into the farmhouse twenty minutes later.

"Nash," Sophie gasped. "What happened to your face?"

"Your cousin punched me."

"Why would Ryan punch you?" Sophie asked, jumping up to look at the black eye.

"Not that cousin. Layne," Nash told Sophie.

"You punched my husband?" Sophie asked, wide-eyed.

"I did a hell of a lot more than that," Layne said with a grin. "I beat the biggest badass of them all."

The uncles, except for Cade, snickered. Her father was beaming. Her grandmother was too as she slowly stood up and made her way to an equally beaming Walker. "Well, now that's all settled, why don't we sit down for dinner and you tell us all about yourself, young man."

"Happy to, ma'am. I believe you'll find we have a common connection."

LAYNE SAT next to Walker at the table that stretched from the dining room into the living room. Her uncles and aunts were on one side and all the cousins were on the other. All of whom were quiet as Walker and Layne filled them in on why Walker was in Keeneston. The uncles, who had already heard this, were interjecting their ideas on how to move forward, while Aunt Annie looked thrilled to be involved in a dangerous mission again.

"Well, it's a good thing we know you can handle yourself," Grandma Marcy said, setting out three apple pies. "But how is this a connection to me?"

Layne reached under the table and squeezed Walker's knee. This was going to be something of a shock for her. He placed his hand over hers and patiently waited until her grandmother took a seat. "Well, ma'am, you know I told you my doctor friend, Gavin, helped me and connected me with Layne?"

Grandma Marcy and the rest of the table except her parents nodded.

"His last name is Faulkner. He's your grandnephew."

The uncles erupted in anger. Grandpa Jake put a hand on Grandma Marcy as she went white.

Layne looked to her father who put two fingers in his mouth and whistled. "Let them finish. There's much more to this story."

Layne smiled at her dad, then turned to her grandmother and explained how she met Gavin and how they found out they were cousins. She left out the part about hitting on him, though.

"My mother hated me so much she told them I was the one who left them?" Tears welled in her eyes and Layne instantly regretted causing her pain.

"It seems the family rift wasn't caused by your brothers

at all. I'm sorry, Grandma. But you have family who want to meet you. They want to meet all of us," she told the table.

"I didn't know they had grandkids. Please, tell me about them," Grandma Marcy requested as Walker filled her in.

"Scott and Kevin are in a nursing home. They both have congestive heart failure, but they're still managing it pretty well. Their children have moved away from Shadows Landing and live in Florida. But, all the cousins stayed in Shadows Landing. Gavin is a doctor. His sister, Harper, owns the local bar and grill. Wade is with the Coast Guard in Charleston and his brother Trent is a furniture maker. Then there's Ryker, who mostly lives in Charleston and owns a shipping company. Lastly there's Ridge, who is a luxury home builder and his sister, Tinsley, who is an artist," Walker explained as silent tears fell down her grandmother's wrinkled cheeks.

"And they want to meet me?" she asked hesitatingly.

"Yes, ma'am," Walker smiled to reassure her.

Jake wrapped his arm around his wife and held her as she cried happy tears. The uncles shifted nervously. Grandma Marcy never cried. Never. The aunts were tearing up as well as they hurried to hug her.

"Thank you so much, young man. It was fate that you came into our lives and brought our family back together," Grandma Marcy said, wiping the tears from her face.

"We have to keep him alive now," Cade muttered.

"You know what you need to do," Aunt Annie said matter-of-factly.

"Keep him hidden?" Layne suggested.

Annie snorted. "Likely chance of that. Riley already blabbed it to Aniyah."

"Oh," was all Layne could say.

"Oh? What does that mean? Who's Aniyah?" Walker asked.

"Son, I have some extra body armor you may want to borrow before you meet her," Miles said with such seriousness Layne actually laughed.

"Steel-toed boots would be more helpful," Layne snickered. "She can't hit an actual target, so she mostly shoots toes off. But, yes, I know what I need to do. I'll send a text out tonight. But now, we need to go. I need to undo all the damage you guys inflicted to Walker's leg tonight."

"I'll drive you home," Piper offered. "It's on my way."

"Thanks," Layne replied as she got up to hug her family goodbye. As they all followed Piper and Walker outside saying their goodbyes, Layne hugged her father. "Dad?"

Her father let out a huff. "You could do worse."

Layne and her mother grinned at the ringing endorsement. "Thank you, Dad." She leaned up and placed a kiss on his cheek before hurrying to the car.

WALKER LEANED HEAVILY on Layne as they entered her house. FP bounded happily around them, and Walker felt a sense of home he hadn't felt since his parents died. It also made him think of his sister—a sister who had been forced to bury him earlier that day. He wanted to call Edie desperately, but he knew Jud was probably counting on that.

"Do you realize what you called me tonight?" Walker asked as they maneuvered to the bedroom.

Layne actually blushed. "Yes. Sorry about that."

"Why?" Walker asked. "I'm not."

"I can't treat you now, and I put a label on something we haven't even discussed."

"I'm pretty sure we discussed it with our bodies if not

with words," Walker said, stopping and pulling her near. He didn't like the worried look on her face. "Layne?"

"Yes?"

"You're fired." Walker leaned down and captured her lips with his. Tonight he had no intention of stopping. For days, their attraction had been building. And when she went toe-to-toe with her shockingly scary and talented family, he had given up trying to restrain himself. Especially when he knew exactly what he wanted, and that was Layne. All of her.

Walker would have loved nothing more than to grab Layne and take her up against the wall, but he couldn't with his leg. Instead, he kept his mouth eliciting moans from hers as he fell back onto the bed, bringing Layne with him. Her body was fully on top of his. He felt the press of her breasts into his chest, the V of her legs cupped his hard-on, and when she sat up he was in the perfect position to peel her top from her body so he could worship the breasts he'd been dreaming about.

"Walker," she gasped as he twirled his tongue around a beaded nipple. Her fingers ran through his hair until she was grabbing handfuls while holding his head to her breast.

Walker pulled away and yanked his shirt from his body before practically shredding Layne's jeans from her body. In a hurried mass of tangled limbs, heated kisses, and fondling hands, they were finally naked. "Oh God, you're beautiful," Walker whispered to her, and she straddled him. She was perfect. It was like she had been made only for him and he for her.

"Condom?" Walker asked as her heat had him practically begging for entrance.

Layne froze. "Don't you have one?"

"Um, no. I don't have anything, not even the clothes now on the floor. Don't you have one?" Walker asked now, saying a prayer to every saint he could think of. Was there a patron saint of safe sex?

Layne groaned and rolled off him. "No. I hardly ever get this far with my boyfriends. My dad usually scares them off by the second date."

Walker sat up and looked at Layne. Her black hair was spread out on the pillowcase, her hazel eyes sad with disappointment and frustration. "Layne," Walker started to say as he brushed back her hair from her cheek. There were plenty of ways to pleasure her without making love to her. "I think I'm fall—"

Knock, knock, knock.

Walker and Layne both shot out of bed and grabbed a gun. "Are you expecting anyone?" Walker whispered.

Layne shook her head as she reached for a robe and tossed it to Walker before wrapping a blanket around herself. They didn't need to communicate. They worked effortlessly together, quietly making their way down the hallway and separating in the living room. Layne went to the door, Walker hid behind a chair with his gun pointed at the door. He nodded and Layne reached across the door, yanking it open and jumping back with her gun raised.

Walker had her in his gun's sight. The most curvaceous African-American woman he'd ever seen. She couldn't be more than five feet, except for the fact she was in five-inch spiked heels. Her short, straight black hair was highlighted red and perfectly swooped over her forehead and behind her ears, which had the largest hoop earrings Walker had ever seen.

"Lordy! What are you doing with that gun pointed at me?" the woman cried as Layne lowered her gun, and the woman strutted into the house with hips swinging. "That's a nice one, though. Do you have another? DeAndre took mine after I shot the mailman. In my defense, he was nosing around my mailbox, and it's not like he needs *all* his toes."

Layne grinned and Walker stood up. The woman's hand fluttered against her chest as she caught sight of him. "It's true! You do have a man. And look at that gun!"

Layne's mouth dropped and Walker looked at the rifle he held out in his hands. "It's the same gun those Delta Force guys use."

"Honey, I'm not talking about that gun," Aniyah said as she began to fan herself. Then what was she looking at? Oh crap.

Walker hadn't closed the robe. He was flashing yet another woman. He put the rifle over his shoulder and hurriedly tied the amethyst colored silk robe that barely covered his gun and ammo.

"It's not that impressive." Walker looked up from tying the robe to see a man in a state trooper uniform standing with his hand on the woman's shoulder. His dark brown eyes were filled with amusement as the woman swatted him.

"Not everyone is packing what you are, Sugarbear, but it's impressive nonetheless." She turned her smile on Walker, even if her eyes still hadn't moved up to his. "I'm Aniyah, and this is DeAndre. Welcome to Keeneston."

"Sorry it has to be under these circumstances," DeAndre said, holding out his hand to shake Walker's. "We stopped by to see if we could help. Sorry for, um, interrupting."

Walker had DeAndre's number in a glance. He was an intelligence operator if he'd ever seen one. He was tall, lean, and strong, but the way he took in every aspect of a room had intelligence written all over him. No wonder he was good at gossip.

"I didn't send out the text yet," Layne said. DeAndre just

smiled and Walker shook his head. This man was completely underutilized as a state trooper.

"You ever think of going to work for Naval Intelligence?"

"Nah, I like it right here in Keeneston. But tell me how I can help."

Walker and DeAndre walked into the living room as Aniyah grabbed Layne and dragged her into the kitchen. Walker took a seat and DeAndre grabbed the blanket from the couch and tossed it at him. "I'm sorry, man, but I just can't talk to you with your equipment just hanging there like that."

Walker put the blanket over his legs and DeAndre took a seat. "Fill me in," DeAndre requested as they got to work.

By the time Aniyah was done with Layne, Walker had filled DeAndre in . . . well, as much as he needed to. The man would make a fortune working for the CIA. He already knew way more than Walker thought anyone could.

"Sure, man. No problem. I'll let you know if I hear anything. And now I know who to look for around town. Once Layne sends out the town text, you'll be covered. It's hard for anyone to sneak into town without someone seeing them. I'm impressed you did. But then again, you had the help of a local, which is a completely different situation."

LAYNE LOOKED to where the men were standing. Aniyah had grilled her about Walker and about their lack of a sex life. Layne bit her lip as Aniyah started to turn to leave the kitchen. Oh, screw it. "Aniyah," she hissed out on a whisper.

Aniyah stopped and turned on the spike of her heel. "What is it, sugar?"

Layne felt her face flush red. "I know by tomorrow

there'll be bets placed at the café, but I do want to keep this as private as possible."

"I'm a freaking vault, sug. You can tell me anything." Layne tried not to roll her eyes. Aniyah was anything but a vault. But right now she was experiencing something stronger than common sense—lust.

"Do you have any condoms in your purse?"

Aniyah didn't blink as she opened up her purse and began to dig around. "Of course I do. And after seeing what that fine man is packing, I know he can handle these." Aniyah pulled out a box of extra large condoms. "And I have these oils somewhere in here. I always have something with me at all times. You never know when you want to get freaky-deaky. Be careful, the oils are flammable." Aniyah pulled out a feather and a pair of cheetah print fur lined cuffs and offered them to Layne.

"No," Layne squeaked. "The condoms are fine. Thank you. And if you value Walker's, um, package, you may not want to mention giving these to me or I'm afraid my dad might—"

Aniyah nodded. "I understand. It'd be a damn shame to lose such a prime example of God's work. My lips are sealed. Oh, speaking of sealed, I have a blindfold that can also be used as—"

"No! This is perfect," Layne said, feeling her face flush. She didn't know if it was from embarrassment or the idea of being blindfolded with Walker's hands running down her body. Either way, she was pretty sure an important line in the sand had been crossed with Aniyah.

"Are you ready to go, baby?" DeAndre called out as he and Walker stood up.

"At least take the cuffs," Aniyah whispered.

"I have my own, thank you." Layne didn't mention they

were actually zip ties her father had given her in a college care package he'd sent years ago. She just didn't seem to need to hogtie intruders as much as her father assumed she did.

"You go, girl." Aniyah shoved the cuffs back into her purse. "I'm ready, Sugarbear. I'm suddenly in the mood to get home quickly."

After DeAndre shut the door, Walker and Layne were shell-shocked. Until Walker turned to her and she held up the box of condoms. Then a slow smile spread across his face as he dropped the robe to the ground.

16

Finally! Layne was panting. Her body was squirming with need. The front door was locked against unwanted guests, the condom fit perfectly, and Walker's mouth had just finished doing wonderful things to every inch of her body. Walker flipped her so he was lying on the bed and she was straddling him once again. She enjoyed the power and the ability to make Walker groan with desire. Walker smiled seductively as he ground against her, urging her to take him inside.

Layne's heart beat wildly and not just from foreplay. When she looked at Walker, she saw someone who really wanted to be her partner. He wasn't intimidated by her. He thought she was sexy when she killed the dummy with a spoon. Plus he hadn't run screaming after meeting her family. Instead, he'd been so kind to her grandmother. Layne might have been looking for a one-night stand back in Charleston, but Walker was so much more. Her heart was telling her what her mind already knew. Walker Greene was someone worth going to battle for. But right now he was all hers, and she couldn't wait another second to feel him inside her.

Layne rose to her knees and a shadow moved on the wall above the headboard. This shadow didn't have breasts. This shadow grew larger as it came closer to the partially open bedroom door.

Layne dove forward, her breasts smashing against Walker's face as she reached for the gun on the nightstand. She rolled off Walker and aimed the gun at the door the same time the barest *creak* came from the hallway. Walker reacted instantly, rolling away from her as she leapt silently from the bed and pressed herself against the wall with the gun aimed at the door.

"Don't move, Walker," the voice said from the hallway. He would have seen Layne roll off Walker, but he wouldn't be able to see her now. However, Walker would be clearly in his sights. "Drop the gun and I won't hurt your lady friend."

Walker's eyes shot to hers and she nodded as she crept closer to the door. "Fine. I'm putting it down. Who are you, and what do you want from me?"

"It's not what I want. It's what a mutual acquaintance wants."

"How much is Jud paying you? I'll double it."

The man laughed as he stepped into the room. Layne hid the gun behind her back and huddled in the corner as he cast a quick, appreciative glance at her before ignoring her. Now that was stupid. Never underestimate a woman, especially a naked one.

More importantly, in that one moment with the moonlight highlighting his face, she knew him. Darrel Snyder. He'd found them. And if he found them, that meant Jud knew exactly where they were.

"There's no way you'll be able to do that. You have no

idea what was on that ship, do you?" He laughed. "And you never will. This is from Jud."

Layne didn't wait. She didn't think. She reacted. Her muscles knew what to do before her mind could register it. Why? Because her father had made her practice so often she'd simply reacted. She raised her gun and fired two quick shots to the head.

The man fell. The room was quiet. And Layne began to shake so hard she slid to the ground. She may have been taught how to kill, but that didn't mean she'd ever taken a life before. And certainly not someone in her bedroom. Someone whose blood was now pooling on the area rug at the foot of her bed.

"Shh, it's okay." Walker checked to make sure Darrel was dead before wrapping his arms around her. In seconds, he had her safe in his arms with his hand holding her head against his chest. "Thank you for saving my life. I know the first one is so hard. Do you need to throw up? I threw up when I killed for the first time."

Layne could barely nod, but Walker had her. He pulled her up and was half-carrying her toward the bathroom. Layne fell to her knees and Walker draped a towel over her shoulders before disappearing. Layne flushed the toilet and took deep breaths as she tried to stop the tears.

"Sir, it's Walker. I'm at Layne's, and there's been an incident. They found me." She heard Walker talking from the bedroom. "No, sir. She's fine. She shot him though. Yes, sir. I'll take care of her."

"Who was that?" Layne asked as Walker hurried back into the bathroom and handed her a cup of water.

"Your father. He's on his way over."

Layne almost choked. "You called my *dad*?!"

"Of course I did. We need to get this cleaned up and

decide on how to act. I respect the hell out of your dad and family. They're my new team. When something like this happens, you turn to your team for help."

Layne gave a slow nod. "Well, if you don't want your new team to castrate you, you better get us some clothes."

WALKER HAD Layne in sweats and he was in jeans and a T-shirt by the time the first car arrived. Walker had helped Layne to the couch in the living room after he had helped her dress. They'd found Fluffy Puppy lying by the door with a tranquilizer dart in him. Layne had lost it then. Big fat tears fell as she cradled her dog.

"He'll be okay," Walker said as he held them both. The little dog was breathing well, which was the only thing keeping Layne from shooting Darrel again.

The front door flew open as Miles and Morgan rushed in. Streams of headlights could be seen down the road coming toward them. "Did you call the whole town?" Walker asked as he reluctantly let go of Layne so her parents could hug her.

"They found out somehow even though Layne hadn't sent out the text yet."

"DeAndre or John must have told them," Morgan said, handing Layne a tissue and sitting next to her, wrapping her in a motherly hug.

Miles stopped and looked at FP. "The bastard killed my dog?"

"Tranquilizer. He'll be fine in a couple hours," Walker reassured him.

"What happened?" Cy asked as he, Cade, and Annie ran into the house.

"What is it?" Ryan and Cole yelled from the porch as they pushed their way in.

"There is a dead man in the bedroom," a stone-cold smooth voice said from behind Walker. Walker turned and found a man with tanned skin, dark eyes, black hair with a sliver of silver in it, and a woman standing next to him armed to the teeth.

"Thanks for coming, Ahmed," Miles said, standing up from where he was kneeling in front of Layne.

"Is this the boy?" Ahmed asked, looking Walker over with cold eyes.

"Yeah," Miles said, not sounding too happy about it.

"He tapped him twice in the head. Almost on top of each other. Very impressive."

Walker stood up and held out his hand. "Walker Greene; it's an honor to meet you. But it was Layne who shot him."

"Then what were you doing?" the woman asked. "I'm Bridget, Ahmed's wife, by the way."

"Nice to meet you, ma'am. I was distracting him so Layne could get the shot off."

Bridget nodded and headed over to talk to Annie as Marshall skidded to a stop at the front door.

"Walk us through it," Miles ordered as he strode down the hall. Walker hurried to follow with Ryan, Cole, Cy, Cade, Annie, Bridget, Ahmed, and newly arrived Deacon following close behind. He gave one look over his shoulder and saw Katelyn and Wyatt, the mother/son veterinary duo working on FP with Morgan. Walker felt his forehead crease with confusion as to why three old ladies had just hobbled up the stairs. The one with big bosoms looked up at him and winked.

When Walker made it into the bedroom, he found Nash

already back there. The window to the bedroom was open. That explained how Ahmed, Bridget, and Nash got in.

"Badass," he heard Cade whisper to Miles.

"Who is he?" Ahmed asked.

"Darrel Snyder. Jud Melville hired him to kill me."

Ahmed didn't respond but sent a text to someone instead.

"So, what were you doing when he came in? How did he get this far into the house?" Miles asked.

"We were in bed." Walker hoped they thought he meant sleeping. The quick punch to the face from Miles told him otherwise. Damn, his jaw was going to be even sorer now.

Annie snickered, and it was then Walker realized they forgot to move the box of XL condoms from the nightstand. That was it. He was a dead man. Miles's jaw worked as he flexed his hand into a fist over and over again and counted to ten.

"Miles, breathe," Cy hissed.

"Oh my. Does that say extra large?" an old voice said from behind him.

"I don't know, Lily. I don't have my glasses on, but I see three X's," another old voice said as the three elderly ladies completely ignored the dead body and zeroed in on the box of condoms.

"I have my binoculars, hold on," the one with the big bosom said as she pulled a pair of binoculars from her suitcase of a purse. "Yup. EXXXtra large, with three X's. My oh my." She winked at him again.

Walker was starting to look forward to Miles taking him out.

"So, before my brother kills you, tell us about the dead man," Marshall said, literally blocking Miles from coming after him.

"Nabi tells me he owns a security company of former special ops guys. All of whom were kicked out of the service for bad conduct. Darrel here was kicked out fifteen years ago for selling drugs on the base. They never found any on him, but the circumstantial evidence was enough to have him dishonorably discharged."

"Which base?" Walker asked as things began to click together.

"Afghanistan. He was a SEAL," Ahmed answered.

"Jud Melville has been a SEAL for sixteen years. His first deployment was a two-year stint in Afghanistan."

Ahmed typed something and a second later nodded. "They were stationed together."

"Okay," Miles said, taking a deep breath. "So we know why Jud has him doing his dirty work. But does Jud know Darrel was in Keeneston?"

Cade bent down and began to go through the clothes on the body. "Here, use these," Ryan said, handing a pair of latex gloves to Cade.

"I see I'm late," Matt Walz said, dressed in his sheriff's uniform. "I had an idea I needed to be on duty for this." He pulled out gloves himself and knelt down on the other side of Cade. They removed a secondary gun and a knife that they handed to Ryan, who put them in evidence bags.

"Here it is," Cade said, pulling a cell phone from the front pocket after they rolled Darrel's body over. Cade used Darrel's thumb to unlock the cell phone and began to pull up the text messages. "Jud knows. Darrel sent a picture of you and Layne to Jud to confirm your identity. Jud then asked for the woman's identity."

"Did he get it?" Walker asked.

"Yes."

Miles and Walker looked at each other. "Get her out of here," Walker ordered to Miles who only nodded.

"Good luck with that," Annie called out, causing Miles to stop in his tracks.

"What do you mean by that?" he asked.

"She's your daughter. You know better than anyone she won't leave the man she loves to go hide."

"No one said anything about love," Miles ground out between a clenched jaw.

"Would you rather it be casual sex?" Annie smirked.

"Sweetheart," Cade said with a warning to his voice, "don't provoke him right now."

Annie rolled her eyes.

"You know she's right." Walker turned to find Layne standing in the doorway. "I'm not leaving. So what's the plan?"

The phone rang in Cade's hand. The quiet vibration seemed as loud as a highest volume ring tone.

"Answer it," Miles demanded. Walker took the phone from Cade and put it on speaker.

"What's the status?" Walker heard Jud ask.

"One dead, unfortunately for you, it's not me."

"Walker," Jud cursed. "I should be impressed. Instead you're turning out to be a huge pain in the ass."

"I'll try to be a little more cooperative the next time you try to kill me."

Jud chuckled. "I'll do that. But you're such a coward you'll probably be gone before I make it to you. Always running away, aren't you?"

"I'm not going anywhere, Jud. Come and get me."

"Oh, I'll get you. But if you run or try to tell anyone what's happening, I'll kill the girl. Layne is her name. Cute little doctor, isn't she? Why, Walker, are you injured?" Jud asked full of fake concern.

"Was it worth it, Jud? Was it worth killing your brothers for money?"

Jud just laughed. "Damn right it was. I'm coming, Walker. And remember, a word about this to anyone, and Layne won't be the only woman in your life meeting her end."

The line went dead and Walker felt the anger pumping his adrenaline. "I have to get to Shadows Landing," Walker said, trying to push his way out of the room. But two iron strong arms stopped him. "Let me go, sir."

"I'm assuming he's talking about your sister. If you go to her now, you'll be walking right into a trap. You want him to come to you. You have us here as your backup. You have an entire town of capable people to help you. There will be no surprise attack. But if you go firing off to South Carolina . . ."

Dammit. He was right. Walker would be running head first into an ambush. No matter how it killed him, he had to wait for Jud to come to him.

"I think it's time to call your sister," Layne said quietly as she slipped her hand into his and gave it a squeeze. "Maybe the Faulkners can help."

Walker nodded as he took Layne's cell phone and dialed his sister's number. No answer. He called Gavin's next.

"Hello?"

"It's Walker. Jud knows where I am. Is Edie safe?"

"Yeah. She's staying at Tinsley's. Why?"

"Jud threatened her, and she's not answering her cell phone."

"Hold on," Gavin said as Miles instructed him to put the call on speaker. Walker did and the sound of a ringing phone could be heard. "I'm conferencing Tinsley in."

"Gav, help me," came the raspy voice of Tinsley.

"I'm on my way!" Gavin yelled as they all heard him grabbing things from the house and running to the garage. They heard the car start as Gavin talked to Tinsley. "Are you safe?"

"I think so. A man broke in. I'm hurt," Tinsley said, her voice filled with pain.

"What about Edie?" Walker asked.

"Walker?"

"Yes, Tins, it's me."

Tinsley began to cry. "I'm so sorry. They took her."

17

Layne wanted to comfort Walker, but the look of pure rage, murder, and pain in his eyes told her not to. Instead, she grabbed the phone from him and began to talk to Tinsley getting information about the man who hurt her and took Edie.

"Who are you?" Tinsley asked with short shallow breaths after describing Jud.

"I'm your cousin, Layne Davies. And my cousins, parents, aunts, and uncles are all here. We're staying on the line until we know you're safe."

Tinsley's breathing hitched and Layne looked around the room and noticed that her father, Ahmed, and Walker had disappeared. "I guess Harper will be mad to know she was wrong about the Davies side of the family. You seem nice after all."

"I'm almost there, Tins," Gavin said, concentrating on driving. "Where are you?"

"In my bedroom," Tinsley said before growing quiet. The only sound was the harsh breathing. "He kicked me in my ribs. I think they're broken. I can't breathe."

"I'm here," Gavin said as the room full of unknown relatives listened in Kentucky. Gavin hung up but through Tinsley's phone she heard him running toward her.

"Jesus Christ." They heard Gavin mutter. "I'm taking you to the hospital in Charleston. Do me a favor, Layne."

"Anything," Layne answered.

"Kill this son of a bitch."

"Consider it done. No one hurts our family," Cy said in a deadly tone Layne had never heard before.

The line went dead and Layne looked around for Walker. She pushed her way through the group as the police and the coroner arrived. Fluffy Puppy was blinking his eyes open on the couch as Wyatt and his mother, Katelyn, took care of him. Relief was short-lived when she didn't see either her father or Walker in the living room. Her mother pointed out the garage door and Layne pushed the door open.

"We need to get the two of you someplace more secure," her father said.

"They can stay at the farm. Mo and Dani will let them stay in the house or there are smaller houses on the property. No one from out of town would think to look for them there. Plus, we have the whole security force there," Ahmed explained.

"If there is an empty house, that would be best. I'm already thankful for their royal highnesses' help, but I wouldn't want to put them in direct danger." Walker looked at the map Ahmed had pulled up on his phone. "Now we just need a plan to draw Jud in."

Layne shut the door quietly and headed back to the living room. Aunt Annie had said Layne loved Walker. As she took a seat on the couch and held a very sleepy FP, she thought about the feelings she had for Walker. She had just killed a man to protect him. That probably was love in

Annie's book. Layne looked to where Walker, her father, and Ahmed were walking back into the house. His eyes instantly searched her out, and her whole body relaxed the second their eyes connected. Love was definitely a strong possibility.

"Are you okay?" he asked, quietly standing next to the couch where she was seated. He reached down and softly stroked FP's head. The little dog pressed his head into Walker's hand and licked.

"Gavin is taking Tinsley to the hospital in Charleston. It was Jud who took Edie."

Walker's other hand moved to her shoulder as he leaned closer to her. "I figured that. I need to think of a plan to stop him. I wonder how long he's going to give me to constantly look over my shoulder."

"You don't think he'll come tonight?"

"No. I think he'll make me wait. He wants me worry about Edie. He'll want to make me jump at every shadow until he tries to strike. And on that note, we're moving to the royal farm."

Layne smiled as she placed her hand over his. "Desert Sun Farm. And no one calls them royalty. It's just Dani and Mo. Their son Zain and his wife, Mila, will be back soon. Their other son, Gabe, and his new wife, Sloane, are on their honeymoon. Now, what can I do to help?"

"Pack whatever you need. We'll leave here as soon as you give your statement to Matt, which consequently can't mention my name. He and Ryan aren't going to input anything into the system until later. We don't want any news outlets to get hold of this," Walker said.

WALKER TALKED with each uncle and discovered Annie and

Bridget had extensive law enforcement and military backgrounds. He watched Layne talk to Matt and FP cuddle with Miles. Walker had already thrown all his borrowed clothes into a small duffle bag and was ready to go.

"Borrow a truck from the farm and come over to my house," Annie Davies said. "My son, Colton, is a fireman. He's not nearly as big as you, so I can't offer you clothing. However, I think I have something you'll like even better than clothes in my special little room." Annie winked and Walker blinked. Um, he didn't really know what to think. What was in the special little room? "Just ask anyone, they'll tell you how to get to my house. See you tomorrow, say eleven in the morning." Annie wasn't asking.

"Yes, ma'am," Walker said, clearing his throat and wondering if he could get Layne to come with him.

The little aunt came up to him next. She looked him up and down and then used both hands to try to encircle his biceps. "My, you're even bigger than my son," she smiled up, way up, at him. She was a tiny little thing with the beginning of a baby bump even though she had a little gray in her hair. "My son's clothes are a little tight but will do for now. I'll drop some more off with you tomorrow. I've never seen anyone larger than Dylan," she said, patting his arm. The mention of her son's name reminded him she was Layne's Aunt Tammy.

"Oh, we all know about how *large* Walker is." The old lady he thought was named Lily Rae winked.

"Don't forget these!" the taller, wiry, white-haired one called out.

The box of condoms went flying through the air as Walker reached up and snagged it before shoving it into his duffle bag.

"It's a pity he was dressed. Morgan said she got to see the

full package," the plumper woman said before shrugging. "Oh well, I guess I'll have to settle for a hug. Come here, young man, and give Miss Violet a hug."

Miss Violet was deceptively strong. Walker had been pulled down so quickly he'd almost dropped to his knees as the old woman smothered him with her bosom. "Violet," he heard someone say from far away. Or maybe it was one of her sisters standing next to him, but right now he was just glad he'd survived enhanced interrogation techniques and could hold his breath for a very long time.

Finally he was released and the woman smiled at him gleefully. "I'm Violet, and this is my sister Lily and my other sister Daisy. You come see us at the Blossom Café and we'll get some meat on those bones."

Walker looked down at the tight T-shirt and then back at the ladies. "Thanks. I have lost some weight."

"Thank you, Miss Violet. I'm sure we'll see you there," Layne said as she smiled at them. "I'm meeting my grandmother there for lunch tomorrow, so maybe Walker can stop by as well."

Walker said goodbye to the old ladies and turned a questioning look to Layne. "The Rose sisters?"

"You got it. Are you ready to go?"

Walker looked around and saw the house starting to clear out. Ryan and Matt were still dealing with the crime scene, but everyone else was now waiting outside.

Walker picked up Layne's bags as she carried FP in her arms. They said goodbye to her family and started the short drive to the farm. She drove past a huge white house and then a smaller, federal-style house. Layne informed Walker that was where Zain and Mila lived.

"Here it is," Layne said at another small house. "Nabi,

the head of security, used to live here before he got married."

"Is it close to the security center?"

"Yup, it's right over there." Layne pointed to a building with two cars parked in front. It appeared to be a barn. But after Ahmed told him about security on the farm, he knew otherwise.

Now he needed a plan. A plan to capture Jud, expose his crimes, and free his sister. He looked at Layne and almost sighed out loud. Unfortunately, getting the girl of your dreams didn't fit into that plan.

THE GYM at Desert Sun Farm was beyond state-of-the-art. Though to be fair, SEALs didn't usually train on state-of-the-art equipment. It was more like load eighty pounds on their backs and run for ten miles.

Layne worked with him all morning as he stretched and strengthened his leg. Ahmed, Nash, Cade, and Miles came in to work out. "Don't even think about it," Layne warned him as she finished rubbing out his leg.

"What?" Walker asked innocently as if he weren't thinking of joining the men who were strapping on boxing gloves.

Layne stood up and shook her head. "You're not going to listen to me, are you?"

"I guess it's a good thing I fired you from being my doctor." He winked, but that only reminded him last night had been interrupted—twice. And he'd ended up sleeping with Layne, only not in the way he really wanted to. He pushed down his disappointment. He needed to focus on healing, not his sexy former doctor.

Ahmed and Miles faced off, and Cade and Nash hit the bags. "Hey, how old is your dad?"

"Sixty-five, why?" Layne asked as Miles hit Ahmed with enough force to send the man's head snapping back.

"He's in better shape than some of the men I work out with." Walker smiled as Ahmed landed a jab onto Miles's chin. Ah, if only it were Walker giving him payback.

"Come on, kid. Let's see what you can do without a girl protecting you," Cade taunted.

Walker looked at Layne who shook her head. "He had to go there," she muttered. "Go get him," she said, giving in. Walker leaned down and kissed her cheek before a boxing glove pelted the side of his head.

"Dad!" Layne yelled as she hurled the glove back at her dad. "I have to meet my grandmother at the café, so knock my uncle out quickly."

Walker grinned and strapped on the gloves. Now this was going to be fun.

18

"I heard you knocked my husband out," Annie said as she greeted Walker at the door.

"I sure did. Hope you're not mad, ma'am." Walker grinned as Annie returned the smile.

"Not at all. If he mentions Nash is the biggest badass one more time, I'm going to knock him out myself. Now, come and see my special toys."

"Shouldn't we wait for your husband?" Walker asked, suddenly a little nervous. What was she talking about? Because whatever her special room with special toys was, it was causing a twinkle in her eye that made Walker a little nervous. Annie was very attractive and would be considered a cougar, if he were into that.

"Nah, he'll be pouting."

Walker gulped and followed the redhead to an office. Okay, everything looked normal. Well, that is until Annie pushed a hidden button and the wall opened. Walker's jaw dropped. "Will you marry me?"

Annie laughed as she walked inside the armory. "I think

you want to ask someone else that question. However, I'll offer you an early wedding present."

Walker didn't get the panicky feeling in his chest at the mention of marriage. Instead, he smiled to himself as Annie handed him a gun.

"All I ask is you get married on January 30th—a winter wonderland wedding. Deal?"

"And for that I get the gun?"

"For that, you get three. I also notice you're not telling me no."

Walker was like a kid in the candy store as he took in the walls of mounted guns and rifles. "Funny, I noticed the same thing."

"Strange when that happens, isn't it? Sophie and Nash, Cade and me . . . when it happens, you just know. Why fight it? Now, look at this sexy thing," she said, handing him a sniper rifle.

Layne was driving to the Blossom Café, the only restaurant in town and gossip central, when her phone rang. She recognized the number immediately.

"Gavin, how is Tinsley?" Layne asked, not bothering to say hello.

"Four broken ribs, a black eye, and a broken nose. She fought, but she was no match for a SEAL. She said Edie fought as well, but Jud just tased her and carried her out when she became too much for him."

Layne felt tears forming for women she'd never met.

Gavin let out a deep breath. "I also stopped to talk to my grandfather and great-uncle. They told me Great-Grammy was the one who told them Marcy didn't want anything to do with them. She always distracted them when they wanted to call and told them not to bother since Marcy wouldn't accept the calls."

"That's not true!" Layne hollered as she slammed her foot on the brake and pulled into a parking spot on Main Street.

"I know that now. My grandfather said he remembers his wife telling him Great-Grammy was mad Marcy had left them because it was her job to take care of them when they got older. The sons fought the wars and earned the money. The daughters did what the parents ordered. My grandmother apparently had issues with Great-Grammy's demanding ways. She wanted to be waited on in her older age and regularly berated my grandmother for not being at her beck and call."

"Grandma Marcy would have taken care of them," Layne said, heartbroken. "She cared for Great-Grandma Helen until the day she died."

"It doesn't make sense to me either, but my grandfather and great-uncle can't wait to hear from their sister." Gavin's response turned things back to pleasant.

"I'm meeting her now and will tell her. And please tell Tinsley we're all thinking of her. She was very brave to fight back."

"I will. Talk to you soon, Layne."

Layne hung up and hurried into the Blossom Café. The Rose sisters had run the café until their much younger distant cousins, Zinnia and Poppy Meadows, moved from Alabama to run the café and bed and breakfast for the centennial sisters. However, that meant the Rose sisters could hold court in the café every day now.

Layne walked in and found the sisters at their table and her mother and grandmother sitting at a nearby table, waiting. Zinnia was cooking, and Poppy was talking to DeAndre and Aniyah at another table.

"You know bets are confidential on the app," Layne heard Poppy lecture Aniyah.

"What's the new bet?' Layne asked, bending down and kissing her grandmother's cheek.

"Why, you are, dear." Grandma Marcy grinned.

"You and that fine muscled man of yours," Aniyah said so loudly the entire café turned and looked at Layne. "You sure move fast. From condoms to marriage. You go, girl."

The door opened and Walker stepped in looking as if he might possibly be lost. Layne felt her mother and grandmother's eyes go from her to Walker and then chaos erupted.

"Twenty on November first!" her mother screamed as she launched herself halfway over Aniyah to hand Poppy a twenty.

"I got the first of November and the original bet of January thirtieth," Poppy called out.

"December twenty-fourth. A beautiful Christmas wedding," Grandma Marcy said, waving the twenty as she patted Layne's hand. "Close your mouth or you'll catch flies. You knew it was coming."

"But ... but ..."

"Hey," Walker said, bending and placing a kiss on her cheek, which only caused the betting to reach frenzied level. "What's going on? And what about January thirtieth?"

Layne swallowed hard. Well, it had been nice having a boyfriend for a day or so. "They're placing bets on when we're getting married. Somehow they skipped right over the engagement. They said it was a sure thing."

"Ah," Walker said, taking a seat as Kenna Ashton shoved

her best friend and princess, Dani Ali Rahman, out of the way to get her bet placed first.

Layne looked at him with shock. He wasn't running. His face wasn't pale. In fact, he didn't seem upset at all. Warmth flooded her at the idea, and her heart skipped a beat as Walker kissed her grandmother's cheek before taking a seat at the table and placing his hand on Layne's thigh as he began to look over the menu.

Layne's mom was at her sisters-in-law's table with their heads huddled together as things finally began to calm down. She knew they had noticed his hand on her leg even though it was hidden under the table.

"I heard from cousin Gavin," Layne said before repeating their conversation. Her heart broke as her grandmother sniffled.

"Oh no she didn't!" Aniyah yelled as she practically shoved her chair to the ground to get to Marcy. She wrapped her in a hug and took the seat next to her. "Why would your mama do such a thing?"

Her grandmother patted Aniyah's manicured hand and let out a sigh. "It was a different time. Daughters were a trial while sons were a blessing. My mother never cared about me. I don't know why, but I was more of a servant than part of the family. I knew I would be cut off when I chose to stay in Keeneston to marry my Jake. It was worth it though. I knew she didn't support my marriage to Jake. I had to wait until I was eighteen to marry him so I wasn't forced to move to South Carolina."

"Why that *Mother Faulkner*!" Aniyah cursed.

"Thank you," Marcy said, patting her hand again. "But that is my mother you're talking about. Dirty language isn't needed."

Aniyah nodded her head. "I know. That's what I said.

You are a mother and you were a Faulkner, but you're no Mother Faulkner." Layne snorted as she tried to hold back the laughter. Aniyah was on a roll. "Trying to take you away from the love of your life. Why if she were here, I'd shoot that Mother Faulkner."

"You mean you'd miss shooting her." DeAndre chuckled as Aniyah leaned back and swatted him.

"That Mother Faulkner needs Jesus," Aniyah said, patting the cross necklace that hung to her cleavage twice with her hand before lifting her hand to God.

"Amen," Walker said so seriously it caused Layne to snort down another round of laughter.

FEELING MORE human after his morning with Annie and the rest of the Davieses, especially after getting much-needed clothes, guns, and a phone, Walker left the farm truck he was borrowing in front of the Blossom Café and headed to Lexington with Layne for an afternoon of physical therapy.

"How are you feeling?" she asked as they drove through the countryside on their way into town.

Walker hadn't felt this much a part of a group since Hell Week. In a way, being the new guy to Keeneston was similar. He never knew when he'd be jumped and interrogated. Only this time, it wasn't instructors yelling an inch from his face; it was little old ladies with cookies or an aunt with a gunroom. Even though he managed to get out of the Blossom Café without admitting his feelings for Layne were becoming more involved, he somehow felt as if he'd failed since the rate of bets only seemed to increase.

However, each person had also vowed to keep an eye out for strangers and had been shown a picture of Jud. Cade walked in with Layne's father and Ahmed after a while and had given him a new cell phone. Cade might have grumbled about the teasing Miles was giving him for being knocked out by Walker, but Cade had still patted Walker on the back and dared him to step into the ring with Layne.

"Not too bad. I can feel the stitches itching and pulling more than anything."

"You're healing. You'll be a whole new man by next week," she said before parking the car in her spot.

"Layne," Walker started. He didn't know exactly what he wanted to tell her, but he felt as if there were things left unsaid. "About last night."

Layne smiled at him then. "Yes?"

"I want you," he said simply. It wasn't a declaration of love, but that didn't come easy for him.

"I'll let you in on a secret," Layne said, lowering her voice. "I want you too." Then, before she let him tell her he didn't know if he could be anything more to her, she was out the door and leaving him to catch up to her.

"Layne," he said again, rushing after her.

Layne hit the elevator button and waited for the doors to open. She turned and shook her head. "Stop it. I can see you thinking. I've seen that look on my cousins' faces too often to not realize what it is."

"And what's that?" he asked her as the doors to the elevator opened.

"It's the *we're just having fun, don't expect anything more, the timing isn't right* speech." Layne gave him a look that pinned him in place. Killing someone with a spoon wasn't the only thing her father taught her. "And I don't play those games. You either want to be with me or not. The rest is about as helpful as a screen door on a submarine."

The doors to the elevator closed, and Layne pressed the

floor button. She didn't push him. She didn't try to talk about it. No, she just looked at the changing floors. She was leaving it up to him. Walker watched numbers change from a one to a two and before it turned to a three he had made up his mind.

He spun and hit the emergency stop button. "You're right."

"What are you doing? Right about what?" Layne asked as they jerked to a stop.

"Worrying about everything else is a waste of time. I know what I want, and what I want is you."

Walker met her lips in a crushing kiss. He used the sheer size of his body to back Layne up against the wall of the elevator as he devoured her mouth with his. Layne wasn't a simple participant. She didn't let him take the lead, and that was one of the things Walker loved about her. Her hands were tangled in his hair, her tongue battling his as their bodies moved against each other. Walker placed his hands against the wall on each side of her head to steady himself as he pressed his body against hers. They were toe-to-toe, hip-to-hip, chest-to-chest. They were equal in every way, which was everything he'd ever wanted in a woman. The timing was horrible. The situation was stressful. He wasn't in a marriage frame of mind. And none of that mattered. He was already in love.

At the realization, Walker pulled his head back enough to look at Layne. Her hazel eyes were greener with desire than they normally were. He liked that he was getting to know these little things about her.

"Well," Layne said primly, "I'm glad we had this discussion. Now, as much as I'd like to carry on, the fire department will be called soon. And if my cousin Colton shows up . . . well, you know Keeneston."

Walker smiled, and she smiled back. He turned off the emergency stop, and the elevator began to move. "As much as I love your breasts, I'm not too fond of the idea of Aaron getting a look at them."

Layne looked down and noticed her blouse was open, then back up at him. "When did you do that?" she asked, buttoning her shirt.

"DeAndre has his secrets, and so do I," Walker said as he sent her a wink over his shoulder before walking off the elevator.

19

Walker paced the house they'd been staying in for the past two weeks. Nothing. No sight of Jud or any stranger for that matter. He'd heard nothing from Edie or from Jud, and he was beyond worried for his sister. Walker took a deep breath to calm himself.

"This is what Jud wants," Miles said from the couch. Layne was at her office. Her cousin Sophie and her husband, Nash, were with her. After physical therapy with Layne at the Desert Sun Farm gym that morning, Walker had stayed and worked out with Miles and Ahmed after Nash promised to keep an eye on Layne. For as much crap as Miles gave him, and a number of bruising punches, Walker liked the guy.

"I know, but I'm worried about my sister. I want to do something. I hate just sitting and waiting."

"You are doing something. You've prepared for his arrival, and you're working hard on healing. You're barely limping anymore."

Walker looked at his leg. The stitches had come out last week, and he'd been stepping up his physical activity.

he's doing things to my leg that hurt, but then a couple hours later it feels fantastic. I can feel my strength returning. Layne's amazing."

"Yes, she is," Miles said quietly. "You know, I don't like this."

"I don't either," Walker said, stopping and dropping into the chair across from Miles.

"No, I mean you and Layne."

"Oh. Is it because I didn't get to the killer spoons?"

Miles cracked a smile. "No. I daresay you even gave Nash a run for being a badass. I won't like any man Layne brings home, but you are the only one who hasn't run . . . yet." Miles shrugged. "But I guess you can't run, being shot in the leg."

Walker smiled at the man he'd come to not only respect but like. "I won't let anything happen to her."

"I know you won't. It's the only reason I'm letting you stick around. Now, my wife has an idea I want to run past you. I thought it was crazy at first, but now I've come around."

"What is it?" Walker asked.

"Morgan runs a PR company. She handles companies in crisis, and that's what you basically are. And you're in this position because Jud has made himself into a hero with the media. They don't know any better because the narrative is only coming from him."

"You want me to talk to the media?" Walker was pretty sure that was the worst idea he'd ever heard.

"No. It means maybe it's time Jud gets asked some serious questions." Miles handed him a folder. "Nabi and Nash put this together."

Walker opened the file. There were pictures, both old and new, both posed and from surveillance, that showed Jud in an unflattering light. "That's him and Darrel in Afghanistan," Walker said, looking at an old picture.

"Look at what's next."

Walker put down the picture and picked up a classified report detailing the drug bust and their suspicion that Darrel was not acting alone. There had been traces of drugs found in Jud's room, but Darrel had claimed he'd been in there borrowing a movie when he dropped his stash. Some must have spilled out. "Where did you get this?"

"It's better you don't know. There's more."

There was a picture of his old girlfriend with a split lip and a confidentiality agreement between them in return for a payout. She had cited disputes over money and drugs as the basis for the fights that led to her beatings.

"Why wasn't he kicked out of the service?" Walker asked, looking over the internal reports.

"Next page," Miles said as Walker flipped to Jud's birth certificate.

"Melville is his mother's maiden name." Walker's gaze stuck on Jud's father's name. "Thomas Rudy is his father," Walker muttered with disbelief.

Miles nodded. "*Admiral* Thomas Rudy. Jud changed his last name when he was eighteen after a drug charge that went away provided Jud enter the military under his father's command."

"Drugs again. Can this whole thing be about drugs?" Walker asked as he continued to read through the file.

"Partly. I think Jud was in with some bad people, and he found a way to make some fast money and get out of the military. He was declared a hero, wrote a book, got a movie deal, and there was no one left on his team to contradict his story. Jud would be the hero who was too famous to serve. He could retire and go on tours, talking about his bravery while sitting on a fortune of stolen items from the ship."

"We need to find those items. Have they hit the black market yet?" Walker asked, handing the file back to Miles.

"Not that we've seen. Ahmed has some people on it. What should I tell my wife?" Miles asked.

"Tell her to go for it. Let's put the screws to Jud and see if that pushes him to make a mistake." Then, hopefully, he could find his sister and finally come out from hiding.

LAYNE LOOKED past Aaron to Sophie and tried to signal for help, but her cousin had put her head together with her husband as they looked at something on his phone. Having Walker in the office daily had spurred Aaron to increase his pursuit, something Layne had told him over and over again wasn't going to happen. She thought he'd understood it, but now she wasn't sure.

"How about dinner?" Aaron smiled down at her from where he'd put his hip on her desk next to her chair.

"Aaron, I've told you, I'm not interested in dating. We have a good thing going here, and I'm not going to mess it up with getting personal."

Aaron bent his head closer to hers. "That's just it, Layne. We are a good team. Can you imagine how much better we'd be as a couple?"

"It's not going to happen. I'm not interested in you like that. I'm sorry," Layne said as kindly as possible.

Aaron's mouth tightened. "I look forward to proving you wrong."

"Wrong about what?"

Layne looked up to see Walker standing with his arms

crossed. Her father stood shoulder-to-shoulder with Walker, his arms crossed too. Both men glared at Aaron.

"Uh," Aaron sputtered as he stood up so quickly he almost tripped over her chair, "I have to get going. Yeah, I have patients."

Layne tried not to laugh as Aaron headed for the door, but neither her father nor Walker moved. Aaron tried to dart around them, but their shoulders blocked the door. Aaron looked like a scared rabbit trying to find a hole to hide in before ducking his head and pushing through the middle of her dad and Walker. The two guys made Aaron push a little before they moved enough for him to get through.

"I thought you were watching her?" Walker shot at Nash, who shrugged.

"We were placing a bet. Besides, I've seen what she can do with a spoon. I figured she was safe from some pretty boy snob."

"What bet?" Layne asked as she got up from her desk to join her father and Walker. In the past week, Walker and her father seemed to reach some kind of truce. Maybe her father knew they weren't sleeping together. Well, they were sleeping together in the most literal form of the word. Every night she asked Walker to join her in bed, and every night he pulled her to his body and fell asleep when sleep was the last thing Layne wanted to do.

"On when the baby is due," Sophie answered with a wicked gleam to her eyes.

"Hasn't everyone already placed their bets on Sienna and Tammy?" Layne asked before kissing her dad's cheek and slipping her hand onto Walker's muscular forearm.

"Oh, it's not Tammy or Sienna. It's a new candidate."

"What the hell?" Miles snarled as looked at the Blossom

Café betting app before he suddenly shoved Walker. Oh. Well, she'd hate to disappoint the betting pool, but there was literally no chance of her being pregnant. And if marriage hadn't sent Walker running for the hills, this probably would.

Walker stumbled back and held up his hands. "Hey, if it matters, I placed my bet for eighteen months from now."

Layne's mouth dropped right as Miles charged Walker. Walker dodged her father and sent her a wink. Nash leapt up as Aaron ran back into the office. He screamed five octaves higher than Layne thought possible when he thought Miles was charging him and looked ready to pass out.

"You got her pregnant?" Miles shouted, bringing Jill running in from the front office.

"You're pregnant?" Jill gasped, ignoring Aaron, who had collapsed to the ground and was now in the fetal position. "No wonder you had me cancel your appointments. But who's the father?"

Aaron's head shot up. "Yeah, who's the father?"

"I am." Walker grinned as Nash and Sophie held on to Miles.

"I'm not pregnant! You of all people should know that," Layne said, wide-eyed.

"Ha," Aaron crowed as he got himself off the floor. "She can't be with you. It's unethical."

"Do I look like someone who cares about ethics?" Walker snarled as he got into Aaron's space and looked down at him. "Besides, I fired her."

Aaron squeaked and her dad chuckled. "Told you he was a wimp," her dad said smugly.

Jill hid a laugh under a cough. "So, baby shower or no baby shower?"

"No baby shower!"

"There better not be," Miles growled at Walker, who only grinned.

"Well then, I'll give you this delivery and let you get back to your family discussion." Layne took the overnight envelope from Jill with a shake of her head and ripped it open. It took a second to comprehend the image. A woman was in the corner of a cement room on a bare mattress on the floor. Her scraggly hair covered half her face as she hung her head. She turned the photo over. *See you soon* was written on the back in red marker.

"Layne's going out with me. What do you have to say about that?" Aaron tried to challenge Walker. Layne's whole world had stopped when she'd looked at the picture, and she'd missed whatever was going on with Aaron and Walker.

"Aaron," she said in a chilling voice, "get out."

"What is it?" Walker asked as Miles was already moving to see the picture. Nash shoved Aaron out the door and slammed it on his pouting face.

"Who is that?" her father asked.

With a shaking hand, Layne held the picture out to Walker. "I think it's your sister."

WALKER TOOK the picture with dread knotting his stomach. "It's Edie." He wanted to punch something or someone. Where did Aaron go?

"Take a deep breath, son," Miles said softly but with command. Walker dragged in a breath, unaware he'd been holding it. "Sophie, go tell Jill to cancel all of Layne's patients and put a notice on the door that Layne will be out of the office for the next week."

Nash came to stand beside him and looked down at the photograph. "She's not injured."

"I noticed that. But she's lost weight and is pretty dirty," Walker said, detached from the whole world right now.

"He won't harm her," Layne said with surety. "She's the only thing keeping you quiet. You lose her, and his cover is blown."

Walker nodded. He understood, but that didn't mean it didn't feel like his heart was being ripped from him. "Let's get back to Keeneston," Walker said slowly, shoving his pain away. He was trained to do that, and now was the time to rely on his training. "Can we see if Nabi or Cade can scan the picture and run it for possible locations?"

There was a small window at the very top of the picture and he wanted to see if they could get any information from it.

"Good idea," Miles said as he opened the door again. Thankfully, Aaron was nowhere to be found. There may have been no holding back. Walker knew he hadn't been pushing it with Layne, but that didn't mean he hadn't already staked his claim. Layne might not know it, but he guaranteed every male in Keeneston did. After his sister was safe, and Layne was safe, and when Jud was dead, then there would be nothing stopping Walker from stripping Layne bare and finishing what they'd started two weeks before.

20

Aniyah fanned herself as she looked at the table. "Firemen! Here in Keeneston. Lord help me!"

Reagan laughed as she shook her head at Aniyah. "Are you going to ask to slide down their pole?"

"I don't need any of that, but Piper sure does. Look at her sitting there getting none. It's sad," Aniyah said before taking a sip of her drink.

"Hey!" Piper disputed then paused as she thought about it. "I can't be the only one not having sex."

Layne saw Reagan, Aniyah, and Veronica casually sip their drinks as their cheeks blushed. Layne chugged the Rose Sisters Special Iced Tea. She wiped the back of her hand against her lips and slammed down the now half-empty glass. Was this her third? The Rose sisters had long ago made their special tea—basically iced tea, some juice, and a hell of a lot of bourbon—for desperate times like this.

"He won't sleep with me," Layne hissed in a harsh whisper to her friends Veronica and Aniyah and cousins Reagan and Piper. "I mean, he sleeps beside me, but that's it."

Her cousins looked horrified. Veronica, Prince Zain Ali Rahman's right-hand woman, looked confused. And Aniyah nodded sympathetically. "Some men only want sex. I didn't take that fine specimen as one of them. Luckily, my Sugarbear wants me *and* sex. That's what you need in a lasting relationship. A man who wants you in and out of the bed. And someone who manscapes. You don't want to be attacked by a wild bush. You never know what'll jump out at you."

Layne shook her head. "No, I want sex. He's not giving it to me. He's just snuggling with me all night."

Veronica blinked her perfectly shadowed eyes with her long black lashes as she took a sip of her drink. Her blonde hair was picture-perfect as was the red suit she wore. "I don't understand men at all."

"I guess it's a good thing you're a lesbian then, isn't it?" Piper teased.

"But right now I'm getting some and y'all aren't," Veronica winked. "And they say women are hard to understand."

"Hold up, did you say you were getting some?" Aniyah said so loudly the Rose sisters didn't even have to turn on their hearing aids to hear that. They suddenly perked up as Veronica innocently sipped her drink and pretended she didn't hear Aniyah.

"Have you gotten naked?" Veronica asked. "Even I know getting naked in front of a man will get things done."

Layne blushed red and leaned forward. "I left the door open when I showered. He walked in and froze. He stared at me for a long time, but then it was just 'Goodnight. Sleep tight' when I crawled into bed."

"Wait," Reagan whispered, "let me understand this. He's seen you naked, he's watched you shower, you two have almost done it, and you're sleeping in the same bed, yet he's not making a move?"

Layne downed the rest of her drink, and Piper poured her some more. "Maybe he really is a virgin," Layne muttered. When Layne tried to pick it up, she saw two glasses, but she couldn't grab one of them. It was quite possible she was drunk. Just a little. She giggled at the idea of being drunk.

"Is he a priest?" Aniyah practically shouted as someone stopped walking and looked at them. He was drop-dead sexy with a lean muscular body and kind eyes.

"Well, yes, I am. Do you need me?" Father Ben asked. *Sometimes it sucked having a priest Layne's own age. Especially when you already hit on said priest once before. And then your cousin.*

Father Ben's throat worked hard as he fought any kind of reaction. "You hit on your cousin? Would you like to come talk to me, Layne?"

Layne looked around her table at everyone staring at her. "Did I say that out loud?"

"You hit on one of us?" Reagan asked. "Please tell me it wasn't my brothers? Porter and Parker are so . . . that's just wrong."

"Oh, maybe she hit on Greer." Veronica winked and then giggled. "I just giggled. Someone cut me off."

"No," Layne snapped. "I hit on Gavin Faulkner before I knew he was my cousin."

"Oh well, you probably won't go to hell for that, right, Father?" Aniyah asked Father Ben.

"Layne's soul is safe, but I can always hear her confession if you're worried."

Reagan looked to Piper and then to Father Ben. "Actually, Father Ben. I know you're probably tired, returning from your priest meeting or summer prayer camp, or whatever it was, but could you do us a favor?"

Piper nodded. "I think we've had a little too much to drink. Could you take Layne back to Desert Sun Farm?"

"That way you could hear her confession and make sure she's not going to hell for hitting on our cousin," Reagan hurriedly put in.

"Of course," Father Ben agreed. "Are you ready to go home now or should I wait?"

Layne looked at Father Ben. "Are you sure you're a real priest?"

Father Ben grinned. "I'm wearing the collar under my jacket, and I distinctly remember taking my vows."

Layne finished off her glass of iced tea. "Too bad you're not undercover or something. Then it wouldn't be so bad that I hit on you," she muttered as she stood up and then fell back down in her chair.

"Okay," Aniyah said, getting up on her five-inch heels and trying to pull Layne to her feet. "Sexual frustration does not suit you. That's something else you can talk to Father Ben about. He'll understand that one."

Layne heard Veronica choke next to her as two strong arms came up under her armpits. Father Ben hefted her from the chair and practically carried her outside as her friends, cousins, and half the café followed to watch the spectacle.

"What was that all about?" Veronica asked Piper. "Aniyah is our designated driver."

"If Walker can't be swayed by naked shower scenes, maybe he needs another kind of push," Piper grinned. Layne didn't know what she meant as Father Ben buckled her into the front seat of his car.

"If nudity won't do it, jealousy will. Priest or not, Father

Ben is a hottie who will have his hands all over Layne getting her inside," Reagan finished explaining.

"You're going to have a priest make Walker jealous?" Aniyah gasped as she made the sign of the cross. "You are so going to hell for that."

Unfortunately, Layne didn't really hear that. Her face was pressed against the cold glass of the passenger door, and as her cousins waved goodbye, Veronica gave her the thumbs up, and Aniyah crossed herself.

MILES ACTUALLY WASN'T a bad guy, Walker thought as he walked from the Desert Sun Farm gym toward the small house he was staying at with Layne. Miles had known exactly what Walker needed after a long stressful day of trying to find his sister. He had taken Walker to the gym and went a couple rounds with him in the boxing ring. It had been exactly what Walker needed to let out his frustrations with his sister and Layne.

Upon close inspection of the photo, Edie was found in good shape. No cuts, no bruises, just a loss of about five pounds—according to Nabi who did a photo comparison from a media picture taken two weeks before. They had a plan. The plan was simple. Wait for Jud. Kill Jud.

Now Layne was a different story. He couldn't count the number of times he'd had to take a cold shower to quell the desire to pin her against the nearest wall and claim her. The trouble was he also didn't want to be a flash in the pan. Walker knew when he and Layne got together they would burn hot, but he wanted more. He wanted something that lasted. Not something that went away as soon as the mission was completed.

Walker had decided the night they'd almost made love

that he needed to take time to get to know her and for her to get to know him. Every night he held her in his arms as they talked. He had learned about her childhood, her love of her family, her time at school, and how much she loved her job. That's how he knew he and Layne needed time. She didn't like that he was a patient, regardless of what she said. So he was going to give it to her.

One thing was clear though. Layne was a woman unlike any he'd ever met before. She was strong, confident, intelligent, and giving. She loved her family, her patients, her dog, the children of her friends . . . she had so much love to give that Walker basked in the attention she gave him. In the love he felt growing for her, he only hoped he could give her as much love as she deserved.

Walker heard the sound of a car stopping and jogged up the slight hill to wave to Layne. She'd gone out to dinner at the café while he'd worked out his mental and sexual frustrations. But it wasn't Aniyah's car Walker saw. And the young man jogging around the front of the car to open the door for Layne also wasn't Aniyah. What the hell?

Walker stalked forward as the man pulled Layne from the car. She giggled and clutched at his arms as she leaned against him. "Can I call you Benny?" She giggled again. "I feel after discussing sex we should be on a first-name basis."

Walker felt his stomach drop as the man bent down and scooped Layne up in his arms. "We have to stop doing this, Layne. This isn't the first time I've carried you home," the man said, pushing open the front door.

Walker saw red. He sprinted through the night toward the house. He darted inside and found Layne lying on the couch and the man kneeling next to her with her hand in his. "Now, Layne, you know how I feel about premarital sex."

Walker roared with hurt, anger, and bloodlust for the man touching Layne. Layne's eyes widened as the man jumped between them. "Oh, you must be Walker. We didn't expect you home yet."

"I bet you didn't." Walker threw a punch Miles would be proud of, catching the man right on the jaw. His head snapped to the side as Layne shrieked.

"Walker! No! Stop!"

The man didn't back down, though. "I let you have that one, but I won't let you have another."

"We'll see about that."

Walker threw a jab and the man ducked nimbly. Walker focused on the man trying to take the one shining light in his life and punched again. The man blocked and danced around the coffee table out of range.

"Walker!" Layne screamed.

"I'll deal with you in a minute. How could you?" Walker's words were like a dagger. He'd never lay a hand on her, but he sure as hell would be out of the house and out of her life as soon as he knocked this man out.

Layne let out a sound of annoyance. "That's Father Ben."

"I don't care if he's a father, brother, or anything else. I'm kicking his ass."

Ben darted, Walker lunged, and Layne jumped. Walker grunted as Layne landed on his back. Her arm wrapped tight around his neck as she locked her legs around his waist. "Stop it right now!" she yelled in his ear.

Walker ignored her as she latched onto his back. He kicked an ottoman toward the door and cut off Ben's escape. Ben ducked a punch Walker threw and tried to dash past him, but Walker's arm shot out and grabbed him by the throat. He shoved him back with a growl, ripping the man's windbreaker in the process.

"What's that?" Walker asked with his hand cocked back ready to unload a fierce punch to Ben's face while Layne hung onto his back pulling at his hair.

Ben looked down. "My collar."

"Why are you wearing that?" Walker asked of the white square appearing at Ben's throat.

"Because I'm a priest. I'm Father Ben."

Walker dropped his fist as Layne slid down the whole length of his body to plop onto the floor. "You don't look like any priest I've ever seen. And I had them stationed with me overseas."

Layne snorted and then hiccupped. "You're not the only one. Nash punched him too. Sophie sat on his lap and hit on him before she got with Nash."

Walker looked at Father Ben . . . really looked at him. The way he moved, the way he easily avoided Walker's punches. "Who are you, really?"

Father Ben smiled as he seemed to relax. "I'm Ben Jacobs. The priest over at Saint Francis."

"Catholic?" Walker asked still suspicious.

"Yes, Catholic," Ben grinned, knowing exactly what Walker was asking. Ben was no threat to his relationship with Layne as a Catholic priest.

"You may be a priest now, but there's something familiar about you."

Ben shrugged. "We all have a past, don't we?"

Walker nodded. It wasn't anything in particular about the way Father Ben looked. It was the way he carried himself. The man had training. What kind of training was something else entirely. Something Walker was willing to let go, since Ben obviously didn't want to talk about it.

"Thanks for bringing her home," Walker said, looking at Layne snoring on the floor. Her hair was over her face and one hand was wrapped around Walker's ankle. "What got into her tonight?"

"I'm sorry. As much as I would like to help, I can't disclose anything someone says to me in confession. Even if it was a drunken confession. But you're a smart man, you'll figure it out." Ben stepped away from the wall and patted Walker's shoulder as he headed toward the front door.

"Some day, if you ever want someone to hear your confession, I'll be here. I may not be a priest, but I have a feeling I'd understand you better than any other priest would," Walker offered as he shook his leg free from Layne's passed-out grip.

Ben paused with his back toward him and his hand on the door. "Thank you. Some day I might take you up on that offer."

Ben walked out the door and closed it behind him as Layne groaned. "Is the room spinning?"

"No, sweetheart, that's just you." Walker bent down and picked her up in his arms. "What made you get wasted?"

"You," Layne slurred as she poked him in the eye with her finger and then giggled. "Let me try that again. *Boink*." She giggled, trying to tap her finger against his nose. She didn't make it.

"What did I do?" Walker asked, setting her on the bed.

"It's what you didn't do." Layne said, ripping off her shirt. Walker swallowed hard. He'd seen her breasts. He'd felt them in his hands as he'd turned her nipples hard with desire, and they instantly affected him. Layne was struggling to undo her bra when she gave up and shoved the bra down to her stomach. "See? Nothing. No caressing, no licking, no kissing, no fu—"

"Okay!" Walker said, cutting her off. "I get it."

Layne got on her knees and Walker had to take a step

back or he'd give in and do all the things he'd been dreaming. He'd take her if he could, but he'd never do it when she was this drunk. "Take me, Walker Greene."

Layne leaned back to arch her breasts toward him and fell back against the pillows, landing with a snore. So, Layne wanted him as much as he wanted her. Maybe the nights of talking were over. Maybe now he needed to *show* her what she meant to him. Just as soon as she sobered up.

21

Walker flipped the last pancake as Layne stumbled into the small kitchen. Her normally silky black hair was a tangled mess as she shoved it out of her eyes, which were rimmed with dark circles.

"I got bits and pieces of last night in my nightmares. I don't exactly know what I should say since I'm not entirely sure what I said last night. So I'm not going to say anything and pretend it didn't happen." Layne poured a cup of coffee and moaned at the first long chug of it.

Walker loaded a plate with pancakes and drenched them with syrup before sliding them across the small bar countertop to her. "It was very enlightening," he said with a grin he hoped conveyed the fact he'd rather be having sex than breakfast. By the way Layne's nipples hardened under the T-shirt he'd put her in, he guessed he'd been successful.

"I must look a fright," Layne said, trying to pat down the tangles as she took a bite of the pancakes. "Ohmygosh! Chocolate chip pancakes; I'm in love."

"If I knew that's all it took, I wouldn't have tried to get

you to fall in love with me this past week." Walker winked at her as she held a fork halfway to her open mouth.

"What did you say?"

"Eat your pancakes, Layne. You'll need your energy."

Walker sent her another grin and then slowly left her alone to eat. He went to the bedroom and checked the phone he'd been given. There was a text message from Miles setting up a time to meet at the gym later that night. There was a message from Nash wanting to see if he was free for lunch. Then there was a message from Deacon wanting to see if he could join them for a workout tonight. And finally, one from Annie to see if he needed anything else from her special room. How, in such a short amount of time, had Walker become part of Keeneston? Folks had opened their arms to him, and it was no surprise to him they were related to the Faulkners. They were all the kind of people who would do anything for a friend.

Walker answered the texts and was putting away the phone when Layne stepped into the room, looking unsure of herself. It wasn't like Layne to not walk into a situation in complete control. He knew that look because he'd been wearing it since he met Layne. Only now he was sure. He was sure he loved her.

"Why don't you take a shower while I get some things done real quick. Then we need to have a long overdue conversation." Walker stopped in front of Layne and dropped a kiss on her lips.

"About what?" Layne asked when the kiss ended.

"Take a shower, Layne. Don't take too long, or I'll come get you myself." Walker ran his hand down her back and felt her shiver in response. Good. He turned and walked out of the bedroom. He heard the shower start and locked the front door. He checked every window as FP happily followed him around.

"Sorry, little buddy, but you need to keep guard duty out here, okay?" Walker scooped up the little dog who happily licked his cheek and wagged his tail. Walker grabbed a chair and set it in front of the window looking out the front of the house. "Here you go. Don't let me down."

The little bow bobbed as FP sat and watched the squirrels running around out front. Walker checked each window on his way to the bedroom, then closed the door and slid a chair under the handle. Every window was locked as he pulled the shades. Finally, nothing was going to interrupt them.

The shower turned off, and Walker stepped into the bathroom. He stood waiting with Layne's towel as she opened the glass door. "Let me help," Walker said as he slowly ran the towel down one arm and then the other.

"About what I may or may not have said last night—"

"Layne," Walker said, running the towel over her breasts and watching as she held her breath in reaction to the sensation, "we've done enough talking. There's only one thing left to say." Walker ran the towel slowly up her legs before standing up.

"And what's that?" Layne asked quietly.

"I love you."

WALKER LOVED HER. He hadn't run in fear from her family. Oh God, her father could still ruin it. "My father—"

"Is a great guy, Layne. But right now, I don't give a damn about your father. I'm more interested in telling you that I love you. I love how you're so sweet yet you can kill someone with a spoon. I love that you stand up for those who need it. I love that you love your family and friends. I love that you're so smart, funny, and one hell of a physical therapist. In fact, you're so good I honestly no longer need your services. I know we joke about me firing you, but Layne, I really am this time. My leg feels great, and I'm working out with the guys daily all because of you."

Layne felt emotion closing her throat as she only nodded. She was going to release him in a couple of days anyway, but now . . . now she was free to love him as well. She wanted him, yes. Wanted him badly. But she also loved him. She was afraid once he was well that he'd leave, and she wanted one time with Walker for her dreams to come true. She was still afraid, but when had fear ever stopped her?

"I love you too, Walker. I have since the night I outshot you. I'd known before then you were a good man. But that night, I saw you were so much more. You're kind, smart, empathetic, brave, courageous, and you let me be me. You don't try to separate me from my family." Layne shook her head with amazement. "Instead, you've embraced them. You didn't try to tell me I shouldn't pull on the gloves and fight. Instead, you encouraged me and were proud of me. Over the past weeks I've learned there's no one I would rather have by my side than you."

Layne wrapped her arms around his neck as Walker pulled her to him. "I know we have a lot to figure out, but we'll do it together. Always together."

Walker kissed her. It wasn't the restrained little peck on the cheek he'd been giving her and it was much more than the couple of times they'd kissed when they first met. This time there was so much more between them, joining them and completing them. This time they weren't two people coming together, but one heart already joined.

Walker tightened his arms around her and lifted her off the floor. His lips never left hers as he carried her to bed. Layne's heart beat faster as he pulled the shirt from his body. Walker wasn't like some of her past boyfriends who worked out at the gym for their six-pack abs. Walker had them, but he'd earned them with every trudge carrying a rucksack and every five-mile swim. And when Walker kicked off his pants and pressed his body against hers, she felt the muscle, the strength, and the energy between them. She felt the brush of the sprinkling of chest hair against her sensitive nipples as Walker kissed his way down her neck toward her breasts.

Layne gasped as his warm lips pulled her firm nipple into his mouth and grabbed his hair when he slid a finger inside of her. Walker looked up and grinned as her body tightened to near explosive proportions. "As I said, we have something to talk about. I've told you how much I love you, but now I get to show you."

Walker slid up her body and reached for a condom. Layne's eyes closed of their own accord as Walker showed her exactly what she meant to him.

LAYNE STRETCHED in bed as Walker casually trailed his finger down her body. It had been worth the wait. Yet guilt remained. How could it not as he fell so deeply in love while his sister was with a madman? All he could think about was how much Edie would love Layne. She'd always wanted a sister. It was one of the reasons they were so close to the Faulkners. They'd adopted Walker and Edie into their family. Just like the Davies family had done with him. Sure, her cousins and uncles gave him crap, but they could take it when he dished it back. It was all good fun, like it had been with the other members of his team.

Fluffy Puppy began to bark and Layne shot up in bed, clutching the sheet to her chest. There was knocking on the door as she practically fell out of bed in her hurry to dress. "Why aren't you moving?"

"How about you just don't open the door. They'll go away."

Layne's mouth dropped. "How long have you been here and you still don't understand my family. Every one of them can pick a lock."

"Oh, damn. You're right." Walker hopped on one leg, trying to get his pants on when they heard Morgan call out.

"Yoohoo! Anyone home?"

"Your mom can pick a lock?" Walker asked in hurried whispered tones.

"Who do you think taught us?" Layne snapped, hurling her uncooperative bra to the ground and pulling on a loose T-shirt.

"Layne? Walker?"

"Coming, Mom!"

Walker snickered as he buttoned his jeans. "Ain't that the truth?"

Layne smacked him in response as she unlocked the door. "And I plan to again tonight."

"Yes, ma'am." Walker grinned, giving up the pretense of hurrying. Morgan liked him. Miles would shoot him. There was a difference in how concerned he would be if it were Miles walking in on them.

"I heard you had a rough night," he heard Morgan say to Layne as the sound of the television came on.

Walker came down the hall with his shirt finally on and

kissed Morgan on the cheek. "Good morning, Morgan. Do you want some coffee?"

"No, thank you. I do have something for you."

Walker raised an eyebrow as Morgan pointed to the interview on the morning show. Jud sat in his uniform next to the news anchor with a solemn look on his face. "I'm not a hero. I just did what my training taught me. Any SEAL would do the same."

The anchor nodded. "You're Admiral Thomas Rudy's son. I'm curious as to why you changed your name."

Jud wasn't expecting that. He froze before clearing his throat. "I, um, wanted to make it on my own so I took my mother's maiden name."

"Or was it because of the drug charges you had mysteriously dismissed after enrolling in the Navy under your father's command? He must have pulled a lot of strings to make a drug charge disappear like that."

"How did they get this information?" Walker asked as Morgan's grin widened. "Gemma, Cy's wife, is a reporter. She's leaking information to different news outlets. The whole story will be out there by the end of the week. While Gemma was doing that, I've been working on this." Morgan handed him a copy of the biggest paper in the country. On the front page was a picture of Walker in uniform in the desert, playing soccer with the local children. Above the picture in big block letters read: *A profile on Walker Greene, SEAL Team Six Hero.*

"Mom, this story is great," Layne said as she read over his shoulder. And it was. It talked about him raising Edie, his love of his country, the work he did with the local children wherever he was stationed, and even had quotes from some of the people he'd rescued over the years.

"How did you get all of this?" Walker asked.

"As I told you, I'm good in crisis. Nabi got me your internal file, and I contacted people to hear the good you've done. They were all to eager to sing your praises. This is only the first story. Tonight on the national news there will be a story about you. Then tomorrow another front-page national story and so on. Each will feature information on how you're a well-loved, respected, and charitable man. Plus, the success of your missions that aren't classified shows what a hero you really are. And I'm not just saying that. You know who I'm married to, and even I'm impressed after reading your file. However, I fear you may not be a SEAL again after all this is over. You'll be too well known. But when you bring Jud down, you'll be the more believable in the press, and we all know a good spin to the story is the most important part of winning the public over. The press will love you and hate Jud by the time I'm done."

Walker flipped the paper over and read a quote from the aid worker he'd helped rescue out of the Congo. His lips tilted up into a smile as he saw a picture of her now holding a newborn. His team had rescued her three years before, and now she was happily married with a baby. She pointed out that the team relied more on Walker than they did on Jud, whom she thought was uncaring during the mission. Walker, she told the paper, talked to her the entire way out of the jungle, sometimes even carrying her, so they reached the rendezvous point on time.

"*His calming words kept me going. If it weren't for Walker Greene, I wouldn't have made it out of there alive.*" Layne sniffed as she read it out loud. "Oh, Walker. I had no idea what you really did. I mean, I had an idea, but to actually hear what you've done. You're so brave."

Walker didn't like talking about himself. Being brave wasn't something he thought about. It was about the mission and the lives that needed saving. His life or feelings never factored into it.

"Jud has several appearances scheduled for this week, but Friday is his last one. So, four more days and then Miles and I believe he'll come here."

"How do you know that?" Walker asked as he processed the information and came to the same conclusion. He would finish his press tour knowing the longer he kept Edie, the more impatient Walker would become and more likely to mess up.

"I called his agent to see about him doing an interview. I was told he's booked all this week, and after Friday will be unavailable so that he might take some time to recuperate from the trauma of the rescue."

Walker nodded. "This weekend it is."

22

"No offense, Walker. Regardless of what the papers are reporting, Nash is still the biggest badass."

Walker rolled his eyes at Nash as he held the punching bag for Walker. Walker wouldn't disagree that Nash was a badass, but Layne had whipped him.

Miles snorted as he circled Cade in the boxing ring at Desert Sun Farm. "No offense, Nash, but my daughter beat you up. So I guess Layne's the biggest badass."

"For now," Ahmed said quietly as he worked the weights.

"What do you mean, 'for now'?" Miles challenged.

"I mean, until Abigail comes back to Keeneston. I taught her personally." Ahmed let the weights clatter to the ground. "And we all know my daughter is doing more than private security. So, yes, Layne is the most badass woman in town . . . for now."

"Well, Dylan isn't too shabby either. I mean, we have no idea what he does, but he looks like he could snap those weights in half," Pierce defended as he ran on the treadmill.

"Why are you even here, Pierce?" Cy asked as he worked the weight machine.

"He's carrying an overnight bag," Marshall pointed out.

Walker and Nash both looked and saw the bag by the lockers. "Shoot me if I turn into Pierce when Sophie gets pregnant." Walker grinned at Nash. For as much as Cade touted his son-in-law, Nash really was a good guy. "But based on the betting at the café, you and Layne may beat us to the baby."

"What?" Walker asked as the Davies brothers and Ahmed continued to outline why each of their children or sons-in-law would be the biggest badass.

"Aniyah told Riley she had to give Layne a box of condoms. Riley told Reagan who told Piper who told Sophie. Apparently that was two weeks ago, so the general consensus is you've run out of said condoms and in nine months a little bundle of badass will be born."

A laugh escaped Walker. "I want a onesie with that written on it when we have a baby."

"*When* we have a baby, is it?" Nash teased.

"You don't punch a priest in the face unless you're serious."

"Dylan could take Jackson down with one hand tied behind his back," Pierce shouted across the gym to Cole.

"And your wife can kick you out of the house while pregnant and not even break a sweat," Cole shot back.

"At least I didn't get my wife a scanner for Mother's Day," Pierce yelled at Cole.

"At least I'm smart enough to never use the word *old* when describing my wife."

"Cole has you on that one," Miles said as the rest of the brothers laughed.

Nash shook his head and turned his attention back to

Walker. "So, you're the one who gave Father Ben the shiner? Been there, done that."

"He's not actually a priest, is he?" Walker asked as he took hold of the bag for Nash to punch.

"I haven't looked into it much. Unlike most people in Keeneston, I believe people should be able to keep their secrets. But from what I can tell, he's really a priest. He was ordained right before coming to Keeneston. But everything before that is hidden."

"Hidden?"

"I could find it, but to be fair I didn't try very hard. I figure Ben has a reason for a past that only starts a couple years ago. He'll tell us when he's ready."

"He's trained. He might be good to have by our side when Jud comes."

Nash nodded and slammed a fist into the bag. "Let's talk to him. And Piper. She has some great technology you and Layne should use to keep you safe. Let's shower, then head over to Piper's lab."

"I had Addison look into what needed to be done to open a government training facility," Cy said suddenly, drawing Walker's attention. While he'd been working out with Nash, most of the room had emptied out until it was only Miles, Marshall, Cade, Cy, Cole, and Ahmed left. But when Cy said that, all eyes turned to Walker and back to Miles.

"What?" Cy asked and then looked to Walker. "Crap, I forgot about him."

Miles stared him down and Walker stared back. There was a moment of silence and then Miles grunted. "He's all right."

"Oh, come on! Nash didn't find out until he was practically engaged to Sophie," Cade complained.

"Condoms," Marshall coughed under his breath, clearly hearing the gossip Aniyah blabbed. Miles heard it through the cough and Walker was sure if he'd been standing closer it would have been Walker who took the punch to the gut instead of Marshall. Marshall bent over and coughed. "I was defending your choice to fill him in. Obviously he's in it for the long haul. He knows we'd all castrate him if Layne didn't get to him first."

Miles grunted with realization that Marshall spoke the truth. "Get on with it."

"Who is Addison?" Walker whispered to Nash.

"She's an attorney. Her parents, Henry and Neely Grace Rooney, are the local defense attorneys. You'll know Henry when you meet him. He constantly spouts some really horrible pickup lines," Nash answered.

"Anyway, she said we can form a private company to train officers and soldiers. The government would contract with us. She can get all the paperwork ready if we decide to do this," Cy explained.

"I know I'm supposed to be silent here, but what exactly are you wanting to do?" Walker asked.

Miles used his mouth to untie his boxing glove and began to pull it off. "See, we're not all the way retired. We like to keep on our toes by helping out every once in a while. And we're trusting you here because our wives and children have no idea we're doing this. However, Gemma, Cy's wife, came up with a good idea. She suggested we start a training facility for police and military. So we asked Addison to look into it for us."

"That's brilliant." Walker was kind of shocked it had taken them this long to do it. "And I knew you all were in too good of shape to not still be active."

"You did?" Miles asked.

"Yeah. It's pretty obvious. I'm surprised your wives haven't figured it out. Anyway, I don't know how it was when you went through training, but we have contracted civilians to teach us some things, especially close combat fighting in different martial arts styles and boxing. And I know lots of guys who went to private pre-training to be prepared for BUD/S selection and training. And many in DEVGRU take private classes all the time in different areas. With all of your specialties, you'd have a wait list a mile long." Hell, why did they think Walker worked out with them every day? He'd learned so much just hanging out and working out with them.

"We don't have a SEAL," Marshall whispered, but Walker heard them anyway.

"Let's see if he lives through this week before we offer him a job," Cade responded.

A job? Walker looked to Nash who shrugged his shoulders indicating it would be possible. Walker was highly trained. He wouldn't be able to be undercover anymore after the PR campaign by Morgan. He would need a job—a job that would keep him close to Layne. And he had the contacts in DEVGRU to get them to put this training facility at the top of their list. As Walker headed back to the house, his mind was reeling with possibilities of a future in Keeneston with Layne.

"How's Tinsley?" Layne asked Gavin over the phone as she cleaned the new gun Sophie had given her this morning after their workout. Walker wasn't the only person who needed his skills sharp. She had no intention of sitting on the sidelines when Jud came to town.

"Healing. We haven't seen anything suspicious here since Edie was taken. And trust me when I tell you, we're looking for clues everywhere. Edie is like part of the family."

"We think Jud will strike this weekend. Hopefully, Edie will be safely back to us in a couple of days," Layne said. Three to be exact.

"Do you have a plan? Are the police involved?" Gavin asked.

"We have a plan. My cousin is the FBI agent in charge of the area, so he's on it. And my cousin-in-law is the sheriff. That's all the law enforcement we will use."

"Don't you need more to take down someone like Jud?"

Layne set down the gun. "The family will take care of it. Look, someone's knocking. I'll call you again soon. And thanks for speaking with my grandma the other night. She hasn't stopped talking about what a nice young man you are."

"I'm glad. She's a very sweet woman. We're all looking forward to meeting her. Goodbye, Layne. Stay safe and call if you need any more family to help."

"I will. Bye." Layne hung up and answered the door. Zain and Mila stood smiling at her as she wrapped them each in a hug.

"When did you get back?" Layne asked.

"Just now," Mila Ali Rahman smiled. "But we've been keeping up on all the news during the conference."

Since Zain Ali Rahman had become the spare heir to the Rahmi kingdom, Zain and Mila had been traveling a lot on diplomatic missions and meeting regularly with Zain's uncle, the king of Rahmi.

"We came by to see if you needed anything," Zain said as they came into the kitchen.

"And to meet Walker," Mila laughed.

"Well, here I am," Walker said, coming in from yet another workout. He was a man possessed. Layne had been worried he would be pushing himself too hard, but he and Nash had gotten into a rhythm of working out and his leg was improving every day.

"Oh my gosh, Layne," Mila whispered with wide eyes before turning back to Walker. "I'm Mila Ali Rahman, and this is my husband, Zain."

Walker reached out and shook their hands. "The diplomats, right? I still need to meet your brother and sister."

Zain nodded. "Gabe and his new bride are touring the world before she starts as the new high school counselor next month. My sister, Ariana, is in DC for the summer. So, if you're still around come next month . . ."

"Zain," Layne groaned as she smacked her friend's arm. "Stop angling for inside information to place a bet."

Zain winked at Layne and Mila rolled her eyes. "You should have let me do the talking. I told you I would be able to get more information than you. Anyway, we just wanted to say hello and offer our help in anyway."

"Thank you," Walker said, "but I think we're stuck in a waiting game for now."

"Well, it was nice meeting you. I'm sure we'll see you around the farm and town. With Gabe's wife, Sloane, and now you, we Keeneston transplants gotta stick together," Mila laughed. "It increases our betting odds."

Walker chuckled as they walked Zain and Mila to the door. The second the door closed, Walker had her in his arms. "I missed you," he whispered in her ear between kisses.

"You were gone for two hours," Layne said, laughing.

"Like I said, I missed you." Walker ran his hand up her

leg and it disappeared under her skirt. As time counted down to Jud's appearance, their lovemaking became more desperate. The night before had been sweet, but that morning had been anything but. And by the way Walker was angling her against the living room wall and kicking off his athletic shorts, she knew he was going to be as frantic as she felt. It was like they both knew their time was coming to an end. Or at least a potential end—the kind death created.

Layne clawed his shirt off over his head and sunk her nails into his back as Walker pulled down the straps of her dress, exposing her breasts to him. "I need you now," he gasped, sliding on a condom before placing two hands on her ass and lifting her to him. She didn't need to tell him she needed him just as much. She needed the reminder that they were alive, and she needed every chance to show him how much she loved him before time ran out.

23

Layne bounced her knee and wrung her hands together as Walker sat next to her on her parents' couch. Jud looked ready to explode during his TV interview. His face was red, his mouth pressed into a tight, thin line, and his eyes narrowed into daggers. The reporter pressed Jud as a picture of his battered ex-girlfriend came onto the screen.

This was his last interview. It was Friday. He was on a prime time news show at what was supposed to be the height of his popularity. But due to the work Gemma and Morgan had done, each interview had only gotten worse for Jud. Questions were now being asked about his drug use, his connection to Darrel Snyder, his abuse of women, and what had really happened on the ship before the drone focused in on him. The pedestal he was on was slowly eroding.

"The communication system you had on your uniforms went down, so the last bit of video and audio footage is of you charging into the bridge. Here at BBN news, we've learned it wasn't only your communication device and video feed that was cut, but the entire team's. Is that normal?" the reporter asked, staring right back at Jud.

Miles turned to Walker with a thoughtful expression. "You had a body cam on?"

Walker nodded. "A helmet cam. My communications pack was shot to smithereens so I couldn't call for help."

"Where's your camera?" Miles asked.

"It's at the house with what remains of my uniform. I tossed the coms pack to swim, and I haven't been able to get the camera to work."

Layne looked back at the television as her father sat in silent thought. "You had previously told us that you lay injured on the bridge as the pirates killed your team, isn't that correct?" the reporter asked.

"Yes, that's correct. I'm not wearing this sling for fashion," Jud said tensely, looking down to his bandaged arm.

"Yet you knew the hero of the night, Walker Greene, had jumped from the bridge and into the water one hundred twenty feet below?"

"Yes," Jud answered tightly. "I was crawling toward Walker to try to save him. I couldn't get to him in time. It was then I propped myself up and took out the pirates and signaled for help."

"Walker Greene's body has never been found."

Jud didn't answer. He stared at the reporter.

"Isn't it true you pushed for his funeral for closure and the government granted you that request? Strange that you wouldn't be out there looking for someone, who by all our research, is shown to be a survivor. Walker Greene has been heralded as a hero, an expert in survival, top of his class in BUD/S, and was rumored to have been promoted to senior chief petty officer of your group until your father, Admiral Thomas Rudy, stepped in and put pressure on to promote you ahead of him. Do you have a response to that?"

Jud snapped. His nose flared, his face flushed, and he stood up so quickly the reporter jumped back. He ripped off his microphone and looked down at her. "*I'm* the hero, not Walker Greene!"

Layne had grasped Walker's hand when Jud snapped and didn't breathe again until Jud had stormed from the stage. Her mother's gleeful chuckle broke Layne's focus on the reporter, now talking to the camera.

"You did all of this?" Layne asked.

"Of course I didn't. Gemma did quite a bit as well. But the reporter, Rebecca, is a friend of mine from college. She was all too happy to be promised the interview that brought down a fake hero."

Layne jumped up and hugged her mother. "Thank you."

"Yes, thank you, Morgan," Walker said, kissing her cheek. "I have a chance to tell my story now."

"I'd like to see that camera of yours, son," Miles said. It wasn't lost to Layne that her father had begun to call Walker *son* more and more often. It warmed her heart to see the two men she loved most in the world working together.

"Do you think we can get something off it?" Walker asked.

"I don't know. But first let's see if I can find a camera expert." Miles sent out a text and looked over at them. "Where's the camera?"

"In the bedroom in a small duffle bag in the closet, why?" Walker asked.

"Nabi is grabbing it. Cody Gray, the deputy sheriff, is coming over to get it. He said he could look at it," Miles explained. "But now we need to prepare. Jud is mad, and he's coming for you, Walker. Are you ready to handle him?"

"You bet I am."

Layne sat back as Walker and her father talked. Jud would be coming the next day. No more taunting from a distance. He would be upon them with revenge and murder on his mind. There was no way he'd let Walker live, and he wouldn't let Edie live either. Not after she'd been held that long. There had to be something she could do to help.

～

TWO HOURS LATER, as Walker was ensconced with her father, uncles, and cousins finalizing their plans, Layne sat at the Blossom Café with her mother, Aunt Gemma, and Reagan. Chocolate was the only answer now.

"What are you thinking?" Morgan asked her. Her mother always did know when Layne was up to something.

"I need to think of a way to find Edie. If Walker kills Jud instead of capturing him, we may never find her," Layne said before scooping up a spoonful of bread pudding smothered in chocolate sauce.

"When do you think Jud will come after Walker?" Reagan asked.

"Since your mom and my mom's bang-up media campaign, I'm guessing tomorrow. He'll want to get his stuff together, stash Edie someplace he can easily get to her, and then come after Walker."

Reagan pursed he lips in concentration. "Is there anything I can do to help?"

"There's something I can do," Piper said from behind Layne. Layne turned and saw Piper holding a large bag. "I know you're not the target, but I'd feel better if you wore one anyway."

Piper pulled out what looked like a windbreaker and

handed it to her. "Thank you." Layne smiled, pulling it on over her head. It looked like any other coat, but it was actually bullet- and stab-proof.

"I have one for Walker, too. I just went off Dylan's measurements, so it should fit."

"Oh, gift time!" Sophie smirked as she pulled up a chair next to Layne. "I also have come bearing gifts." Only this time it was a briefcase that she placed on the table instead of a bag. Layne looked at the metal case that was protected by a fingerprint and code lock. Sophie pressed her finger against the reader and then entered a code and the case unlocked.

"Wow," Layne whispered, looking at the array of weapons.

"Now my gift seems puny," Piper teased, sitting down next to Reagan.

"These are two of my newest inventions," Sophie explained, picking up a very compact little gun. "It's made out of plastic—very strong plastic that isn't available to the public yet. It makes the gun undetectable at all metal detectors. Plus, its small size allows it to be concealed easier. But don't let the size fool you. It's just as strong as a 9mm."

"Dad is going to be so jealous," Reagan joked as her mother nodded her agreement. Cy always liked to play with whatever weapons Sophie developed after she'd shown her father, Cade.

"This is also made from the same plastic, so it's undetectable," Sophie said, pulling out a folding knife. She unfolded it and the blade was more needlelike than swordlike. "This thin blade can slip between ribs, puncture the heart, the neck, or whatever and the person may not even realize it until they fall down dead seconds later. Plus the side is serrated, so you can cut things as well."

"Won't it break?" Layne asked, holding the ultra lightweight knife gently.

"Shouldn't. This plastic is crazy. It has a super-high melting point, is undetectable, sharp as metal, and very durable. That's why I began crafting some weapons out of it," Sophie explained. "Go ahead, put them on. You won't even know you're carrying them."

Layne reached down her shirt and hooked the knife to the underside of her front bra strap and then looked at the gun, trying to decide where to put it.

"You can put it between your breasts and attach it to your bra, or you can put it on the inside of your waistband. Hell, you can hide it in your underwear," Sophie said, handing her a small leather holster for it.

The gun was small, and it would be undetectable hidden in the small of her back. Using the holster, Layne secured the weapon and already felt better being armed with Sophie's weapons and protected by Piper's jacket.

"Thank you both. And now I'm going home in a sugar-induced coma to find a way to sleep. I know tomorrow I won't get any."

Layne stood up and her mother, Gemma, and Reagan joined her as Sophie and Piper took their table and began to pass the word that everyone needed to be hyper aware tomorrow.

Layne pushed open the door to the café and stepped out onto the sidewalk. The night air was warm as it danced around her. She looked into the night sky at the twinkling stars. She felt small and useless in that moment. She was a pawn in a massive game going on all around her.

"I'll drive you home, dear," her mother said, sensing her mood. Layne hugged and thanked Aunt Gemma and Reagan before turning and meeting her mother.

"Where are you parked?" Layne asked as Morgan put her arm around her shoulder and pulled Layne to her side.

"Just down here," she said as they began to walk past the alleyway leading behind the café. "I see you have a lot on your mind. Would you like to . . . aah!"

Morgan was thrown forward, her arm ripped from Layne's shoulder as a man emerged from the shadows behind them. "Dr. Layne Davies, a pleasure to finally meet you."

"Layne!" She heard Reagan yell as footsteps pounded behind her. Layne stared into Jud's evil twisted face and decided then and there what her plan was.

"Don't hurt me, please!" Layne begged. Her mother's eyes widened in surprise from the ground as he pulled her hand from her head. Layne saw blood covering it as her mother staggered to stand.

"Let go of my daughter." Her mother managed to stand on wobbly legs as she lunged for Jud. Jud smashed his fist into Morgan's stomach, sending her to her knees, gasping for breath. Layne saw red but kept her cool as she leapt between them.

"I'm sorry, Mom, but little Layne is needed elsewhere." Jud snatched Layne's arm painfully as Reagan closed in on them. Her mother lunged, but Layne blocked her.

"It's okay, Mom. I love you," Layne said, only this time the tears were real. "Tell my *sister* I'll see her soon," were the last words she got out before Jud yanked her into the alley and into the trunk of a waiting car she hadn't seen before.

Layne went willingly as gunfire erupted. Sophie must have had some others following her. It was likely half the café were packing guns. Layne heard her mother's screams as the car took off into the night. She tried not to think about her mother's cries or her cousins' desperation. She had protected them by going. And if she was right, she'd be able to protect Edie as well.

24

"Why the hell didn't she fight back?" Reagan yelled as she and Sophie hurried to her car. Morgan and Gemma were trying to find the car that took her while Piper was calling in the troops—literally and figuratively.

"I don't know, but hurry up," Sophie said with desperation to her voice. She hadn't gotten there in time. She'd let her cousin be taken by a madman. How could she live with herself if something happened?

"*Tell my sister I'll see her soon.* What does that even mean?" Reagan asked as she pressed the gas pedal to the floor. For anyone else, it would be dangerous to drive those back roads at ninety miles per hour. But Reagan and her cousins grew up on these roads and knew every inch of them.

"Oh my God. I got it!" Sophie screamed as she told Reagan her theory.

Reagan's car didn't slow for the gates of Desert Sun Farm. They were expecting her and would be open. "You tell the others," Reagan ordered as she slammed on the brakes. The car skidded through the grass and came to a rocking stop yards from the helicopter. Nabi stepped from the cockpit, his dark hair reflecting the lights from the landing pad.

"Find her!" Sophie yelled against the sound of the blades as Reagan nodded to Nabi and leapt into the private helicopter of the Ali Rahman family and took off.

"Jud has Layne."

Three simple words had the power to destroy Walker. "What?" Walker asked a white-faced Miles.

"He has my daughter," he said though clenched teeth even as his hands shook.

"Where is he?" Walker was grabbing his gun and heading for the door. Cade and Cy pulled him back.

"We don't know," Cade said gently.

"I'm gathering all the information now," Nash explained. "We need to move to security."

Silently, Walker followed as the group left the house and walked to the nearby security complex on Desert Sun Farm. He turned his head as he heard a helicopter taking off.

"Reagan," Cy said without looking back. "Gemma and Morgan haven't had luck finding the car, so Reagan is our eye in the sky. She'll find them."

Miles's phone rang, and he answered it before the first ring was complete. "Honey, are you okay?" Walker held his breath as he watched Miles go from pale white to flushed red. His hand fisted at his side as he listened. Everyone was quiet. And everyone's heart broke at the sobbing they could hear over the phone.

"It's okay, Morgan. You're so brave. You did everything you could," Miles said gently. "Have Gemma bring you to the security complex at Mo and Dani's. Do you want me to stay on the phone with you?"

"Find our daughter," Walker heard Morgan order before Miles hung up.

"What can we do?" Mo asked as he, Dani, Zain, and Mila rushed into the office. "We got the text Piper sent."

"Dylan will arrive in two hours," Pierce called out as he slid into the room. "I figured you all were here."

Cole looked at his phone. "Ryan will be here in fifteen minutes. Jackson will be here with his partners, Talon Bainbridge and Lucas Sharpe, in two hours as well. They're FBI hostage rescuers," Cole told Walker.

"Abby will be here in an hour and a half," Bridget reported, hurrying in and stopping by Ahmed's side.

"Have everyone meet here," Mo said as Nash sent out the text.

Two hours seemed like an eternity. How could Walker sit there for two hours waiting for backup? Didn't they have enough backup already?

"We need a plan, you know that," Miles said quietly, so no one else heard them. As they were all talking, Miles had moved to Walker's side. Walker nodded, not trusting himself to answer. The pain of losing Layne was so strong he thought he'd throw up.

Sophie was the next one to run into the building. Nash put his arms around her, but she shrugged him off. "Something wasn't right," Sophie said, raising her voice to get their attention. "And I think I figured it out."

"What?" Walker asked as he pushed forward to be able to talk to Sophie.

"I had given Layne two weapons that she'd hidden on her body. And Piper had given her a bulletproof jacket. We all know Layne can fight. But she didn't. Not even when Jud hit Aunt Morgan," Sophie said. Everyone looked to Miles and the pain was clear in his eyes.

"Instead, Layne told Aunt Morgan 'tell my sister I'll see her soon.'" Sophie stopped talking and looked expectantly at Walker.

"She let herself be taken on purpose." Walker ran a hand over his hair.

"What? Why?" Pierce asked.

"To save my sister, Edie. Dammit!" Walker slammed his hand against the nearest wall.

"It was a smart move," Nash said quietly but confidently. "You're going to kill Jud. And when you do, you'd never be able to find your sister. Now she has Layne to protect her, and you can focus all your attention on Jud."

It may be the truth, but Walker didn't want to hear it. All he could think about was Jud had the two women he loved the most.

LAYNE COUNTED. She counted in five-minute increments as they drove. So far they had driven forty minutes. The road had been bumpy at first, as if Jud had cut across a field. Then there had been some twists and turns and then she could finally tell they were on a highway of some kind. There were plenty of places to hide within thirty minutes of Keeneston. She could be headed in any direction. Either way, she knew with each minute that passed they were getting closer to Edie. She just needed to keep her wits about her until then. So she counted.

"I FOUND her and have been following the car. I think we're getting close to stopping," Reagan's voice crackled over the intercom and into the room. Everyone gasped as Walker and Miles looked at the map showing the GPS of the helicopter.

"Are they still moving?" Walker asked.

"Affirmative. They're heading into Western Kentucky. They're fifteen minutes from Elizabethtown and are getting off the interstate onto a small country road heading south."

"What's in Western Kentucky?" Walker wondered. He wasn't familiar with the region.

"Caves," Jace said from the back of the room. "The whole state sits on limestone, but we have massive underground systems in that area. Jud could be hiding Edie in one of them, which would make finding her almost impossible unless Reagan can find the entrance."

"That has to be it," Colton agreed. "We explored them all the time as teenagers."

"I'd forgotten about that," Cade said.

"Do you know where they could be going?" Walker asked as Jace shook his head.

"No, but if you can find a map of the cave systems to underlay with the street maps and Reagan's GPS, I can probably narrow it down."

"Then what?" Morgan asked as she clutched her husband's hand.

"Then we divide and conquer," Walker said coldly. He knew what he'd have to do. He would have to stay here and take on Jud. Not going after Edie and Layne would nearly kill him, but Jud had to be taken down. "I'll stay here and take care of Jud while Miles and his brothers rescue my sister and Layne."

"Here you go, Jace," Nabi said as the group looked up at the large screen hanging on the wall.

"There's an extensive cave system here," he said, pointing to a section on the map. "It was used for mining and it's private land. That's all there really is in that direction. At least according to the maps."

"They're slowing down," Reagan reported over the coms.

"Are you flying lights out?" Nabi asked her.

"Sure am. And I'm high up. They shouldn't be able to hear me," Reagan responded. "Okay, they're pulling into what looks like an old driveway, but I don't see a house of any kind. I do see plenty of cars about a mile up that dirt road."

Nabi was already working the computers. In seconds, he had the deed and the map for the property pulled up. "It's part of those mines you were talking about," Nabi said to Jace. "But it's hundreds of acres."

"The entrance will be near where they're parked. Who are the owners?" Jace asked.

"Dead. An estate owns the property, and the executor lives in California. They haven't paid taxes on it in three years. It's essentially abandoned," Nabi responded.

Walker nodded to himself. "It makes sense."

"What does?" Miles asked.

"Jud would have done a records search for abandoned property when looking for a place to keep Edie. I thought it would be closer, but it seemed like an easy drive. He would never bring Edie to me. It was never his intention, but he'd have to have someone with her, just in case he needed to show me he was going to kill her to get me to do whatever it is he wants. If he were in Keeneston, then you all would have found him too soon. This way he feels he's safely out of reach. He's been planning this the whole time. I thought he wouldn't move Edie until tonight, but he probably moved her right after he sent that picture to Layne."

"We have movement," Reagan said and the room went

still as they looked up at the map. "Nabi, I'm going to video in with my phone."

"Go ahead," Nabi confirmed as he connected his phone to the large screen. Reagan's call came in and the screen turned dark as Reagan pointed it toward the cars pulling to a stop.

Walker was used to looking at drone footage, so it was easy for him to read the images. The lights from the car showed a door built into a mound of earth. It would have been near impossible to see from the air without the cars parked there.

Walker watched as someone, probably Jud, got out of the passenger door and went around to the trunk. It was hard to see in the dark what was going on, but soon they all saw a timid and stumbling Layne being pulled into the headlights. There was a knock on the door, and Layne was shoved inside. Walker's heart broke. He wanted to fight. He wanted to get there and save her, but he had to force himself to observe.

Jud and a passenger stood talking to someone at the door before the door was pulled open wide and six men hurried out to meet Jud and his cohort.

"What's going on?" Morgan asked.

"They're talking. I see nine men," Reagan responded. The Keeneston group silently watched as Jud and his men talked and looked at a large piece of paper spread out on the hood of the car. Men moved from behind the door to outside, carrying bulletproof vests and weapons. Jud was preparing to make his move.

25

Layne whimpered as she was dragged from the trunk. She didn't fight. Instead, she cowered. The men didn't look at her twice as Jud shoved her through the hidden door in the hillside with her arms tied behind her back with a zip cord. The smell of earth, rock, and stagnant air hit her hard as another man grabbed her arm.

"Who do we have here? She's a pretty one, too."

"She's Walker's flavor of the month. He always did like the pretty ones. Dumb as rocks, but they knew their way around a bed," Jud responded with a chuckle. "Gather the men. It's time to go over the plan one more time, and then we'll be set for life. Dumb bimbos on our arms as we sit on our own private island."

"Hooyah!" the man holding Layne yelled, echoing down what looked to be a mining corridor. Lanterns lit the way as the man dragged her deeper into the caves. The walls were lined with old beams, and her feet hit mining cart rail tracks as they went farther down.

A man reading a book came into view, lit by lanterns on each side of the thick door he was leaning against. He looked at Layne and grinned. "Walker is going to be pissed. We have both the women in his life, and he'll have to die knowing they're at our mercy."

"Screw mercy." The man holding her laughed as he squeezed her arm tight. "Is your name Mercy?"

Layne shrunk back and turned to escape his grasp as he laughed. Her muscles bunched and her adrenaline rose as she suppressed all her instincts to fight. She needed to find Edie first.

"Come on." Layne heard someone yell from the entrance of the mine. "Boss is ready for us."

The door opened and Layne was shoved inside. "Sit tight and maybe I'll show you some mercy of my own when we finish our operation."

Layne stumbled inside, and the door was slammed shut. She looked around the dark room; only one lantern was inside it. There were shelves and a massive six-foot-tall steel safe in the room. Layne squinted, thinking she saw something in the shadows.

"Edie? Edie Greene?"

The shadows moved as a dirty woman stepped into the glow of the single lantern in the middle of the room. "It's Edie Wecker. Who are you?"

"I'm Layne Davies. Your brother sent me."

Fifteen minutes later, Reagan broke into the conversation Walker was having with Miles and Ahmed. "They're on the move."

Walker turned to the screen and watched the men break into two groups before getting into two SUVs—four in one and five in the other. A man came out of the tunnel, watched them leave, and went back inside, shutting the door leading to Layne and possibly Edie. The cars turned and headed down the dirt road toward the main road and Keeneston. They were coming for him, and he was more than ready.

"What do you want me to do?" Reagan asked.

"Is there a place you can land?" Cy asked his daughter.

"I'd have to land a couple miles away. I'd lose eyes on the door. If I land here, they'll know it," Reagan replied.

"Stay in position. We'll report back in a minute with a team to help you," Cy said before turning to Walker and Miles. "It's your sister and um, girlfriend, and your daughter. You two have the final say. I suggest sending Marshall and me in to rescue them."

Walker looked to Miles. They both knew it wasn't going to be Walker. He had his own battle to handle.

"WALKER? WALKER SENT YOU?" Edie gasped, her voice harsh after many days of silence. "Is my brother alive?" Edie stumbled forward and clutched Layne's arm. Her hair was so dirty and tangled Layne couldn't tell if her hair was really brown or if it was the dirt. Her face was streaked with dirt as well. Her clothes smelled, and her white shirt was stained with the clay color of the dirt floor. But from what Layne could see, there were no bruises or signs of beatings.

"Yes, he's alive. He survived Jud's attempt to murder him by jumping from the bridge of the boat and finding a life raft. He was afloat at sea for a week until a Greek shipping boat found him. He went to Shadows Landing where Gavin helped him."

Edie began to sob as she collapsed to her knees, holding

tight to Layne's upper arm. "I knew he couldn't be dead. I just knew it. But they forced me to bury him. Why didn't Gavin or Tinsley or *someone* tell me?"

"They were trying to protect you. Walker was going to call you, but these men were in Shadows Landing. I'm from Keeneston, Kentucky. It's fifty minutes from here. Gavin is my cousin, and he found me at a conference in Charleston. He knew Walker had to get out of town, so I brought him to Kentucky to recuperate from the gunshot wound to his leg."

Edie looked up; the dirt on her face was streaked with tears now. "Is he okay?"

"He is. But now we need to get out of here."

Edie shook her head. "I've tried. This room appears to be where they kept the gold, or gems, or whatever it was they were mining for. There's a guard outside the door and I'm sure there are others. I haven't left this room since I got here except to go to the bathroom in the next room over. It's horrendous in there."

"I'll take care of that. But first, will you please reach down my shirt? Attached to my bra strap is a knife. I need you to get it and cut me free. They may be mercenaries, but they've completely underestimated me." Layne grinned. "Don't make the same mistake, okay?"

Edie nodded and stood up. She found the knife and opened it. "I could kill them for what they've put Walker and me through."

Layne turned her back toward the light so Edie could see to cut the tie. "Don't worry, I'll make sure they pay."

With a satisfying snap, the plastic zip cord broke and Layne was free. She turned and smiled at Edie as she took the knife from her. "Your brother is a SEAL. Your husband was a SEAL. I need you to be as tough as they are for me. Can you do that?"

Resolve and determination filled Edie's face. "I can."

"Does the guard open the door when you ask to go to the bathroom?"

Edie nodded. "Yes. Do you need me to do that?"

Layne shook her head. "No. I need you to scream, then bang on the door. Tell them I tripped in the dark and hit my head when I fell. Do exactly what he says, and I'll handle the rest. Can you do that?"

Edie nodded. "Tell me when you're ready."

Layne looked around the room for the darkest point. She pushed up the sleeve of the jacket Piper had given her and sliced the soft skin of the underside of her forearm. She wiped the blood with her hand and smeared it onto her forehead by her hairline and then lay down with her head next to the stone wall. Layne held the knife in her hand behind her and took a deep breath. She wasn't looking forward to what she had to do, but she'd be damned if that stopped her.

"Okay, Edie. Go."

Edie screamed her head off and ran toward the door. She pounded against it with more strength than Layne thought she had. "Help! The girl hit her head, and she's not waking up!"

The door was unlocked and it slowly opened as Edie began to cry. "Help her! Oh, God, there's so much blood."

The man had a gun pointed at Edie as he looked into the room. Edie pointed to where Layne was. "She tripped with her hands tied behind her. She couldn't break her fall. She went head first into the wall."

"Sit against the wall. There," the guard ordered as Edie backed up to the far wall. "Sit down and put your hands on your head. And shut the hell up."

Edie gulped down her cries and did as ordered. Layne

waited until she felt the man kneel next to her. She heard him transfer his gun to his left hand as he used his right to feel for a pulse at her neck.

In a swift motion, Layne used her left hand to grab the gun and with her right she shoved the blade up through his ribs and into his heart. His eyes bugged, his mouth opened, and Layne twisted the blade. With a shove, she pushed him back as she ripped the gun from his hand. He fell on his back with the knife, buried to the hilt, sticking up from his chest.

At least this time Layne didn't throw up. Adrenaline shoved her to her feet as Edie slowly stood and looked at the open door. "You did it."

Layne leaned down and pulled the knife from the man's chest. "One down. You doing okay?"

Edie took a deep breath. "I'll do anything to get to my brother."

"Good," Layne answered, handing her the man's gun. "Do you know how to use this?"

"I'm a SEAL's wife and sister. Of course I do," she said, taking it and doing a quick check to see if it was loaded. "But don't you need it?"

Layne grinned as she reached behind her and pulled out Sophie's gun so small she could palm it. "I have my own. Let's go."

Layne took the lead, and Edie followed close behind. Silently they closed the door and pressed themselves to the rough cold wall as she slowly turned off the lanterns to allow them to hide in the shadows. It seemed to take hours as they quietly made their way toward the exit. Layne held up her hand and Edie stopped walking. She wasn't sure how to pull this next one off. There was a man sitting against the wall where the door to their freedom was securely latched.

The distance was questionable on whether the bullet would kill him, but right now she didn't see any other option.

Layne looked down at the gun and hoped Sophie was right. It needed power to take him out from twenty-five yards. She motioned for Edie to lie on the ground. As soon as Edie was down, Layne lined up her shot. It was different from the targets at home, and Layne wrestled with killing the man. That thought probably made her shot go an inch too high.

The bullet slammed into the man's collarbone, knocking him into the wall. Layne cursed as she took off running toward the man. She needed a clear shot as he pulled his gun. Layne didn't give him a chance to fire it. Instead, she slid to a stop, raised her gun, and fired off three more shots. The man dropped to the ground and Layne rushed toward the door ready to battle whoever came through it.

"Come on, Edie!" Layne called as she bent down and retrieved the man's gun. She shoved it in her waistband as Edie caught up. She was breathing heavily after two weeks of captivity but showed no signs of giving up. "Okay, you open it, and I'll go through first."

"Do you think there're more people outside?" Edie asked as she took a deep breath.

"I have no idea, but now isn't the time to quit." Layne moved against the wall next to the door as Edie prepared to unlock it and then flung it open. It was now or never. "Go!"

26

"Are you sure you know what to do?" Walker asked the Rose sisters one more time.

"Are you kidding?" Miss Lily asked.

"Yeah, we've been doing more than this way before you were an itch in your father's pants," Miss Daisy snorted.

"It's a shame my arthritis is acting up. I would feel better if I had my crepe pan with me," Miss Violet said to no one in particular as she rummaged through her purse.

Walker's eyes narrowed in confusion. "Why would you need a crepe pan?"

"One good thwack with a crepe pan to the head, and they're down for the count. It's a tried-and-true method. Ah, here it is."

Walker jumped back as Miss Violet pulled out a Sig P238 micro-compact gun. "It's purple," he said with astonishment.

"Oh, Vi, you remembered your gun. I have mine in here somewhere," Miss Lily said before digging out a similar pink gun.

"I got one too!" Aniyah called out as everyone dropped to the floor or ducked behind a desk except for Walker.

"If she shoots toes, isn't the ground the least safe place to be?" Walker asked as he stepped behind a desk to shield his toes.

"Hey, I've been practicing, and last week I shot the shin of the dummy." Aniyah set her hands on her curvy hips. Walker shook his head and looked to where the Rose sisters were standing off to the side.

"Do you know how to use those?" Walker asked the Rose sisters.

"Better than she does, bless her heart," Miss Violet answered with a nod to Aniyah.

"Baby, who gave you a gun?" DeAndre asked, holding out his hand.

"I bought it from a nice man on the corner of the street in Lexington. He said it was his mama's, and you're not taking it. I've been practicing, and I'm hitting shins now," Aniyah said proudly as she shoved the gun back into her purse.

"That's real good, baby. But maybe this time don't try to help by shooting someone," DeAndre said as he held out his hand for the gun and motioned with his fingers for her to give it to him.

"The door is opening," Reagan said, cutting into the conversation. "I'm getting video up. And by all that is holy, take the gun away from Aniyah."

Aniyah huffed as the video came onto the screen. Walker and everyone else leaned forward as the open door cast a small glow in the darkness of the night. He saw a figure appear and then disappear into the darkness.

"Mo, doesn't this fancy helicopter have any night-vision

binoculars in it?" Reagan asked as she obviously was feeling the same frustration as Walker.

"They're in the bag behind the copilot's chair," Nabi responded. Walker heard some rustling and then the phone moved as Reagan set it down.

"I'll be damned," Reagan said with a lightness to her voice that gave Walker hope. She moved the phone to the binoculars. "Let's see if this works. Can you see?"

"Yes," Walker said as the screen turned to a green hue and images he couldn't see before became visible, one woman with long hair moving back toward the door. He'd know that body anywhere.

"Layne," Miles said with relief.

They watched as Layne motioned to the door and another woman appeared. "She has Edie," Walker said, filled with awe and pride in Layne.

"I'm not seeing anyone else," Reagan said, removing the night vision and setting the phone up on the dash. "I'm going to land and bring them home. If I hurry, we might beat Jud and his men back to Keeneston."

Morgan grabbed Walker's hand. When he looked to his left, he saw her in the middle of himself and Miles, holding tightly onto both of them as Reagan began to fly closer to the caves.

"They're running for the woods," Reagan reported as she turned the helicopter toward the woods and hit the interior and exterior lights.

Walker saw Layne holding Edie's hand and running with a gun in her other hand as she looked back at the now illuminated helicopter. Layne slid to a stop and stared as the helicopter landed before breaking out into a grin that everyone cheered to see.

"Layne!" Reagan shouted as Layne sprinted for her cousin. In the video, they watched as Layne and Reagan wrapped each other up in a tight hug. Walker's heart broke as Edie came into view with a tentative smile on her grimy face.

Reagan pointed to the helicopter, and Layne waved as Edie looked to Reagan who nodded her head. Edie rushed toward the helicopter before going outside of the camera's view. "Walker?"

"I'm here, Edie!" Walker called out with relief and joy. Morgan tightened her hand on his before letting it go so he could rush to Nabi's phone as Edie reversed the camera. Her face filled the large screen and he heard some people in the room sniff as they watched the reunion.

"You really are alive," Edie cried as she covered her mouth with her hand and sobbed.

"I am. I'm so sorry I couldn't tell you, Edie. I should have been there when you learned about Shane. I'm so damn sorry, Edie." All the guilt, the worry, and the pain Walker had been carrying around poured out as he saw his sister's thin, dirty face.

"I knew you weren't dead. I knew it. This woman, Layne, saved me. She told me you were alive. I can't wait to see you and pinch you to see that you're real. Oh, Walker, how could Jud do this? Why did he do this?"

"Money and fame. Don't worry, he'll never hurt you again."

"Come on, Edie. Let me take you to your brother," Walker heard Reagan say gently. Edie nodded and wiped the tears from her face.

"Edie, can I talk to Layne for just a minute? We'll be together before you know it," Walker asked his sister.

"I love you, Walker," Edie said before handing the phone

to Layne as Miles and Morgan rushed to join Walker at the computer.

"Now don't be mad, Walker—" Layne started to say, but Walker was so happy to see her that being mad hadn't entered his mind.

"You saved my sister. I'll never be able to repay you," Walker said before Morgan hurried past him to grab the phone.

"Layne," her mother gasped. "You're hurt!"

"I'm fine. It was a ruse. How are you? I'm so sorry I didn't stop Jud from hitting you." Walker saw her break then. A single tear fell down her cheek as she turned away from the camera and took a deep breath.

"I'm stronger than that, and so are you. I'm perfectly fine. Better now that I know you're safe," Morgan replied before stepping back from the camera and letting Walker and Miles take over the screen.

"Your cousins are on the way. They'll get here when you do, and shortly after we expect Jud and eight other men. How did you get out?" Miles asked.

"Luckily they underestimated me. I had Sophie's weapons on me. Dad, I'm sorry. I killed two men."

Walker knew how this upset her and wanted to be there to comfort her.

"We'll take care of it, honey. I'm so proud of you. You used your brain and saved Walker's sister. We'll see you shortly. I love you."

"I love you too, Dad. And Walker, I love you."

"I love you too, sweetheart. Now make Reagan get my two girls back to me ASAP."

Layne smiled and Walker finally exhaled.

"See you soon," Reagan called out a second before the screen went black.

Walker took a deep breath and turned to face Miles, currently buried on his phone. "You're not going to hit me again?" Walker asked.

"Not unless you break my daughter's heart. Then you won't have to worry about me hitting you because I'll kill you," Miles answered as Morgan looked over at his phone.

"Oh good, you put twenty on tonight. I'm putting twenty on tomorrow."

"Tonight?" Walker asked as he looked around at everyone frantically texting. "You all know a baby can't be born tonight, right?"

"Oh, we're not betting on that. We're betting on when you'll propose." Nash grinned.

"Don't you think we should worry about coming out of tonight alive?" Walker asked as he shook his head.

"*Pfft*," Miss Lily said with a wave of her hand. "That's at one to two odds right now. And the baby in nine months bet has shot up to three to one."

"*Psst*," Aniyah whispered as she nudged him. "Just in case you haven't put a bun in that oven, I brought you some more condoms."

Aniyah slipped a mega-sized box from her purse that was almost the size of a shoebox. "Here, just put it under your shirt. I know how passionate my Sugarbear and I get after I shoot someone," she said with a wink, leaving Walker standing next to Miles, holding a massive box of condoms in his hands.

"Oh!" Miss Violet exclaimed. Her head perked up from her phone as Miles took a deep breath and flexed his hand into a fist. "The odds of Walker living just went down from one to two to two to one."

"Um, let's get ready for Jud's arrival," Walker said,

shooing the Rose sisters from the room and getting as far
away from his future father-in-law as he could.

LAYNE AND EDIE sat in the luxurious cabin of the Mercedes
helicopter Reagan was flying and used the last bottle of
water and some paper towels to clean up. Edie had already
chugged two bottles. They hadn't talked as they worked, but
Edie opened up the second Layne leaned back and took a
deep breath.

"So, you disobeyed my brother to come rescue me, and
then he tells you he loves you. I think you may have
misrepresented your relationship a little."

Layne opened her eyes and saw Edie grinning as if the
harm of two weeks of captivity had simply fallen to the
wayside. Of course, Layne knew better. Edie would need
help recovering but being able to smile was a good sign.

"Maybe just a little," Layne said with a smirk.

"Why don't you tell me what's really going on between
you two?" Edie drank the rest of the bottle of water and
consumed a bag of peanuts they found in the storage
compartment.

"Well, it all started when I met my cousin for the first
time." Layne started. By the time they landed at Desert Sun
Farm, the story was complete, and Layne was pretty sure
she'd gained a sister.

Walker was opening the door before the blades had
turned off. Layne stayed in the helicopter as Edie launched
herself into her brother's arms. Edie was crying, and Layne
felt tears pushing for escape. She smiled happily as she
watched brother and sister reunite.

Walker finally set Edie down. She looked at her brother

and smacked him on the shoulder. "You better marry this woman or I'll kick your ass."

Layne laughed in surprise. They hadn't talked about marriage. They hadn't talked about their relationship at all until they told each other they loved one another.

"I believe you're right, Edie. I may have to do that," Walker said as he reached for Layne with a smile that reminded her of someone who knew something she didn't. What had happened while she was gone?

Layne's breath caught as he pulled her from the helicopter and into his arms. His lips met hers with reverence as she lost track of how long he kissed her. "I love you, Layne," Walker said softly after reluctantly ending the kiss.

"I love you too," Layne whispered before placing one last kiss on his lips. She slid down his body and her brow knit. "Um, what do you have shoved in your waistband?"

"A little gift from Aniyah." He chuckled.

"Oh no. It's not her fur-covered handcuffs, is it?"

Walker smile grew as he shook his head. "No. Remember I'm a Navy man. I don't need handcuffs. I'm rather talented with knots." Walker winked and stepped back at the sound of someone running toward them.

"Honey!" Her mother and father tightly embraced Layne before she introduced everyone to Edie.

"Abigail!" Layne cried as Ahmed's daughter moved to hug her. "What are you doing here?"

"Piper sent out the alarm, but it looks like you took care of it yourself."

Layne shrugged. "I had a good teacher."

Abby winked at her and dropped her voice. "We'll let your father pretend you're talking about him."

"Don't forget your favorite cousin," Jackson joked as he

casually rested his arm on Abby's shoulder. Two giant men with sniper rifles hung across FBI bulletproof vests flanked him. "How you doing, man?" he asked Walker who shook his hand.

"Edie, this is my cousin, Jackson. And Walker, you haven't met his teammates, Talon Bainbridge and Lucas Sharp."

Edie and Walker shook hands with them all, and then Edie's arms widened. "I thought you were big," she whispered to her brother as a man stepped from the shadows to join them. He rested his arm on Abby's other shoulder and nodded over Abby's head to Jackson.

"The three amigos ride again." He smirked.

"He's not even wearing a vest, and he's that big," Edie whispered to Walker, who rolled his eyes.

"Hey," he said to Walker. "Nice shirt. I have one just like it."

"That's because it's yours, genius," Piper teased. "Walker, Edie, meet my other brother, Dylan Davies."

Walker held out his hand and shook it. "Nice to see you again."

Dylan's hard face split into a grin, completely changing the way his tough face looked. Suddenly Layne saw the handsome man women drooled over. Apparently Edie did too, since her mouth was hanging open. "Wait, you two know each other?" Layne asked.

"No," they both answered with a glint of mischief in their eyes.

Piper looked between them as if she were trying to figure it out. "You know, I give up. I know you do something dangerous, so it may be best if you just don't tell me."

"So, what's going on?" Jackson asked as they moved to the security building.

Walker had slipped his hand into hers and so far hadn't let Layne go as he explained what happened with Jud, Edie, Layne, and now the nine men coming for him.

"You asked the Rose sisters for help?" Dylan asked with one raised eyebrow.

"Yeah, they're more likely to break a broom over Jud's head and capture him at the café than to follow the plan," Jackson added.

"Aniyah is with them," Walker said as Dylan, Abby, and Jackson shook their heads.

"That's not making it any better," Abby said, trying not to laugh. "But what do you want us to do?"

"I want Jud alive," Miles said, prowling toward them with his brothers behind him.

"I think it may be best to keep as many alive as possible," Ahmed said, joining the group. "Not that I can't bury a body or ten if need be. But we may want to find out exactly what Jud took and where it ended up. Walker has come up with a plan." Ahmed rolled out a map of the farm for the newcomers to hear their parts.

27

The Blossom Café was still full as Reagan and Piper sat with Aniyah at the table next to the Rose sisters. It had been decided the café was too crucial a place to leave Aniyah in charge. The entire Main Street was closed down and half the town was in the café, awaiting the life-and-death battle about to occur as if it were a theater production.

"With all this action going on, I bet we'll have another panty dropper incident," Aniyah said with a nod. "You know how a little shoot-out gets the blood pumping."

"I wish," Piper said with a huff and then looked to where Reagan was suddenly very interested in her glass of sweet tea. "You and your mystery man are the panty droppers, aren't you?"

"What? No!" Reagan shouted. "What man? I don't have a man."

Aniyah gave a *yeah right* look to her. "For your father being a spy, you are a horrible liar. Everyone knows you're getting some. The only question is from whom."

"Shouldn't we be looking out for Jud or his men?" Reagan deflected.

"You know it's only a matter of time before the truth comes out. Secrets have a shelf life in Keeneston," Piper reminded her.

"Why don't you date someone?" Aniyah asked Piper. "You're pretty, smart, and your father is the only Davies brother that's not scary."

Piper looked sadly down and ran her finger around the lip of her glass. "That's the trouble. I'm too smart. The men I've gone on dates with barely get through a drink before they're running for the door. As soon as they ask me, 'So, what do you do for a living?' their eyes glaze over as if they're zombies."

"Then you're dating the wrong men. You need someone smart and into science like you are. You have to have things in common. My Sugarbear and I have lots in common, but enough different interests to make it work."

Reagan nodded her head. "I actually agree with Aniyah on that one. You need someone who respects how smart you are, not intimidated by it."

Piper let out another long-suffering breath. "I've dated scientists. Really smart ones. They're even worse. They like to tell me all the ways I'm wrong and they're right. And heaven forbid I tell them something they said was wrong. I'm almost thirty, and I feel like a spinster already. It's been two years since I've had sex," Piper whispered.

"Heavens to Betsy!" Aniyah gasped. "Your poor doodah. We need to get you laid."

Piper shrugged. "Got any suggestions? I know everyone in town, and I'm not having any luck finding someone in Lexington."

"Don't you worry about a thing. Aniyah will take care of your doodah. Smile," Aniyah held up her phone and snapped a picture.

"I wasn't even smiling," Piper said as she looked to Reagan, who was shaking her head.

"I don't need your face. I was taking a picture of your cleavage. This here app is all about hooking up. You just click the smiley face or the frowny face. If you both click a smiley face, then you can meet up. If you want the most smiley faces, you gotta show what the good Lord gave you."

"Wow, and I didn't think I could feel worse about myself. Now I'm going to be solely judged on my boobs."

"Yeah, but you already got a smiley face. And look at this hottie." Aniyah said, turning the phone around. Piper and Reagan both went wide-eyed.

"I haven't seen a pecker that big since the sixties," Miss Lily said as the entire room turned to see what was going on.

The door opened and Jud walked in. Piper exhaled. "I've never been so happy to see a murderer before," she whispered to Reagan who laughed.

"Why hello there, sonny. I'm sorry, we're all filled up tonight," Miss Violet said sweetly. "It'll be about twenty minutes for a table."

Poppy hurried over with her notepad. "I can take your name if you'd like to wait for a table. It shouldn't be too long."

"That's awfully kind of you, ma'am, but I was hoping to surprise a friend of mine," Jud said, giving her a wink. Poppy blushed and was everything a simpering woman from Alabama was thought to be.

"Lucky friend. Who is she?" Poppy asked with a bat of her eyes.

Jud's grin widened in pleasure. "It's a he. He's new to town. Around six foot one, scruffy-looking with brown hair and bright blue eyes."

Poppy's face fell. "Oh, it figures. You're gay. All the good-looking men are."

Piper snorted and covered it up with a cough as she and Reagan pretended to talk.

Jud's face turned red. "I'm not gay. He's a friend of mine."

"Oh." Poppy smiled again and Jud's anger instantly faded.

"Bright blue eyes you say?" Miss Daisy asked.

"Yes, ma'am." Jud nodded respectfully.

"Lily, doesn't that new farmhand out at Desert Sun Farm have brown hair and blue eyes?" Miss Daisy asked her sister.

"Sure does." Lily answered. "I'm sure he'll be so happy to see a friend. He really keeps to himself, that one."

"And where is Desert Sun Farm?" Jud asked Poppy.

"Oh, real easy to get to. Just continue through town and go four or five miles. The farm will be on your left. They have large stone posts at the driveway with Desert Sun Farm written on them. Turn into there and then veer to the left at the house."

"Poppy, can I get a refill?" Aniyah asked, calling Poppy away and letting Jud slip from the café as Piper sent word that Jud was on his way.

"So, what about AnacondaMan725?" Aniyah asked Piper as she flashed the dick pic once again. Piper was tempted to ask Jud to come back and take her with him. Anything would be better than slowly dying of embarrassment.

"They're on their way," Walker said, looking at the message from Piper. Sienna and Tammy were forced to stay at Will and Kenna's house at the farm next door. Will and Kenna swore to watch them, but Pierce had stayed with his wife along with a loaded gun. A select group had been chosen to help, and the rest were in Mo and Dani's giant house as backup. Before Walker could give his order, people peeled off into the darkness. It was like he was working with his very own special ops group.

"Here, put on the jacket Piper gave you," Layne said once they had a moment alone. Walker lifted his arms and slipped the jacket over his head. "Walker?"

"Yeah?" he asked, tugging the jacket into place.

"Why do you have a giant container of condoms shoved down your pants?"

Walker just shook his head. "One word. Aniyah."

"Ah. Why don't I take those?"

Walker pulled the box from his waist and was finally able to button his jeans again. "Don't lose them. I have plans for each one of those. And that's just for tonight."

Layne laughed and rolled her eyes before growing serious. "I'll be right behind you. Be careful, Walker."

"Are you sure I can't get you to wait in the house?" Walker asked, running the back of his finger over her cheek.

"You know I'm the best shot. I won't get in the way unless I have to."

Walker didn't like it. She'd already killed three people, and all Layne wanted to do with her life was help people. It went against everything she believed in. Bridget and Annie, they were different. Abby was different. But Layne, while trained to kill, wasn't destined for it.

"I know you'll watch my back. I love you, Layne." Walker slid his hand to the back of her neck and brought his lips to hers.

"I love you, too. I know you're angry with Jud. I know you want to kill him, but focus on keeping calm. The calmer you are, the smarter your decisions will be. And the less injured you are, the more of those condoms we can use tonight."

Walker chuckled as Layne sauntered away with her father's rifle over her shoulders. He watched as she climbed a fifteen-foot mountain of hay bales and then buried herself in them at the top. She was invisible, but that didn't mean Walker wasn't worried about her. He didn't want her to see what he had to do. For all of Miles's talk about keeping Jud alive, Walker wasn't so convinced it was the best idea.

Walker's phone buzzed. It was DeAndre. Jud and his crew were a couple minutes out. Walker looked around, and even though he knew where people were, he couldn't see them. Colton and Landon were in trees. Miles and his brothers were with Ahmed and members of the Rahmi Services lying in the grass and behind water troughs in the surrounding pastures. Paige was on the roof of the mansion with a sniper rifle. Dylan, Jackson, Talon, Lucas, Matt, Ryan, Nash, and Abby were the closest at hand. They would be his initial backup, along with Layne. He hoped he knew Jud as well as he thought he did, or this whole operation would be up the creek without a paddle. Especially if Jud decided to immediately shoot him in the head and be done with it.

All the lights in the main house went out. The outdoor lights were turned off, leaving only the glow from the sole light over the barn door casting an eerie yellow glow on the area they planned to ambush Jud and his men.

He heard the sound of the car engines before he saw the headlights. Now was the time for Walker to exact his revenge, not only for himself, but for Edie as well. He checked his weapons one last time. Abby had been quite inventive on where to hide them. With everything clear, Walker took a deep breath. Headlights appeared in the distance as he took his position near the barn door. The faces of his team flashed through his mind along with Edie and Shane's wedding. One thing was sure: Jud was never going to walk out of here a free man. He'd either be in custody or in a body bag. Walker only hoped he wasn't in the body bag next to Jud.

28

Layne's heart beat so loudly against her chest she was afraid everyone could hear it. The two black cars she'd seen at the caves came to a stop exactly where her team wanted them. Their headlights illuminated the open farmyard area and pierced the darkness around them for several yards. Layne didn't move as she worried that the tip of her rifle barrel could be seen. Though her scope, she saw Jud and his men get out of the car. Walker had frozen while he was closing the barn door. He turned toward the cars and raised his hand to shield his face from the lights, leaving the door open five feet or so.

"I told you I would come for you," Jud called out as his men backed him up with weapons drawn.

Behind the cars, Layne saw Talon and Lucas take position with their rifles. Flattened against the dark side of the barn were Abby, Jackson, and Dylan. Behind the barn door were Ryan, Matt, and Nash. From deep in the pastures, her father and uncles, Ahmed, Nabi, and the rest of the Rahmi guard were moving forward to surround Jud and his men. Inside the security room, Cody and Deacon were working on repairing the footage from the camera to be able to turn over to the authorities.

"I wondered when you would get here. What took you so long? You're making me late for a date," Walker called out, full of a cockiness that Layne had never heard before.

"Oh no," Jud said with mock sadness as his men chuckled. "I'm afraid you're going to have to miss your date with the lovely Layne. She's with me tonight."

Walker tensed and stopped walking toward Jud. "Leave her out of this," he threatened.

Jud only smiled as he continued to taunt Walker. "It appears you can protect the women in your life as well as you could protect your team."

"What do you want, Jud?" Walker asked. Layne waited to hear Jud's response. Everything was being recorded, but they needed to know Jud's actions and motives before they could move in.

"You, dead and buried."

"Just like you killed our whole team?" Walker said through clenched teeth. "Why did you do it, Jud? Why kill our team in cold blood? They were your *brothers*."

"Brothers?" Jud questioned with disbelief. "They barely listened to me. They all looked to you for confirmation of the orders I gave them. They were no brothers of mine. Especially when faced with the opportunity that I was given."

Walker shook his head. "What opportunity? To become a media star? To get your fifteen minutes of fame?"

Jud tossed his head back and laughed. "These are my brothers, and they'll reap the rewards for being loyal—rewards worth millions. That wasn't an ordinary ship. I only read what customs knew was on that boat. Do you have any idea how many millions of dollars of drugs were also on that ship?"

"Drugs like you and Darrel used to sell before he got kicked out of the SEALs?" Walker spat.

"Someone has been doing his research. Who else knows about this?" Jud asked, moving closer to Walker.

The barn door opened as Nash, Ryan, and Matt strode out. "We do."

"So do we," Abby said in a voice so dangerous it reminded Layne of Ahmed's. Abby, Jackson, and Dylan moved to Walker's left as Nash, Ryan, and Matt moved to his right.

"Hey, mate, we know too. Not a very well-kept secret," Talon called out in his slight Australian accent.

"Who the hell are these people?" Jud asked, looking frantically around.

"My friends. Now, drop your weapons. You're surrounded," Walker ordered.

The hired men looked at each other, unsure of what to do until Layne squeezed off a shot, hitting the hand of one of the men. He yelped and dropped his weapon as the others quickly followed. From a distance, the second wave of reinforcement could barely be seen approaching.

Jud looked panicked as he turned his head from left to right. "If you kill me, you'll never find Layne or your sister."

"Who, me?" Layne asked, standing. She shook off the hay and slowly made her way down the rectangular bales stacked like a pyramid. "I wouldn't worry about me. I would be more worried about making it out of here alive."

Jud's look of shock was priceless. Although Walker's look of anger wasn't so amusing. Layne was supposed to have stayed hidden. Lucas moved in and collected the weapons as her friends and family encircled them. Jud was the only one still armed.

"I believe Walker told you to drop your weapons," Layne said, coming to stand next to Walker.

"You can't shoot me. I'm a hero," Jud taunted, although his voice waivered.

"Okay," Layne said, strapping her gun to her back. "I won't shoot you."

"Shoot them now!" Jud yelled as he pulled a gun from his waistband and fired.

It seemed as if everything was in slow motion. The bullet slammed into Walker's chest, sending him flying backward and collapsing to the ground. Layne was already moving forward as she launched herself at Jud. Fighting erupted around them.

Walker rubbed his chest and sucked in a lungful of air as he rolled onto his side. Layne disarmed Jud in an impressive move as Nash and the rest of his friends moved into hand-to-hand combat with the guards. From the fields, Walker saw Miles and the others sprinting toward them.

Walker moved to his knees as Layne slammed her fist into Jud's nose. "I got this," Walker called out as he leapt into the fray. Layne ducked a punch and Walker was there to slam his fist into Jud's nose. The feeling of it crunching was beyond satisfying.

"Layne!" Miles yelled as the reinforcements formed a circle around the fighting. "Are you okay?"

"I'm *pissed*," Layne yelled back before she grabbed a man by the neck from behind, allowing Abby to knock him out with an uppercut.

"I told you my daughter was a badass," Miles teased his brother.

"Yeah, well, Nash has already taken two men out," Cade yelled from the other behind Walker. "Bad. Ass."

Walker saw Jud pull a knife as he got ready for Jud's attack. Jud lunged and Walker jumped to the side. Using Jud's momentum, Walker shoved him in the back, sending him sprawling to the ground right as one of Jud's men jumped onto Walker's back.

Walker wasn't under the delusion that these men were simply security guards. These men were all special ops trained. Abby and Layne worked in tandem, taking a second man down as Walker felt the man try for a chokehold. This was the most fun he'd had during a mission.

Walker pulled out his knife, stabbed the man in the thigh, and grabbed the man's arm. As Walker bent at the waist, he threw the man over him, sending him careening into Jud.

"Who has the most badass son-in-law now?" Miles yelled over the fighting.

"Doesn't count. He's not your son-in-law yet!" Cade argued back.

"Well, I don't need a badass son-in-law, my daughter is a bigger badass," Miles called out with pride in his voice.

Walker looked to where Layne and Abby high-fived each other. Dylan had a pile of men at his feet, Jackson one, and Nash two, and then the one Walker had stabbed. Talon, Lucas, Ryan, and Matt had been ready to jump in if needed, but they seemed instead to be placing bets on the fights.

"I can fix that, sir!" Walker yelled to Miles as the man he stabbed pulled the knife from his leg and charged while Jud scrambled to his feet.

Walker pedaled backward until he was near Layne.

Facing her, he ignored the man coming toward his side. He watched the man out of the corner of his eye, and when the man leaned forward to attack, Walker went down on one knee. He reached out to the side, grabbed the man's arms, flung him like a sack over his body, and he crashed down on the other side. Abby and Talon immediately grabbed him and dragged him away.

"Layne, not only are you caring, compassionate, smart, and sexy as hell, you're my soul mate. There's no one else I'd rather have by my side during a fight or during life," Walker confessed, looking into her eyes as he held her hands in his. "My heart and my life are full with you in it. I'm in awe of your strength and courage, and I love you more than I ever knew was possible."

"Oh, Walker," Layne whispered as her eyes teared up. She was smiling though, so that gave Walker hope.

"You son of a—" Jud yelled as Layne and Walker both slammed their fists into Jud's face with a cross. Jud weaved on his feet before his eyes rolled back in his head, and he fell to the ground. Instantly, Nash was there, pulling Jud's body away.

"Layne Davies, will—?" Walker started to ask as he knelt back down onto one knee.

"*Wait!*"

Walker froze as he heard Edie's scream from the window of the mansion overlooking the pasture. "Edie?"

"Wait!" Edie yelled one more time before she disappeared from view only to reappear out the side door as she sprinted toward them with the entire houseful of people behind her. Cy and Marshall moved out of the way as Edie, now clothed in clean jeans and a light blue blouse ran past them and over to Walker. She was breathing hard and had her right hand tightly clenched. "You can't propose without a ring. Mama left it to me, and I want you to have it."

Edie opened her hand to reveal the emerald-cut diamond she'd worn on her right hand ever since their mother had passed away. Walker didn't think he could become any more emotional as he took the engagement ring from Edie.

Taking a deep breath, Walker looked into Layne's hazel eyes and held out the ring. "Layne Davies, I love you so much. Will you make me the proudest and happiest man in the world and marry me?"

Walker didn't breathe as Layne reached forward and cupped his cheek with her shaking hand. "Yes, I'll marry you." Layne bent and placed a soft kiss on his lips. Walker wrapped his arms around her and kissed her back as her feet dangled off the ground and everyone cheered.

Walker pressed his forehead to hers. "You're my life, Layne. I swear I will spend every day showing you how much you mean to me," Walker said for her ears only.

"Eat it up, Cade! My future son-in-law is a physical *and* romantic badass!"

Layne and Walker laughed as he set her down and placed the ring on her finger. He wanted more time alone with her, but he wasn't about to tell Miles that as Miles held out his hand to Walker and a tearful Morgan hugged Layne. Walker shook Miles's hand and was surprised when Miles pulled him in for a hug. "I knew one day she'd find the right man who I couldn't scare away."

"It wasn't for the lack of trying," Walker laughed.

Miles leaned in close. "Remember, Froggy. I'll take you out and have your body buried before anyone even knows you're gone if you hurt her."

"I wouldn't have it any other way," Walker said with a smile.

"Oh, no," Layne muttered, causing Walker and Miles to look at her. She was standing next to her mother and holding hands with his sister.

"What is it?" Walker asked full of concern.

"If we have a daughter, she'll never get married with Walker as her father and my dad as her grandfather."

"And would we be experiencing that event in say, nine months?" Morgan asked as Walker threw his head back and laughed.

29

Edie slipped away from the crowd after offering her congratulations. The scariest man she'd ever seen had taken Jud away, and she needed to have a word with him. She was happy for her brother and Layne, but right now happiness wasn't something she could feel with a broken heart.

The lights were back on, and she followed the road a short way to a building that looked impenetrable. This had to be it. She made her way to the steel door and pressed the buzzer. She looked around and saw a video camera and waved.

"Yes?" a voice said from the intercom.

"My name is Edie Wecker. I'm Walker's sister. I need to see Jud Melville before he's turned over to the FBI."

"One moment."

Edie waited as she heard cheers, laughter, and joy from the crowd a short distance away. The minutes ticked by, but after two weeks as a hostage, three minutes of waiting didn't seem like a lot. Finally, a guard opened the door.

"This way, please. He's with Ahmed."

Edie followed him into the building. As the steel door

closed behind her, so did her heart on what she had to do. She was led underground and down a hall until she reached another steel door. This one had a small envelope-sized window at eye height. Inside, she saw Ahmed alone with Jud.

"Where are the others?" Edie asked the guard.

"One in each holding room," the guard answered as he motioned to the other doors lining the hallway. "Ryan and Matt will take them into custody once we have all the information we need."

The guard tapped softly on the door before Ahmed answered it. He stepped out into the hall and the guard went back upstairs on a silent command. "What can I do for you, Mrs. Wecker?"

"I'd like to see Jud Melville, please." Edie tried to hide the tremor from her voice, but Ahmed heard it nonetheless.

"I don't think that would be wise. If you tell me what you'd like to know, I will be sure to acquire that information from him before I hand him over." Ahmed was so calm as he talked about Jud.

"He killed my husband and tried to kill my brother. I *will* have a word with him. Now." Edie was shaking, but she wasn't a coward. She'd survived two weeks with Jud and his men. She wasn't about to back down now.

Ahmed observed her, and she forced herself to keep eye contact. With a nod of his head, he opened the door and allowed Edie to walk in. Ahmed followed and silently closed the door. Jud's bloodied face split into a grin.

"Couldn't stay away, love?"

"Why did you kill my husband? Shane would have followed you to the ends of the earth," Edie asked, moving in front of Jud.

"You husband was a sheep. A mindless and expendable

means to an end." Jud spat, sending bloody saliva spraying across her cheek. Ahmed made a move to intervene, but Edie stopped him with a simple raise of her hand.

"And what was that end? Was it really just a robbery like Walker told me? Where did you possibly put the merchandise you stole before the drone could see through the smoke?"

"I'm not telling you shit, Edie," Jud laughed.

"How much was my husband's life worth?" Edie asked softly as she flicked her fingers open. The knife she'd been hiding up her sleeve slid out and she tightened her hand around the ornate handle. She had found it in the mansion. The knife was the size of a letter opener and had wicked, sharp point in contrast to the beautiful jeweled handle.

Jud's eyes widened. "Aren't you going to stop her?" Jud demanded of Ahmed.

Ahmed shook his head. "I wasn't planning on it."

Edie looked at Ahmed leaning against the wall, and with the slightest inclination of his head, she knew he was giving her permission—permission to take her pound of flesh.

"How much was my husband's life worth?" Edie asked again, placing the tip of the knife's blade against Jud's cheek.

"You crazy bitch!"

Edie's mind wasn't on the present. It was on the past— the love, the laughter, and the dreams she and Shane shared. A hurricane of emotion raged inside of her. Slowly, she dragged the knife down Jud's cheek.

Jud screamed in pain and thrashed against his bindings as Edie made the long cut. "Tell me, Jud. What was my husband's life worth?"

"More millions than you can count!"

"Where is it?" Edie asked sadly. It was true. It was only

about money. The love she and Shane had, the future they had planned, all ripped from her over money.

"I'm not—"

Edie didn't let him finish. She moved the knife up and cut across his cheek. She and Shane were trying to have a baby. He'd even bought a onesie before he left on his last mission and swore when he got back they'd make a little baby for it.

"Where?" Edie whispered through tears of her broken heart.

"I sunk it!" Jud yelled in pain. "Threw it overboard with a marker to let me know where it is."

Edie looked down at the large *T* on Jud's cheek. "Now everyone will know you as the traitor you are. I hope you rot in hell."

Ahmed moved silently and opened the door for her. Edie walked out as the first tear broke from the dam of her eyelids and poured down her cheeks. In the quiet of the hallway, Edie collapsed into Ahmed's arms and cried. She cried for her love, cried for their unfulfilled future, cried for Shane, cried for his teammates, for her brother, and finally for herself.

The man she had thought was so scary never said a word as he held her tight. He pressed her head against his chest and held her safely in his arms until she could cry no more. Exhaustion and grief buckled Edie's knees, but Ahmed had her in his arms, carrying her from the basement.

"Call Dr. Emma and my wife. Have them meet us at my house," Ahmed ordered to someone. "And tell Walker the stolen items were sunk at the site of the attack."

Edie gave into the abyss that had been threatening her since two soldiers had come to her house to tell her Shane was dead. Finally, she'd fulfilled the promise she'd made to Shane that night. She'd have made him proud. Letting go, Edie slipped into the darkness.

EDIE'S EYES fluttered open at the jab of the needle. Standing over her was a young woman whose eyes were filled with concern. Next to her, an older woman with curly hair pulled messily back into a ponytail was hooking up an IV.

"Hello, Edie. I'm Ava Miller and this is my mother, Dr. Emma Miller. How are you feeling?" the young woman asked with concern in a calm and soothing voice.

"I can't believe I fainted. How long have I been out?"

"Just ten minutes. I'm more surprised it took you so long to faint. You're severely dehydrated," Dr. Emma explained as she turned the fluids on full blast.

Edie heard the cheers off in the distance and the merry laughter. "No, I can't stay here right now. I need to be celebrating with my brother."

Ava put a gentle hand to Edie's shoulder and smiled down at her. "And you will be. Give us twenty minutes to get you as hydrated as possible while you eat something. The Rose sisters arrived at the impromptu engagement party, and I snagged a sandwich. I want you to eat slowly and drink as much as you can stand. Then you can head off to the party."

"Isn't that a drink for toddlers when they get sick?" Edie asked taking the large bottle and taking a gulp. She almost spit it out. It was disgusting.

"Yup," Dr. Emma said, patting Edie's knee. "But it restores things your body has been missing. It'll help balance your system out. Try your best to drink it. Dani has a room prepared for you in the main house. Ava and I will see you after the party for a more complete exam and probably some more hydration."

"Main house? I'm staying here?"

"Of course you are, dear."

Edie looked past Dr. Emma and saw two women standing there. One she'd been introduced to, Danielle Ali Rahman, Princess of Rahmi. She had insisted on being called Dani. The other she didn't recognize. Her light red hair was in a ponytail, and she was dressed in all black, but she smiled kindly at her and stepped forward.

"I'm Bridget Mueez. My husband, Ahmed, brought you here."

"He's awfully nice for someone that looks that scary," Edie said before taking a bite of the sandwich and moaning with pleasure.

"That's why I married him. He's a nice guy. He also told me what you did. You got the information he was trying to get. Jud's already been handed over to Ryan, and now it's time for me to make some calls to help our guys get to the finish line of this mission."

Edie nodded. She was too busy eating the sandwich to answer.

"Good. Then I'm going to answer this phone and get it in motion. I'll inform Walker you're eating and receiving treatment for dehydration and will rejoin the party shortly."

"Thank you," Edie said through a mouthful of food.

"And now it's my turn to see what I can do for you," Dani said with a smile as she took a seat on the side of the bed.

"You've done enough. Thank you for letting me spend tonight at your house and for your daughter-in-law's clothes."

"Sydney, Deacon's wife, will be over tomorrow with a sampling of clothes to get you through the week. She owns a clothing company and said she has plenty stashed in storage that you can have."

"The week?" Edie asked, making herself drink the nasty baby drink.

"Why don't you stay the week and visit with your brother? You can also get to know Layne and the rest of us. There's an empty house on the back side of the farm if you wish to stay longer. Or you're free to stay in the house with us. We love having company."

"Thank you," Edie said as the tears threatened again. "With Walker here and Shane gone, I don't really know my place in the world right now."

"You will always have a place in Keeneston," Dani said caringly.

"I wonder if I can get my parents' house back in Shadows Landing. That has always been home to me and home is where I need to be to start over," Edie thought out loud. She went to take a bite of the sandwich only to discover it was gone.

"You're ready to head back to the party if you want," Dr. Emma said. "You're holding down your fluids and food well. Don't go crazy and eat a bunch of sweet stuff. But you can eat other things if you'd like."

"Yes, please. I want to be with Walker and Layne. There's been so much darkness. We need to celebrate the light."

Dani stood up and held out her hand as Dr. Emma removed the IV, leaving the port in, but covering it with Edie's sleeve.

"Then why don't we head over together? You're right. Good should always be celebrated." With a lightness Edie hadn't felt in weeks, she took Dani's hand and walked to the party. Shane and the future they had planned were gone. But she could start again in Shadows Landing.

30

Atlantic Ocean near Nigeria, three days later . . .

IT WAS SO different from the last time Walker had been here. The sun shone brightly. The sky was a perfect blue. The water shimmered. He would never have recognized it as the place his life had been turned into a nightmare.

"So, let me get this straight," Walker asked his future father-in-law. "I'm supposed to say we're on a guys' fishing trip?"

Nash chuckled next to him. "I guess we're technically fishing. I mean, we have a reel, and we're casting it into the ocean. Only we're fishing for a treasure."

"You're part of the family now, son," Miles said seriously. "And that means there are certain things you don't tell your wife."

"Like the fact you're still active duty?" Walker asked. They had landed in Africa only to catch a military helicopter out to a naval vessel. Walker was forced to wear a disguise, but they weren't on the ship very long. They were given an RIB and were on their way to the location of the sunken treasure within ten minutes. The Navy had simply handed over a boat to Miles, Cade, Marshall, Cy, Nash, and Ahmed with no questions asked.

"Technically not *active* duty," Marshall hedged. "That would imply we are enlisted."

"Yeah, we're more like contract workers," Cade said with a shrug as he tested the wench. "Okay, Froggy. You're up."

"I don't think Layne would believe me even if I told her. How are we going to explain coming back with no fish?" Walker asked, pulling his scuba mask into place. He had a small air canister attached to his mouthpiece and tested it out. He wasn't intending to be down there long.

"That's what Pierce is for. He didn't want to be far from Tammy, so he's fishing at Cedar Creek catching some bass for our cover." Cy chuckled.

"Now hop to it, Froggy," Miles ordered.

Walker turned his back to the water, gave the Davies brothers the middle finger, and fell back into the ocean. He surfaced, grabbed the hook from the winch, and dove under. Twenty-five feet down he saw the marker Jud had left. It was a bright yellow buoy with a rope attached. Walker hooked the rope and tied it security to the winch before swimming back to the surface. Nash leaned over and helped haul him onto the boat as Cade turned on the winch.

"So, rumor has it you were Army Rangers. I must admit, I'm slightly disappointed," Walker teased as he stripped the wet suit from his arms so it hung at his waist. "I thought you were more than that."

"At one point, we were Army Rangers," Miles grinned. "But would Army Rangers be able to get all this?" Miles pointed to the boat and winch.

"Shit, Miles. I'm in DEVGRU, and I wouldn't be able to get this."

"Exactly." Miles and his brothers laughed as the large object broke the surface.

Walker turned to help haul it in. It was a large rectangular box close to ten feet tall and four feet wide wrapped in plastic. It took four of them to get it on board since it was so heavy. Walker used his knife to tear away the plastic, revealing an airtight trunk made out of thick plastic. It took another ten minutes to open it. When the contents were exposed, Walker gave a low whistle.

"That's a lot of drugs," Cade said, opening one of the plastic-wrapped bricks. "It's pure opium. I can't even guess at how much heroin this could make."

"And don't forget these," Nash said, opening one of the gallon-sized Ziploc bags full of raw diamonds.

"Jud was right. This trunk on the black market would bring in three hundred million or so," Ahmed replied.

"Let's put it all back in there and get home," Miles ordered. "Apparently we have a farewell party to plan for Edie."

"When's your sister going back to Virginia?" Cy asked.

"She's not. She put her house on the market and had the movers pack and ship everything to Shadows Landing. She'll leave at the end of next week," Walker said as Marshall turned the boat toward the Navy ship.

They were going to have a hell of a time getting the trunk onto the helicopter, but Walker would let them worry about it. He had other things to think about. Like coming back from the dead. Edie wasn't leaving until Walker was legally alive again and the first frenzy of the press was over. She'd bought their parents' house, but the deed wouldn't be filed for at least a month to help give her some privacy. She was healing slowly, but she was going to make it. They had each other, a new family in Keeneston, and their friends back in Shadows Landing.

LAYNE HAD JUST FINISHED with the Thoroughbred professional football players she treated for physical therapy when her phone buzzed. She couldn't contain the excitement she felt reading the text from Walker. He was home and cooking her some of the fish he'd caught on his guys' trip.

Walker had only been gone a couple of days. However, it felt strange after being constantly together for weeks. She missed him. As she drove back to her house, she thought about all she'd gotten done while he was gone. There were long hours at work with a backup of patients to see since she had taken time off. Her cousin Sydney had measured her for a wedding dress and was hard at work designing a one of a kind dress. Nabi and Grace's daughter, Faith, was all signed on to be a junior bridesmaid in charge of walking Fluffy Puppy down the aisle.

It was amazing the amount of work her mother and aunts had gotten done in only a few days. And it was equally amazing how much was left to do. Layne was armed with a binder full of venues for the reception, caterers, musicians, photographers, and more. It had also been fun spending time with Edie and getting to know her soon to be sister-in-law.

Edie had slept most the day after the rescue and then had been bombarded by the Rose sisters, Violet's chef husband, Anton, Poppy and Zinnia, and what seemed like half the people from Keeneston. Cakes, pies, casseroles, fried chicken, pot roasts, and soups arrived one after another. The first one had surprised Edie. The tenth one sent her into grateful tears. After Walker left for the guys' trip, Edie and Layne had talked about their lives, their loves, and their futures while eating a whole red velvet cake.

Layne wished Edie would stay in Keeneston, but she understood the feeling of safety that returning home provided. During their cake eating marathon, Gavin had called from Shadows Landing with Tinsley. They were ecstatic to hear about the engagement and even happier to have Edie coming back to town. Tinsley told them it was all the small town was talking about.

As Layne parked in her garage, she picked up her phone that'd buzzed. It was an email from Gavin listing all the addresses of the Faulkner cousins. Walker and Layne had already decided to invite them all to the wedding. Layne's grandmother was excited to meet the family she thought she had lost and was pushing for a quick wedding. But before they could have a wedding, the groom needed to be declared alive. And her groom was very much alive.

Layne smiled up to Walker as he leaned against the garage door with FP held like a football in his left hand. It was crazy how right love felt. "I've missed you," Walker said in his slow and deep southern drawl before lowering his lips to hers as she stepped in front of him. She'd missed the warmth of his skin and the masculine feel of his body pressed against hers.

FP was running on air to get to Layne, but the second Walker's lips met hers the world around her vanished and her heart overflowed. "I missed you, too. I still can't believe you went on a guys' trip with my family and came back alive." Walker chuckled as he stepped back so she could walk into the kitchen. "Oh, dinner smells delicious."

"Thanks. Four-cheese risotto and fresh fish."

Layne set down her purse and snagged a bite of risotto. She moaned with pleasure as the taste exploded on her tongue. "This is out of this world."

"So is this." Walker laughed, holding up the massive wedding binder she'd left on the kitchen bar.

"Who knew we'd be thrown into wedding planning so quickly," Layne said with a sigh as she snagged another bite of the risotto.

"Getting cold feet?"

"No!" Layne instantly denied. And she wasn't. It just didn't seem right to be planning a wedding without the groom. "I just want a groom to help plan the wedding."

"I guess it's a good thing I'm here then. And a good thing we head to DC tomorrow to get me declared alive. Let's eat and go over the plans. I got a voicemail from Grandma Marcy, informing me she wasn't getting any younger and she couldn't die happy without holding her great-grandchild. And in order to do that, we needed to get married right away." Layne felt her eyes go round in horror, but Walker seemed amused.

"You're okay getting voicemails like that?"

Walker laughed as he made up Layne's plate. "That was nothing compared to the one I got from Grandpa Jake."

The fork Layne picked up fell to the counter. "My grandpa called you?"

Walker nodded. "I hope we're like them after decades of marriage. He told me to rush you to the altar. Something about knocking you up if it would hurry it along."

"No way he would say that!" Layne said in disbelief.

"Oh, yeah. And he ended it with a bit of marriage advice about keeping your wife happy, getting apple pie, and never giving an iron as a gift. I got the happy wife part, but he lost me on the iron." Layne was still staring as Walker shrugged and opened the binder. "Oh, I like the idea of getting married at your grandparents'. After all, that's where I became part of the family. We could have shooting competitions for who gets the first piece of wedding cake. That oak tree with your grandparents' initials on it has to be three hundred years old."

"I am so in love with you right now," Layne said as she wrapped her arms around him.

"So, wedding planning turns you on?" Walker asked seductively. "Then what do you think about the script invitations along with the local country band?"

Layne's lips quirked up before splitting into a smile. "I think all this wedding planning is making it hard to keep my clothes on." She slowly untied the drawstring on her scrubs and winked at Walker.

"Really?" Walker asked, his voice dropping to a low rumble as he leaned forward and kissed her. "Then how are the colors navy blue and gold for the theme? They are the Navy's colors after all," he whispered in her ear.

"That's so hot my pants just fell off. Talk food choices to me," Layne said as she kicked off her pants and teasingly began to lift her shirt.

"Southern cooking all the way. How about barbeque and chicken and waffles?" Walker suggested before lifting Layne's shirt the rest of the way off for her. "With an Amaretto cream wedding cake and a chocolate peanut butter groom's cake."

Layne's bra dropped to the floor along with her top. Dinner was forgotten as Walker hooked a finger in the waistband of her lilac satin panties and slowly began pulling her toward the bedroom.

"You'll be beautiful in white, and I'll wear my dress

uniform," Walker murmured against her lips as Layne began to unbutton his shirt.

"And early the next morning, we'll board a plane and spend our honeymoon on a private beach somewhere," Layne said, attacking the button of his jeans.

"Nash already told me about where he and Sophie went. It sounds perfect. A week with no clothes, no one out to kill us, and no chance of anyone interrupting us." Walker kicked off his pants and fell back onto the bed, pulling Layne with him.

Layne let out a squeak of surprise as she landed on top of Walker's hard body. "Did you happen to call that resort to see if they have any openings in say, two weeks?"

Walker grinned up at her as he slid his hands under her panties. "Not even married yet, and we know each other so well."

"I'll show you just how well we know each other." Layne pulled her panties off and tossed them on the floor as she reached for the giant box of condoms Aniyah gave them. It was so large it didn't fit in the nightstand drawer.

"I look forward to a lifetime of it," Walker said a moment before he flipped Layne onto her back and showed her exactly what she had to look forward to.

31

Washington DC

"I DON'T BELIEVE IT," Lieutenant Commander Stephens said in shock as he took in a very alive Walker and a roomful of people who had come to the Pentagon with him. "You're a dead man."

"Not so dead after all. But not for lack of trying," Walker said to his commander as Stephens wrapped him a tight hug before stepping back and thumping Walker's back for good measure.

Stephens, along with Admiral Thomas Rudy, had been called to Washington for a secret meeting. With Miles, his brothers, Bridget, and a royal family, they had a top-secret meeting scheduled with the top brass along with members of the president's cabinet and a federal judge. In return, Ryan and Matt were in a holding room deep within the Pentagon with Jud and his crew, ready to hand them over to the federal authorities.

Stephens's brow knit in confusion and worry. "Are you the reason I was summoned to DC? What's going on, Walker? Who are all these people?"

"My family," Walker grinned as he held out his hand to Layne. She stepped forward and placed her hand in his. "This is my fiancée, Layne Davies. And you know my sister, Edie."

"Ma'am," Stephens said, shaking Layne's hand and turning sadly to Edie. "I'm so sorry that Shane didn't come back."

Edie smiled sadly as she gripped Walker's arm. "At least I have my brother back, and I have answers."

"Would you like to explain now, Walker?" Stephens asked.

Walker gave his commander the succinct timeline of events as if he were debriefing him on a mission. "Layne's father, Miles Davies," Walker said, nodding to where Miles stood, "and his brothers, Cade, Marshall, and Cy Davies all helped. We also had help from Ahmed Mueez and Nash Dagher on behalf of the Rahmi royal family."

"Royal family?" Stephens stuttered with wide eyes. "Not *the* Ahmed and Nash?"

"So, you have heard of my men," Mo said proudly. "I am Prince Mohtadi Ali Rahman, and this is my wife, Princess Danielle, and my son, Prince Zain."

Walker fought the smile as Stephens looked around the room. "Are you to thank for this meeting?" he asked Mo.

"No, she is," Mo grinned as Bridget stepped forward.

"This is Bridget Mueez. She's Ahmed's wife. You probably know of her father, General Richard Ward." Walker introduced her as Bridget shook his hand.

"The former commander of Special Ops and then Chief

of Staff of the United States Army, Richard Ward? Where did you find all these people?" Stephens asked dumbfounded.

"Keeneston," they all answered as one.

There was a knock on the door and an aide came in. "We're ready for you all now. If you'll follow me to the hearing room."

Walker never let go of Layne's hand as the large group walked down the halls of the Pentagon to the room set up like a congressional hearing. Inside was a long table sitting on a platform. Behind it was the chief of naval operations along with the rest of the joint chiefs of staff, the secretary of defense, the attorney general, and someone Walker guessed was a judge.

"Where the hell is Keeneston?" Stephens whispered behind him.

"Chief Petty Officer Greene, please take a seat with your attorney," the chief of naval operations ordered, sending everyone to their seats. Layne squeezed his hand once before letting go and sitting in the row of chairs between her parents.

Walker pulled the seat back and stood next to Addison Rooney, the young prosecutor from Keeneston who had been helping him get everything in order to declare himself alive.

"We are here today to determine if the man standing before us, is in fact, Chief Petty Officer Walker Greene, who was declared dead after the Nigerian Waters Operation. Ms. Rooney, does your client have an opening statement before you call your first witness?"

"He does," Addison responded, nodding to Walker. Walker stood and delivered his statement of facts. He told about his history in the SEALs before joining DEVGRU. Then he told of the night in question and the night he "died." The panel whispered among themselves as he talked. Then they peppered him with questions. He saw it dawning on them that the man they'd all held as a national hero was, in fact, anything but.

"Call your first witness," the chief ordered once Walker was permitted to sit.

Edie was called to the stand first. She described being notified about her husband and brother's deaths and how she was pressured to declare Walker dead, even when she refused.

"Who pressured you?" the Secretary of Defense asked her.

"Jud Melville and Admiral Thomas Rudy, who I only later discovered was, in fact, Jud Melville's father."

"Is that true?" the attorney general asked as the chief of naval operations silently affirmed it with a nod of his head.

Edie then proceeded to tell of her kidnapping at Jud's hands and Layne's rescue. She ended with swearing that the man standing in front of the panel today was her brother, Walker Greene. Next, Layne was called to the stand and Walker watched as his brave fiancée told of killing Darrel Snyder, receiving threats from Jud Melville, and then going along with her kidnapping in order to rescue Edie.

"Where did you learn skills like that?" the commandant of the Marine Corps asked in disbelief.

Layne smirked and Walker almost laughed as Layne looked at her father. "From my father, retired Lieutenant Colonel Miles Davies of the U.S. Army."

"Miles Davies?" the chief of staff of the Army asked. "As in the Davies who worked under General Ward?"

"Yes, sir," Miles confirmed, standing up. "General Ward's daughter, Bridget, is who notified you of this meeting."

There was a lot of whispering now and Walker wondered which one of them knew that Miles and the row of his brothers seated next to him were not retired.

"Thank you, Miss Davies. Miss Rooney, any other witnesses?" the chief of naval operations asked a minute later.

"One last witness, sir. Keeneston's Deputy Sheriff Cody Gray."

Walker watched as Cody stepped forward and was sworn in as Addison handed a thumb drive to an aide.

"Mr. Gray, can you tell us about the video we are about to see?" Addison asked.

"Chief Petty Officer Walker Greene, upon arriving in Keeneston, was in possession of a damaged body cam. I was able to recover the video." He held up the camera for everyone to see. "This is the camera I am happy to hand over as evidence."

Addison took the body cam and passed it to the panel who agreed before pressing play. On the screen, Walker saw his team as they rode in the RIB. He heard Edie's gasping cry as Shane laughed on the screen. All too soon, the happy pictures of a band of brothers turned into a nightmare as Walker plunged into the ocean.

The room was completely quiet for several long minutes.

"Thank you, Mr. Gray. You may be excused. I also have this to present into evidence." Addison hooked up the television and a picture of Keeneston came into view. Jud's capture played out as the panel quietly whispered among themselves. "My client is willing to perform a government-ordered DNA test if the one we provided from Davies

Laboratory is insufficient. But at this time, I request that my client, Chief Petty Officer Walker Greene, be declared alive and all his paychecks, retirement, and standing within the Navy be retroactively brought to current and reinstated. Thank you."

Walker held his breath as Addison took her seat next to him. The panel gathered close and the microphones were muted as they talked. Finally, they turned to Walker.

"I'm Judge Joyce Monk, and I hereby rule that upon the evidence presented, Walker Greene is alive. All back pay, social security, government benefits, and identifications will be immediately effective retroactively from the date of death." There was a rap of a gavel as his friends behind him whispered their congratulations.

"Where is Jud Melville now?" the attorney general asked.

"Here in a holding cell. He is in the custody of the Keeneston sheriff and the Lexington office of the FBI. Providing the government is ready to press charges, the town of Keeneston is prepared to waive their right to prosecute Mr. Melville and hand him over to you right now."

"I believe we will be glad to take him off your hands, and we thank the town of Keeneston for their help in catching such an evil perpetrator," the attorney general said as the others nodded. "Bring in Mr. Melville and Admiral Rudy," she ordered the aide.

"We are sorry for what you went through, Chief Petty Officer. Thank you for your heroism. I will be personally recommending you for the Medal of Honor," the chief of naval operations informed Walker.

"Thank you, sir."

The chief of staff of the Army smiled. "Then Lieutenant

Commander Davies won't be the only Medal of Honor recipient in Keeneston. Bridget, tell your father I said hello. I'm also hearing a rumor of a private military training facility in Keeneston. Are the rumors true?"

Miles and his brothers stood. "Yes, sir. We hope to be up and running in six months."

"You're putting together a training facility?" the chief of staff of the Air Force asked. "Who will be your instructors?"

"We are in the process of hiring. So far it will be my brothers, retired FBI agent Cole Parker, Ahmed Mueez of the Rahmi Special Forces, his wife, Bridget, who is a renowned K-9 handler that supplies Special Ops with their dogs, and myself. Hopefully, even a DEVGRU man." Miles winked at Walker.

Walker felt his chest puff with pride. Miles wanted to work with him.

"Hooyah," Walker answered with a smile. He would be a trainer in Keeneston. He would be able to do what he loved and be with the woman he loved without long and dangerous deployments.

"Oh, come on, Froggy," Cade groaned under his breath.

Morgan leaned behind Miles and looked at her brother-in-law. "Uh-oh. Someone else has a badass son-in-law now," Walker heard Morgan whisper before standing upright again with a sweet smile on her face.

"When are you accepting trainees?" the chief of staff of the Army asked. "I have a group of Special Ops guys to send to you as soon as you're open."

"I'll call you to schedule them," Miles said as the aide came back into the room with Jud. Another aide came in from the opposite door with Admiral Rudy. The father and son looked surprised to see each other.

"Thank you for your service, Chief Petty Officer Greene.

We'll take it from here," the attorney general said, interrupting the talk of a training facility. With a nod to the panel, Walker turned and held out his hand for Layne. He walked out with the woman he loved by his side and never turned back. There was too much to look forward to for him to ever look back again.

EPILOGUE

Marcy Davies stood nervously in front of her bedroom mirror and checked her hair for the fourth time in five minutes. Her family would be here any moment. Well, the family she never thought she'd meet. Her sons, daughter, their spouses, and all their children were already here for the sunset wedding of her granddaughter and Walker.

"How are you doing, darling?" Jake asked as he came up behind her and looked at her in the mirror.

"I'm so nervous, Jake. What if they don't like me? What if it wasn't Mom who kept them away from me?" Marcy fiddled with her pearl necklace as she felt the familiar pain of being a disappointment to her family assault her. At least she'd thought that was the reason for their separation. However, her grandnephew Gavin had told her otherwise.

"Oh, Marcy. You've always been the only family I need. I've lived a long life. If they hurt you, then I'm pretty sure Matt won't arrest his grandfather-in-law for hurting them back." Jake placed a kiss on her cheek and slipped his hand into hers. The decades had gone by. The once young and invincible man had gone through war, poverty, loss, love, fatherhood, and now to the patriarch of a family with more love for each other than he knew possible. He looked out the window as his family was gathering below and smiled.

"What is that smile for?" Marcy asked, stepping to the window next to him.

"It just dawned on me. We're responsible for all this—all of them."

"Oh, Jake," Marcy whispered as she rested her head on his shoulder. They stood silently watching as Sienna rubbed her slightly swollen belly with their first great-grandchild inside to where all their children stood lovingly by the side of the spouses. Tammy glowed as she was given the gift of a late-in-life pregnancy. Although unexpected, it wasn't unwelcome. He or she would be their eighteenth grandchild who would grow up surrounded by the love Marcy's family never gave her . . . but maybe even that was about to change.

"They're here," Miles said from behind them. Marcy turned to see her oldest child, now in his sixties, looking ready to defend her if someone dare upset her.

"Have you met them?" Marcy asked as she and Jake moved toward the door.

"Yes. I saw them coming and hurried them inside before the crowd could descend on them. They seem very happy to be here." Miles stepped aside so she and Jake could walk past them. Marcy raised her hand and cupped her son's cheek.

"You're a good son, Miles."

"It's only because you've been such good parents."

Marcy took a deep breath and headed down the hall to the living room with Jake's hand in hers and Miles offering his silent support behind her.

WALKER HUGGED his friends from home. He couldn't stop smiling as the Faulkners were all talking at once. Gavin and his sister, Harper, had driven their Grandfather Scott. Ridge and Tinsley had similarly driven their Grandfather Kevin while Wade, Trent, and Ryker all flew there together.

Walker could tell they were nervous. Kevin and Scott sat in their wheelchairs with their heads together as they talked. Walker saw their hands wringing in their laps. It wasn't just Kevin and Scott who were nervous to see their sister. Their grandchildren couldn't stop looking at all the pictures hanging on the wall and asking Walker about a family they'd only heard of in passing.

"Ah, here they are," Walker said as he hurried over to Marcy's side. In just a matter of weeks, she and Jake had become the grandparents he'd never had, and he felt protective of them as they faced the family they thought had abandoned them.

The room went quiet and Walker could feel Miles growing tense. "Marcy Belle?" Scott whispered and Marcy broke at her childhood nickname. Tears streamed down her face as Gavin and Ryker pushed their grandfathers forward.

"I thought you'd forgotten about me," Marcy said tearfully as Jake led her to her brothers.

Walker saw tears in Kevin and Scott's eyes as Marcy stopped in front of them both and held out her hands. Soon the three Faulkner siblings were linked once again, hand in hand. There wasn't a dry eye in the room as Kevin struggled to stand and wrapped his sister in a hug. "We never forgot you."

"We're so sorry, Marcy Belle. Ma told us you didn't want anything to do with us. That you thought you were too good for us after marrying Jake," Kevin confessed as Ridge hurried to help his grandfather sit back down in his wheelchair.

Marcy shook her head as she bent and hugged her brother Scott. "Never. I only wanted a family. A family Ma apparently didn't want me to have. I'm so sorry. I should have tried harder. I should have reached out more."

Scott squeezed her hand. "No. None of this was your fault. But now we have a chance to right this wrong. You have to tell us all about your life. Has it been a happy one?"

Marcy looked back to Jake and Miles and smiled. "It's been the absolute best. Jake, Miles, come meet our family."

Scott held out his hand. "My dear Debra passed away a year ago. Kevin's wife, Brenda, passed on three years ago. Deb and I had two sons who moved with Kev's two sons to Florida last year to start a small hotel on a private island. Luckily we have our grandchildren with us still. Though I would really like to hold a baby in my arms before I die," Scott said, giving his grandkids and grandnephews and - nieces a glare.

Miles snorted and covered it up with a cough. Walker didn't bother hiding his laugh. He still had the voicemail saved of Marcy saying the same thing.

"I will have my eighteenth grandchild in five months and my first great-grandchild in six months. Y'all knew Jake but haven't seen him since you left. And this is my oldest son, Miles."

Jake and Miles shook hands and smiled. Jake rested his hand on Marcy's back and Walker couldn't help but sit back and hope he and Layne would have such a long and happy marriage as Jake and Marcy.

"And these are my grandchildren," Scott said, motioning for them to step forward. "This is Gavin. He's a doctor. And his sister, Harper, owns the best bar and grill in town," Scott said proudly.

Harper looked distrusting but still shook Marcy's hand. Gavin hugged her and Walker thought Marcy would cry with joy.

"And these are my other grandchildren. Wade, he's in the Coast Guard. And his brother, Trent. He makes the most exquisite furniture."

Wade and Trent both hugged Marcy and shook Jake's and Miles's hands. "It's nice to meet y'all," Trent drawled.

Kevin held out his hand for Marcy, and she happily took it. "And these are my grandkids. "Ryker is an only child and now runs a shipping company in Charleston."

"Mrs. Davies," Ryker said, shaking her hand.

"Would calling me Aunt Marcy be too much to ask?"

For once, Ryker smiled kindly. Ryker was always the dark and brooding kind. But when he smiled, his whole demeanor changed. "Not at all, Aunt Marcy." Marcy sniffled and launched herself at Ryker, wrapping the surprised man in a hug.

"And this is Ridge. He's a builder. Went to school to be an architect, but now he designs and builds luxury homes and buildings. And this sweet little lady is his sister, Tinsley. She's a beautiful artist," Kevin said proudly.

"I brought you this, Aunt Marcy," Tinsley said shyly. She handed Marcy a wrapped package that Marcy tore into.

"Oh! Oh, Jake, look at it! It's beautiful." Marcy began to cry at the painting of an old oak tree with the initials M + J in carved in the trunk. "How did you know?"

"Walker told me about the tree they're getting married under. When I asked for a picture he sent it to me," Tinsley said as Marcy wrapped her in a hug.

"I'll cherish this. Thank you." Marcy took a deep breath.

"Now are you ready to meet all your uncles, aunts, and cousins?"

"And any single ladies and gents of Keeneston, too," Scott called out as Gavin began to push his wheelchair toward the party out back.

"*Grandpa*," Gavin groaned as the rest of the kids all rolled their eyes.

$\sim$

"You may now kiss the bride," Father Ben said under the massive three-hundred-year-old oak tree. The lower branches were entwined with soft white lights as the warm glow of the sun setting behind them turned the wedding into a fairy tale.

Layne couldn't stop smiling as Walker, more handsome than she'd ever seen him in his dress uniform, wrapped her in his arms, bent her back, and kissed her. Her friends and family cheered.

"I love you, Layne. Today is just one of the happy days we will have."

Layne kissed Walker one more time before he brought her upright, and they walked arm-in-arm up the aisle.

They stood off to the side as they received good wishes and congratulations from their friends and family. Layne couldn't have been happier to meet her cousins and felt as if the shy Tinsley was already her friend after what they went through to find Edie. Layne laughed as she grabbed Ryker and introduced him to Dylan. The two looked at each other with stone faces before they finally started to talk. They were definitely two peas in a pod—tall, dark, and quiet, but with a lot going on beneath the surface.

And what warmed Layne's heart more than anything

was seeing the utter joy on her grandmother's face. As Layne and Walker talked to their guests, the oak was turned into the center of the reception. A dance floor was set up under the edge of its outreaching branches and tables were grouped all around it.

Grandpa Jake clinked his champagne glass to get everyone's attention at the trunk of the oak tree. "My lovely bride and I carved our initials into this tree the day of our wedding. We didn't know what the future would hold. I was off to war, and she was left to run a farm, but we had faith, and we had love. Now, as we look around, we see so much love we no longer think we should be alone on this tree. Walker, Layne, I'm sure one of you has a knife on you. Come up here and be the first to put your initials on the tree next to ours. Then we ask for all our children and grandchildren to do the same. For long after we're all gone, our love will be known to anyone that visits. To Walker and Layne, and to a forever love."

Layne hiked up her dress to reveal a knife held in place by a blue garter. "Your knife or mine?"

"That's my girl." Miles chuckled as he slapped Walker on his back. "Welcome to the family, Froggy."

Layne hugged her father. When he hugged her tightly in return and told her how proud he was of her, Layne knew now what Sydney and the rest of her cousins were talking about. She was complete. She was loved.

"Thank you, Dad."

"Even if you did marry a Navy man. At least he's a badass," Miles dipped his head and whispered. "But we both know who the real badass in the family is. After all, you are Daddy's girl."

∾

THE MUSIC WAS LIVELY. The tree, now filled with the initials of all the happy couples, shined as Walker pulled Layne from the dance floor and into the night.

"What are you doing?" Layne giggled as she followed him toward the shooting range.

"Getting a couple minutes alone with my wife. It's been killing me not to touch you. Sydney is evil, that's all I can say."

Layne looked down at her dress. It was stunning, but it also gave a very seductive view of her cleavage. Walker hid her behind the straw dummy and backed her up against it with a searing kiss.

"I've been wanting to kiss you like that all day," Walker confided as he ran his hands down her side, skimming the sides of her breasts before resting at her waist.

"Soon we'll be all alone on a private beach. Until then, I guess this kiss will have to do," Walker said, kissing her again before pulling back with a look of puzzlement on his face. "What are these doing out here?"

Layne looked up as Walker plucked the purple thong from the straw dummy's head above her. "Why would you leave your panties out here?" Walker asked, dangling the garment from his fingertips.

"Those aren't mine!" Layne gasped.

"They look like yours."

"The panty dropper has struck again."

Walker dropped the panties. "If they're not yours, whose are they?"

"I don't know. The whole town has been betting on it."

"Now I'm kinda bummed. I thought they were yours, which would mean you're not wearing any right now," Walker said, using his finger to trace a path down her bodice.

"Just because they belong to someone else doesn't mean I'm wearing anything underneath my dress. I guess you'll just have to love me for the rest of my life to find out."

"That's the easiest order I've ever received." Walker leaned forward and thoroughly kissed his wife.

~

"CHEERS, LADIES," Morgan said to her friends and sisters-in-law as they sat around the table under the tree. They sipped champagne as they watched Walker and Layne emerge from the shadows with a besotted look on their faces.

"Do you think you'll be a grandmother by next year?" Katelyn asked.

"Not if Aniyah keeps giving them condoms," Morgan grumbled.

"Oh, look at that, ladies," Dani said with a wriggle of her eyebrows.

Morgan laughed as Lucas Sharpe and Poppy boogied their way across the dance floor while Talon Bainbridge stood stoically by with Zinnia looking at him with stars in her eyes.

"Maybe they'll be next instead of one of ours," Tammy sighed. "I wish Piper would get her head out of her lab goggles and look at the men around her. But she is working on something she says will change the world, so I guess I can't begrudge her that."

Tammy then laughed as the women turned to see Captain Kyrkos and his medic, Costa, dancing with Addison Rooney and Ava Miller. The two Greeks looked as if they'd died and gone to heaven. As a surprise to his son-in-law, Miles had tracked the two men down and flown them to the wedding.

"Cheers to them!" Morgan toasted.

"Honey!" Pierce yelled, running up and slapping the glass from her hands. "You can't drink that! You're pregnant. And being so old, your body doesn't metabolize alcohol—"

Tammy made a move to grab Annie's gun that was hidden under her dress, but Annie shoved her own glass in her hands instead. "It was sparkling apple juice," Tammy said through gritted teeth as she splashed Annie's drink into his face. "It's a damn good thing I love you. You are testing me, Pierce Davies. If you remind me how old I am one more time, I swear I will shoot you. And not an Aniyah type shot, but a Bridget type shot."

"But honey—" Pierce stopped and looked down at the notebook sitting between Dani and Kenna. "Why is our daughter's name in that book? What is under Piper's name?"

Kenna slammed their matchmaking notebook closed as they all blinked innocently at Pierce. "Honey," Tammy said, lowering her voice, "I believe the perks of the second trimester are hitting."

"Huh? Oh!" Pierce grinned. "I'll, um, go inside and get you a sweater. You look cold. Maybe you should come with me to make sure I get the right one."

"I'll meet you in just a minute," Tammy said sweetly as she watched Pierce run off. "I'm too old to have a baby, but not sex," she said with a roll of her eyes. "Carry on, ladies. These hormones are hitting, even if he says the wrong thing over and over. He's still so hot in that suit that I'll forgive him instantly."

Morgan shook her head as Tammy hurried after her husband. "I think Reagan is hiding something," Gemma informed the table.

They looked to where Reagan was talking to a group of people. "Ask DeAndre," Morgan suggested.

"*Hmph*," Gemma sighed. "We don't have a good candidate for who is next."

"Abby's shown no interest in settling down," Bridget said.

"Neither has Ariana," Dani agreed.

"Same with Greer," Paige added. "But, Jackson—"

"Or Carter," Kenna smiled before her face dropped. "But he's shown no interest in serious dating either."

"Wyatt's another possibility," Katelyn said, sitting up straighter.

"Now we're cooking." Annie grinned, leaning forward to set the wheel of romance in motion.

REAGAN STOOD with her cousins and friends as Walker and Layne danced so closely on the dance floor she was sure Uncle Miles would explode. Instead of causing a scene like her father, Cy, would have done, Uncle Miles was happily lost in his wife's eyes. Layne thought she had it bad with Miles as her father. Uncle Miles was nothing compared to Reagan's father.

Reagan made a snort that caused Piper to look at her. Reagan smiled back and Piper went back to telling about her new experiment. Reagan's father was driving her crazy. He still regularly threatened to castrate her brother-in-law, Matt, and he and Riley had been married for over a year now.

It was a good thing her dad was a spy because that was the only way she had survived the past sixteen months. He'd taught her survival, surveillance, and how to fight. What her dad didn't know was that he was teaching her how to keep her life private from him. What had started as friendship had blossomed into something so much more and she was fiercely guarding it with every lesson her father had taught her.

Their relationship had started off slowly. They'd always been friends. Then she'd flown with him, and he'd spent the entire flight talking to her as a woman, not just some girl he'd played with as a kid. When Reagan had landed her horse transport plane, they knew their relationship had changed forever. Reagan glanced around and saw him dancing with Poppy. So many weddings, so many events, so many nights . . . she wished she didn't have to hide. She wanted to dance with him, to kiss him, to feel his hands on her, but he was different. He wasn't Matt, or Ryan, or Nash, or Walker who knew how to handle a scary-ass father. Therefore, it was up to her to protect him.

The dance ended and he came toward her as the strands of a slow dance started. "Dance with me, Reagan."

"We shouldn't. My dad is watching."

"I don't care. I'm done hiding." He held out his hand and Reagan looked up into his dark brown eyes. He smiled at her. His dimples shone and she was lost. She wanted what her sister had. She wanted what Layne had. She wanted it all.

Reagan's hand shook as she placed it in his. His smile held the promise of a future—one that Reagan was finally ready to fight for. He pulled her so close that her breasts pressed against his hard chest. Reagan should have pulled back, but she was lost in his eyes. He was smiling down at her with love in them. Love was not something they'd talked about, but it was as clear as day. Then, right there in the middle of the dance floor, he lowered his lips to hers. This wasn't a dance. This was a statement of his feelings—a statement that he was no longer going to hide.

"What the hell do you think you're doing, Carter?" her father bellowed over the sounds of the wedding.

The End

New Release Notifications for Kathleen Brooks, Sign Up Here:

www.kathleen-brooks.com/new-release-notifications/

Subscribers will be the first to learn about the new Forever Bluegrass series coming soon.

Please visit the retailer's product page if you have enjoyed this story to leave a review. It helps me to know which characters and story lines the readers enjoy so I can make future books even better. Thank you!

Bluegrass Series

Bluegrass State of Mind

Risky Shot

Dead Heat

Bluegrass Brothers

Bluegrass Undercover

Rising Storm

Secret Santa: A Bluegrass Series Novella

Acquiring Trouble

Relentless Pursuit

Secrets Collide

Final Vow

Bluegrass Singles

All Hung Up

Bluegrass Dawn

The Perfect Gift

The Keeneston Roses

Forever Bluegrass Series

Forever Entangled

Forever Hidden

Forever Betrayed

Forever Driven

Forever Secret

Forever Surprised

Forever Concealed

Forever Devoted

Forever Hunted - coming April/May of 2017

Women of Power Series

Chosen for Power

Built for Power

Fashioned for Power

Destined for Power

Web of Lies Series

Whispered Lies

Rogue Lies

Shattered Lies

ABOUT THE AUTHOR

Kathleen Brooks is a New York Times, Wall Street Journal, and USA Today bestselling author. Kathleen's stories are romantic suspense featuring strong female heroines, humor, and happily-ever-afters. Her Bluegrass Series and follow-up Bluegrass Brothers Series feature small town charm with quirky characters that have captured the hearts of readers around the world.

Kathleen is an animal lover who supports rescue organizations and other non-profit organizations such as Friends and Vets Helping Pets whose goals are to protect and save our four-legged family members.

Email Notice of New Releases
kathleen-brooks.com/new-release-notifications
Kathleen's Website
www.kathleen-brooks.com
Facebook Page
www.facebook.com/KathleenBrooksAuthor
Twitter
www.twitter.com/BluegrassBrooks
Goodreads
www.goodreads.com

36880706R00177

Made in the USA
Middletown, DE
19 February 2019